Love and Theft

Also by Stan Parish

Down the Shore

Love and Theft

Stan Parish

DOUBLEDAY  NEW YORK

Book design by Maria Carella
Jacket images: (diamond) BlackJack3D/E+ and (cityscape) Jay Speiden/
EyeEm, both Getty Images; (motorcycle) VGstockstudio/Shutterstock
Jacket design by Jaya Miceli

Library of Congress Cataloging-in-Publication Data
Names: Parish, Stan, author.
Title: Love and theft : a novel / Stan Parish.
Description: First Edition. | New York : Doubleday [2020]
Identifiers: LCCN 2019047823 (print) | LCCN 2019047824 (ebook)
Subjects: GSAFD: Mystery fiction
Classification: LCC PS3616.A74314 L68 2020 (print) |
LCC PS3616.A74314 (ebook) | DDC 813/.6—dc23
LC record available at https://lccn.loc.gov/2019047823
LC ebook record available at https://lccn.loc.gov/2019047824

ISBN: 978-0-385-54524-2 (hardcover)
ISBN: 978-0-385-54526-6 (ebook)

MANUFACTURED IN THE UNITED STATES OF AMERICA

1 3 5 7 9 10 8 6 4 2

First Edition

For Philip and Margaret Parish

And in memory of Jim Salant

Love and Theft

Prologue

Officer Rob Sullivan of the Las Vegas Metropolitan Police Department is responding to a possible 413 when the second call comes in. It's a Hispanic woman on the line with 911 this time, but the details are the same: white male, late teens to early twenties, wandering the streets in broad daylight with a weapon in his hands. The first caller, who hung up after giving a description, mentioned an assault rifle. "Big gun" is the second caller's phrase. The suspect is supposedly six blocks from Officer Sullivan, who's roaring into his second shift on twenty milligrams of Adderall and half a diet Red Bull. His mind circles the dispatcher's description as he scans the streets. Sullivan has a two-year-old white male at home, and twelve years from now his kid will enter Ed W. Clark High School, where the LVMPD has responded to two bomb threats in the past three years. The school has monthly active shooter drills, and Sullivan wonders what makes these teenage gunmen snap. Their parents seem normal enough when they go on TV asking for America's forgiveness. There's only so much—Jesus Christ, Sullivan thinks, fucking focus. This is why he takes the Adderall. And how it works against him. Sullivan draws his pistol and pulls the slide back to reveal the bright brass of a chambered round.

SARA KOH, emergency services dispatcher with the LVMPD, gets her nails done near the first reported sighting of the gunman. She's friendly with the salon's manager, Shannon Jacobson, who comped Sara's last French manicure. Sara does something she's not supposed to do on shift and sends Shannon a text: *Hey stay inside if ur at wrk . . . smthng may b going on by u* ☹

SHANNON JACOBSON is not at work. At 4:25 p.m. she's halfway through the line for a boozy Sunday pool party hosted by Encore Las Vegas at the Wynn hotel and casino. A Swedish DJ goes on in an hour, and it seems like half the UNLV student body is crammed inside the velvet rope that snakes toward the entrance. Frat boys in tank tops and flip-flops share to-go cups with sorority girls wearing almost nothing over their bikinis. Shannon loves the music and tolerates this hormonal day-drunk mob of people half her age. In the coin pocket of her jeans is Ecstasy shaped like a hand grenade, a gift from her coworker at the salon. Shannon dry-swallows the pill and tilts her head back to draw it down her throat. Her phone buzzes with a text.

THERE'S A white male walking north on Fairfield with something in his hand, but Officer Sullivan can't tell what it is at fifty yards.

"Dispatch, this is one-six-two, possible suspect heading north on Fairfield toward Chicago, over."

The suspect is loping down the sidewalk in an oversize Steelers jersey. If he hears the car, he pays no mind. When he stops suddenly, Sullivan taps his brakes. His hands feel hollow as he puts the car in park and grips his pistol. The suspect turns. In his right hand is a leash attached to a small dog.

Another cruiser rolls through the intersection of Fairfield and St. Louis, ignoring the stop sign. It's Russell Pratt and his partner, the newish guy from Phoenix. Windows come down.

"You call something in?" Pratt asks.

"Guy walking his dog."

"Where is this asshole?"

Sullivan shrugs.

"Nobody's seen shit except whoever made those calls," Pratt's partner says. "You'd think this guy'd be hard to miss."

SIX BLOCKS west of the Wynn, a fifteen-foot U-Haul pulls over on a quiet stretch of Lisbon Avenue. The driver, in a black leather racing suit and full-face helmet, jumps down from the cab. At the back of the truck, he throws up the container door, lowers the loading ramp, and disappears inside. The thin walls of the trailer shake as engines cough and growl inside. Two motorcycles roll slowly down the ramp and into the street. Each bike holds two riders and all four wear full-body racing leathers, their faces hidden behind tinted visors. Both passengers wear backpacks and they crouch down as the motorcycles pick up speed until the riders resemble giant insects with pebbled skin and gleaming eyes. The truck, stolen but still unreported, is abandoned with open doors and hazards blinking weakly in the golden afternoon light.

KAI PRESTON and Anna Levine drove from L.A. to the Wynn Las Vegas last night on a whim. The young, blond, dreadlocked couple won next month's rent at blackjack before losing it at craps. At 4:36 p.m., Kai reminds his girlfriend that they haven't eaten anything since breakfast. They leave the casino floor and wander the Wynn Esplanade, a gently curving corridor lined with luxury boutiques.

"Holy shit," Kai says. "Baby, check this out."

In the window of Graff jewelers is a brooch shaped like a peacock with plumage made from precious stones. Anna smiles at her boyfriend.

"Can't hurt to look," she says.

The marble floor inside looks clean enough to eat from, and

jewels in the display cases sparkle like flitting fish as the couple moves around the store. Anna is examining engagement rings when a petite woman with a platinum bob appears beside her.

"Welcome. Can I help you?"

"I'm in love with that one," Anna says, tapping the glass.

"It's a lovely piece. Would you like to see it? I'm Cynthia, by the way," the woman says, pulling on a thin white glove to unlock the case and extract a six-carat yellow diamond set in platinum. These whiskey-breath surfer kids do not strike Cynthia as likely buyers, but she's seen stranger things here. Anna slips the ring onto her finger and stares down at her hand.

"It's unusual to find a yellow stone in that size and clarity," Cynthia says.

"What's the color from?"

"Trace elements of nitrogen." Cynthia leans in. "You know, for a long time, colored diamonds were considered flawed. But Mr. Graff spent years educating people about stones like that one. They're much rarer than white diamonds. And now they're much more valuable."

Kai laughs. "What's that expression? One man's trash?"

"Well," Cynthia says, "that's one way to think about it."

"How much are we talking here?" Kai asks.

"I believe that one is $225,000, but I'll have to double-check." Anna holds the ring up to her face.

"Not bad for the flawed stuff," Kai says.

BRIAN DALMORE, valet attendant at the Wynn, is ten dollars richer thanks to the driver of a red Corvette who asked Brian to take special care of "Cindy" when he slipped him the bill. Brian is about to duck into the driver's seat when he sees his colleague, Marty Stetson, locked in conversation with a tall man in a motorcycle helmet. The scene strikes Brian as tense.

"Marty," he calls out. "Hey, Marty, everything okay?"

Marty nods enthusiastically. Brian puts the car in drive, still unconvinced. He adjusts the rearview mirror for one last look, but Marty vanishes behind an Escalade packed with kids dressed for the pool party. Brian is dreading their release five hours from now. That, he thinks, will be the worst part of my day.

MARTY STETSON expected a question about parking when the helmeted rider hopped off the back of his friend's bike and approached the valet stand. Instead, the man lifted the backpack slung over his shoulder to give Marty a glimpse of the compact assault rifle hidden underneath.

"Is your friend gone?" the rider asks, as Brian drives off.

Marty nods.

"I need your radio."

Marty hands it over and the man—whom the FBI will designate as Rider 1—tucks the earpiece up into his helmet, switches over to the channel monitored by Wynn security, and calls in a brawl outside the Margeaux Ballroom, at the opposite end of the property, eight minutes away on foot. Rider 1 asks all guards to respond.

"Hands," he says to Marty.

A thick zip tie binds Marty's wrists to the valet stand. Rider 1 opens one of six tall doors to the Esplanade and inserts a locking steel wedge above the bottom hinge. Heads turn as dry heat and car exhaust pour into the perfumed resort. Marty is saying an urgent prayer for all the folks inside when a second bike rips through the arrivals area and stops behind the first. Rider 1 lays a hand on Marty's shoulder.

"If this gets called in from out here, by you or anybody else, I'm coming back to put a bullet in your head. Okay?"

Marty nods.

Rider 1 saddles up and the bikes roll through the open door, engines throbbing in low gear.

———

IN THE Wynn's security command center, three guards scan the ballroom feeds for the reported brawl, ignoring camera 17, which shows two motorcycles moving slowly down the Esplanade, past carousel horses covered in flowers and through a grove of bare trees wrapped in strings of lights. Guests stop and turn; parents hurry children into stores. A knot of college kids whip out their phones and snap pictures while two New York publicists guess that this is a PR stunt, some kind of viral marketing campaign in which the whimsical, colorful world of the Wynn is thrown into sharp relief by racing bikes and riders in black leather. No one dials 911.

JEREMY DUNCAN has always been a little different. Tall for a fifth-grader, he walks with shoulders hunched and eyes fixed through thick glasses on his Velcro sneakers, which his mother buys him to assuage a crippling fear that his shoelaces will come undone at the worst possible moment. Jeremy loved fire trucks until he discovered that their job is to extinguish fires, not to start them. These days he's into motorcycles, and spends hours clicking through old superbike races on YouTube. He loves watching a pack of riders fly into a turn and lay their bikes down so far that their knees scrape the track. Jeremy loves motorcycles. He's also terrified of them. When his father lifted him onto a Vespa parked outside their local Safeway, Jeremy jumped off so fast that he cut his elbow and ripped his favorite sweatpants with the blue stripes down the sides.

The Duncan family is heading to an early dinner at the Wynn Buffet when engine noise becomes audible over the Esplanade's smooth jazz soundtrack. Jeremy lights up at the sound. His dad says motorcycles aren't allowed inside, but Jeremy knows an exposed inline four-cylinder engine when he hears one. His mom says he can run ahead and see, but just around the corner and no farther, which is fine with Jeremy. Around the corner is exactly where the sound is coming from. As Jeremy vanishes into the crowd, Andrea Duncan puts a hand on her husband's arm.

"Kyle," she says, "why is everyone running this way?"

CYNTHIA IS showing Anna a pale pink princess-cut stone when two motorcycles pull up outside Graff. The men on back dismount, remove their packs, and shift their automatic weapons to their hips. In comes Rider 1, telling everyone to put their hands up and lie facedown on the floor. The voice is male and the helmet makes it sound as if he's shouting at them from another room. With a flick of the wrist, Rider 3 unleashes an expandable baton and whips it into the rib cage of Rashad Lyons, Graff's armed guard. While a writhing Rashad is disarmed and zip-tied, Rider 1 scans the store and stops on Cynthia, who knows exactly why he's here.

The package arrived this morning with an armed escort. Cynthia signed for the delivery, which is how she knows the single item was insured for seven million dollars. The guards showed her the necklace before they placed it in the safe: a cascade of white and Champagne diamonds with a twenty-carat pear-shaped stone hanging at the bottom like ripe fruit. The piece was shipped in from the Paris store, a birthday gift for the second wife of a Shanghai developer. Li Jianrong insisted on an in-store pickup because his new bride, who grew up in Zhejiang Province without running water, loves shopping almost as much as the things she buys. Mr. Jianrong likes privacy and anonymity, but he's making an exception here. The armed delivery and in-store guard are on his tab. Another guard is due at 6 p.m. to transport the necklace to the happy couple's suite, which won't be necessary now.

Cynthia is shaking. Rider 1 spins her gently and steers her toward a mirror-paneled door that leads to the stock room, one gloved hand on his gun, the other on the back of her neck. Cynthia unlocks the door and goes straight for the safe, a head-high custom piece in green and gold. She knows the combination like her date of birth, but somehow gets it wrong.

She whispers, "I'm so sorry."

"Relax," the man says. "Breathe."

She's retrying when his hand moves from her neck to her arm. Cynthia whimpers and shuts her eyes, but then the man gives her shoulder an encouraging squeeze. It's almost enough to make her turn around. She gets the combination right this time. The steel bolts in the door retract, and Rider 1 brushes her aside. Out comes the necklace and the tray below it, which contains thirty-six diamond rings arranged by color and weight. Cynthia sees the neat rows in her mind's eye as the rings rain down into the bag. Outside in the showroom, glass display cases shatter at five-second intervals. The buzz of a zipper is followed by the creak of leather as Rider 1 exits the stock room. Cynthia sits down beside the gaping safe. She'll stay here until the cavalry arrives. She can still feel the man's hand on her arm.

WHEN JEREMY sees something that excites him, he takes a video with the iPhone he got for his tenth birthday. The behavioral therapist at Lakeview Montessori says Jeremy does this to create distance between himself and things that over-stimulate him. Jeremy's phone is out when he spots the two modified 1200cc racing bikes with matte-black gas tanks and thick Michelin Commander tires that sit—and this thrills Jeremy the most—on the big red rug outside a jewelry store. He hears his mother yelling but feels certain she would drag him backward by the collar if anything was really wrong. All he wants is a good look at the aftermarket front suspensions. He stops ten feet away, as close as he'll get to a live engine, and hits record three times with his trembling thumb before the red dot on the screen begins to flash. The riders don't seem to mind. And then they do. They turn to him in unison, and Jeremy can feel their eyes burning into him from behind the tinted visors. His mother has gone silent. Jeremy stares at the image on his screen and sees the guns for the first time.

SHANNON JACOBSON is finally poolside, dancing with a college kid who introduced himself by asking for a lighter. They shared a laugh when he relit her cigarette with a white BIC from his pocket. He's clearly doing this for kicks, to scratch an itch for older women. Shannon doesn't mind. He's not obviously crazy and the kid can dance. The pressure of his hands on her back sends heat waves through her body as the drug kicks in. The opening DJ is wrapping up his set when two security guards almost mow down Shannon and her new friend as they sprint toward the exit.

"Hey!" college boy yells. "Get some fucking manners, pigs!"

SARA KOH is struggling to understand the woman on the line with 911. The call is coming from the Wynn. The caller is hysterical.

"Ma'am? Ma'am," Sara says, "I need you to speak slowly and tell me exactly what's happening, okay? Who has your son? Are they holding him hostage?"

"He's taking a video—right in front of them—my son is—they're on the motorcycles—and the other ones—they're robbing the store and—"

"Who is, ma'am? Is your son being robbed?"

"No, he's just—he's close—he's right next to them and they're with the other ones—the ones robbing the store. Are you sending help? Where are you? Where are the police?"

"Can you describe the men to me, ma'am? The police are on their way, I promise."

———

BYRON SHERMAN and Mark Janowski are the first guards on the scene. Initial reports have been confusing: a fight near the Margeaux Ballroom, a distress signal from Graff, some assholes using the Esplanade as a racetrack. Mark goes first through a growing crush of guests, then stops short and says, "Fuck me." Two riders strapped with compact assault rifles sit on racing bikes outside of Graff. Neither Mark nor Byron draws his sidearm. Guards with guns are mainly a deterrent here. In an armed-robbery scenario, their job is to get the perpetrators off the property as quickly and quietly as possible. Every poker chip, Swiss watch, and ounce of gold here is insured, and killing guests in a gunfight does not create value for the shareholders. Mark and Byron shepherd the gathering crowd away from Graff, pushing people into the surrounding stores and back the way they came, clearing the Esplanade.

"Holy shit," Mark says, as three women duck into Cartier for cover.

A kid is standing ten feet from the bikes, between the riders and the exit, filming with his phone. Three guards and two undercover cops arrive at a run, pistols pointed at the floor in front of them. Riders 2 and 4 raise their rifles.

JEREMY IS frozen. People scream behind him as the men on bikes bring up their guns. Another armed man in a helmet emerges from the store and, after a brief pause, walks straight toward Jeremy, reaching for the phone. And then, as if he willed it, the boy is swept up and yanked backward by his mother. Rider 1 misses the phone by inches. He turns on his heel, adjusts his backpack, and mounts up. Engines roar. Jeremy is still filming as the riders accelerate toward the exit, scattering the crowd. He captures the receding yell of the engines before his mother wrestles the phone from his hand.

———

WITH HIS keychain Swiss Army Knife, Brian Dalmore saws frantically at the zip tie that binds Marty Stetson's wrists. Engines scream inside the Esplanade, and Brian looks up as two bikes blow through the open door, their draft tugging at the polyester fabric of his shirt. A squad car and a SWAT truck come screeching around the left side of the landscaped center island as the riders make a sharp right turn and hit South Las Vegas Boulevard without touching their brakes.

THE CREW splits up. One bike rips around a ramp onto Spring Mountain Road while Riders 1 and 2 head north, using all three lanes and the shoulder. The glamour of the Strip fades quickly, name-brand resorts giving way to chintzy gift shops, liquor stores, and cheap hotels. A hundred yards ahead, two patrol cars block an intersection, bringing northbound traffic to a halt. Officers Pratt and Sullivan leave their vehicles, sprint between stopped cars, and fan out in the empty street, guns drawn, screaming for the riders to dismount and drop their weapons. The bike is twenty yards away and closing fast when Sullivan fires a shot that stiffens the right arm of the man behind the handlebars. The front wheel wobbles, and both officers dive for cover as Rider 2 locks up the rear wheel and sends the bike into a low-side skid. The men in the saddle are about to come unstuck when the motorcycle somehow rights itself, pulled up as if by invisible strings. Pratt and Sullivan scramble to their feet as the bike bangs up the curb of the center divider and shoots a gap between two palms. A quick ninety-degree turn brings the riders face-to-face with drivers stopped at a red light. The light turns green and horns blare as the bike flies straight into oncoming traffic. Rider 2 leans into a hard left turn that misses the front bumper of a Cadillac by inches. Half a mile later he turns right on Rancho Drive, weaves through a quiet residential neighborhood, then opens up the throttle one last time before releasing it completely. The bike coasts noiselessly for two blocks and turns into the driveway of a foreclosed ranch-style home. The garage door just misses Rider 1 as it comes down. A bald and bearded man, heavily muscled and tattooed, stands beside the silver pickup parked inside. Rider 1 dismounts and disappears into the house while Rider 2 rips off his helmet, eases the bike up a ramp into the truck bed, and lets it fall onto its side. The bald man spreads a fitted bedsheet over the motorcycle.

"Lose the leathers," he says.

"Mate, my arm's fucked."

The bald man unzips the racing suit and strips it to the waist, revealing a Kevlar vest and a deep gash in the shoulder from the bullet. The garage door jerks open as Rider 2 climbs into the truck, removes his vest, and starts the engine with his good hand. He backs down the driveway and speeds off.

Rider 1 is pacing in the empty living room, slapping the insides of his arms against his ribs like a swimmer on a starting block. The bald man grasps him by the shoulders, sits him on the low stone hearth, and takes a knee. One hand cups the rider's calf while the other unlaces the left boot, grips the heel, and frees the foot. He's gentle but purposeful, like a trainer tending to a thoroughbred after a race. Once both boots are off, the bald man reaches under Rider 1's jaw and unsnaps the chin strap. The helmet comes off easily, its pads slick with sweat.

"Everyone's home safe," the bald man says as he helps Rider 1 to his feet. "Let's hit the road. I want to beat the traffic."

REBECCA RYAN, the LVMPD's forensic photographer, is on her knees in the Graff boutique when she spots the ring, a dome of pavé diamonds buried under bits of broken glass.

"Looks like they missed one," she tells Detective Hector Ramirez, standing up to show her camera screen. "That's, what? A fifty-thousand-dollar screw-up?"

"It's a rounding error on this haul," Ramirez says. "Can you ask Jon to bag that up?"

Ramirez is an amateur middleweight boxer, compact and athletic, his black hair slicked back above a boyishly handsome face that still gets him carded at the age of thirty-six. In a sharply tailored navy sports coat, bright white shirt, and polished loafers, he could be a Graff customer if not for the badge and gun. He pretends not to notice Special Agent David Harris of the FBI's Las Vegas field office as the stocky silver-haired man unbuttons his ill-fitting tan suit jacket to duck under the crime scene tape that blocks the door.

"Christmas in July," Harris says as he approaches.

Ramirez looks up from his notebook. "Not bad for three minutes of work. You're Agent Harris?"

"Call me Dave."

Ramirez knows the FBI has jurisdiction in a case likely to cross state lines and international waters. As head of the LVMPD robbery squad, he'll assist with an investigation led by Harris, who ran the bureau's Jewelry & Gem Theft program before transferring to Vegas. Ramirez knows the man by reputation: a formidable investigator and, in the words of another detective, kind of a dick.

"Do we have a number?" Harris asks.

"Someone's doing inventory now. The assistant manager says twenty million on the low end."

"Am I correct in thinking that's a record for this town?"

"I fucking hope so," Ramirez says.

"Is there an injured list?"

"The Graff guard has a few cracked ribs but he'll be fine."

"Where are we with the traffic cameras?"

"Someone took out two cameras on Sahara Avenue ten minutes before these guys showed up."

"Took them out?"

"Sorry, shot them out. From the back seat of a black Yukon with no plates. Small-caliber rifle, probably a .22."

"And they used Sahara to get on and off the Strip."

"Correct."

"So we have no idea where these guys went. Or came from."

Ramirez shakes his head.

"Four men on bikes with automatic weapons materialize outside a casino and disappear into thin air."

"We're double-checking everything," Ramirez says. "But yeah, the headline writes itself. Looks like they called in a bullshit 413 to draw our guys downtown. Two calls, both from burner phones."

"What about this kid who filmed them?"

"He's pretty shaken up. The parents turned the phone over, but the father sent the video to at least three people."

"Do you have a copy or should we watch it on YouTube?"

Ramirez pulls the video up on his phone.

"Wired for sound inside those helmets," he says, as Riders 2 and 4 spot Jeremy for the first time. "No one heard them say a word, but watch the head movement. They're discussing what to do about this kid."

"Did anybody hear them talk?" Harris asks.

"The girl who opened the safe said the tall one sounded American, but the helmet made it hard to hear. And she was scared shitless. Still is."

"Odds that she was in on it?"

"We're looking into her. I'd say zero if I had to lay a paycheck on it."

When Rider 1 emerges from the store and walks toward Jeremy, Harris presses pause.

"One thing I'd lay a paycheck on," he says. "This guy right here's in charge."

AT 7:25 P.M., Shannon stands outside The Griffin, an old-school cocktail bar downtown. She came here with college boy and his friends when the pool party ended early due to an incident next door. People gathered on the sidewalk where word of the robbery rippled through the crowd. Strangers huddled and gossiped, drawn to each other as if they'd flown through a lightning storm and landed safely. No one wanted to go home so Shannon suggested The Griffin, where college boy ordered a round of Irish car bombs. As she dropped a shot into her pint of Guinness, Shannon decided on an Irish goodbye. When her new friend hit the men's room, she slipped out the door.

The Ecstasy hasn't quite worn off, and Shannon craves the heat and pressure of a body against hers. She scrolls through her texts, weighing several friends with benefits before messaging a tall and much younger Australian who her friends call Captain Kangaroo behind his back. He's rough around the edges—questionable manners, bad haircut, worse tattoos—but handsome enough, cut like a classical sculpture, and remarkably good at going down on her, which is the deciding factor tonight. Behind her, a bouncer discusses the robbery with a bachelor party from Seattle.

"Unreal," one man says. "Fuckin' Wild West out here."

Shannon smiles to herself and lights a cigarette. Captain Kangaroo is not a great communicator, but minutes later he responds to her *hey mister* with *hey what's up w u?* He's watching the game at a mate's place, he says. Does he want to watch at hers? He does. He can be there in an hour. Shannon hails a cab.

Craig Hollinger knocks on the door to her condo ninety minutes later, helmet in one hand, sweating bottle of Champagne in the other.

"Wow," she says as she accepts the wine. "Are we celebrating?"

"Why not, right?"

"I like it. Come inside."

In the kitchen, she takes two wineglasses from the dishwasher and rinses them out in the sink.

"Do you want to put the game on?" Shannon asks.

"The game?"

"The one you were watching."

"That's all right. Reckon it's over now."

"Guess where I was earlier."

"On the golf course."

"No, silly," Shannon says. "At the Wynn."

"Yeah? Did you win big?"

"Did you not hear what happened?"

Craig shakes his head.

"These guys on motorcycles robbed the place. Made me think of you, actually. You and your big fast bike."

"Robbed the cashier?"

"No, they rode into the Esplanade and cleaned out Graff."

"What's Graff?"

"Obnoxiously expensive jewelry. Stuff you should buy the women in your life when you get your act together."

Craig smiles. "How'd they ride out after they robbed the place? Someone hold the door for them?"

"I don't know," Shannon says. "They did, though. It's all over the news."

"That," he says, pressing his body against hers, "sounds like a bullshit rumor."

Shannon pushes him away and peels the foil off the cork.

"Take your coat off," she says. "Stay a while."

Craig gingerly removes his jacket, wincing as he frees his right arm from the sleeve. Even the loose waffled cotton of a long-sleeve Henley can't hide his swollen, bandaged shoulder.

"Holy shit," she says. "What happened?"

"Took a bad spill at the track this morning," Craig says. "Nothing serious."

"Are you sure it's not broken?"

"Broken? Nah. It's just a bump."

"You should be icing it."

She's halfway to the fridge when her phone buzzes with a text.

"There's a video," she says. "Of the robbery. My friend just sent it to me. Are you ready to be wrong?"

"You want to watch that now?"

"Definitely," Shannon says. "Don't you?"

She holds her phone between them. On-screen, a local news anchor is shuffling his papers between segments.

". . . and the ranchers say they're looking forward to their day in court. Finally this evening, we have exclusive body-camera footage from the officers who confronted a pair of thieves near the Wynn hotel and casino after four armed men made off with an estimated twenty-two million dollars in jewels earlier today. Take a look."

The body cam is trained on East Sahara Avenue through the windshield of a cop car. A call comes in over the radio, and Officer Sullivan jumps out of the vehicle and sprints between two lanes of stopped traffic, his pistol pointed down the Strip.

"Told you," Shannon says, as the bike comes into view.

The image jerks when Sullivan fires his gun. The man behind the handlebars is obviously hit, and the scene blurs as the two officers dive for cover.

"The LVMPD is asking anyone with information about the suspects you just saw to call the number on your screen," the anchor says.

The clips ends. Craig and Shannon stand side by side, staring down at the still image on her phone. The tension feels like rising water. Shannon slips the phone into her pocket, slides her hands over Craig's hips, and presses her nose into the tendons of his neck. She's shocked but not offended to learn that he's mixed up in this. For her own safety, she needs Craig to know she doesn't care.

"I lost four hundred bucks at blackjack last time I was at the Wynn," she whispers. "And the service sucks. Let me see your arm."

Craig takes off his shirt and peels back a corner of the bandage.

"Jesus," Shannon says, "how'd you get stitched up so fast?"

"These boys had a doctor standing by." Craig tilts her head

back with a finger underneath her chin, looks down into her eyes, and says, "This never happened."

"What never happened?" Shannon asks with a coy smile.

When he opens his mouth, she covers it with hers. Craig grabs the hem of her shirt with his good arm and Shannon raises her hands as he pulls it over her head.

One

A small suburban gathering, six cars parked in the gravel drive-way of a large brick home. Alex Cassidy is the last to arrive. The monthly invitation gives a start time of 8 p.m., but the hour before the main event has become the kind of freewheeling social occasion that Alex avoids. At 7:56 p.m., he parks his late-model Volvo station wagon across the street and sits, listening to talk radio. A chance of thundershowers tonight, apparently. Alex makes a fist with his left hand. His wrist aches where the bone broke years ago, a childhood injury that sometimes feels this way before a storm.

The July air is thick with humidity and the buzzing of cicadas. Alex recognizes all the cars parked in the drive except a freshly waxed white Mercedes truck with Pennsylvania plates. He scans the house as he crosses the street and peers through the driver's window of the Mercedes: file folders, tangled cell phone chargers, packs of gum. Stuck to the rear window is a platinum Policemen's Benevolent Association badge, the kind reserved for friends and family, husbands and wives.

Dr. Mallory answers the door himself.

"Mister Punctuality," he says, opening his arms. "Come in, come in."

At six-foot-three, Alex stands a full head taller than his host. Their embrace is awkward but customary; the two men share a history that leads Dr. Mallory to believe there are no secrets between them. Alex follows the doctor to the sunken great room, a recent addition to the Civil War–era Colonial, its walls covered in books and abstract paintings. Tall windows look out on Lake Carnegie, but tonight the blinds have all been pulled.

The other guests are seated on low sofas around a marble coffee table. Mark Willard, a local money manager, salutes as Alex enters. Next to Mark is Dr. Raymond Klein, an orthopedic surgeon at Princeton Medical Center, where Dr. Mallory is head of anesthesiology. The driver of the white Mercedes sits alone on an ottoman.

"Alex," Dr. Mallory says, "this is Ralph Imperato, orthopedic sales rep at the hospital—artificial hips and knees."

This does not explain the PBA medallion or put Alex at ease. Ralph wears polished loafers, dark jeans, and an untucked purple dress shirt—an outfit for entertaining surgeons at Manhattan nightclubs. If Ralph came to party, Alex thinks, he's in for a surprise. Ralph looks Alex up and down as they shake hands, taking in the paint-flecked chinos, denim shirt, and canvas high tops—clothes for yard work, errands. No fancy watch, no wedding ring. Ralph wears both, but this is Princeton, where families with historic fortunes keep their clothes and cars for decades, shop at Costco, raise chickens in their yards.

"Hey, nice to meet you," Ralph says. "And what do you do, Alex?"

"Events," Alex says. "Event production."

Before Ralph can dig further, Alice Mallory emerges from the kitchen with a silver tea tray in her hands.

"Mr. Cassidy," she says, smiling warmly as she sets the tray down on coffee table. "I was wondering if we'd see you."

"Wouldn't miss it," Alex says.

Ralph is transfixed by the tray. "So, what does this feel like?" he asks.

"It's like a freight train, at first," Dr. Klein says. "Knocks you right on your ass. That's when things get interesting."

He's interrupted by the doorbell. Alex, it turns out, was not the last arrival. Alice disappears down the hallway and returns with a woman on her arm—trim and tan, her dirty-blond hair wet at the ends. White sneakers, white jeans with threadbare thighs, a faded navy Joy Division tee shirt. Her face is bare and beautiful.

"Sorry I'm late," she says. "Hope I didn't hold up the show."

"Not at all," the doctor says. "Everyone, this is our friend Diane."

Diane waves and smiles as she scans the room. When she spots Alex, she cocks her head and narrows her green eyes.

Dr. Mallory rolls up his sleeves and says, "Should we get started?"

Mark Willard, a man accustomed to going first, stands and unbuttons his suit pants. He wears baggy white briefs underneath, an unselfconscious choice that Alex admires. Mark resumes his seat, and Dr. Mallory kneels on the floor in front of him. Ralph watches intently as the doctor pulls on latex gloves and fills a short syringe from a small glass vial. His left hand steadies Mark's knee while his right hand holds the syringe like a dart. Mark winks at Ralph as the doctor sinks the needle into his thigh.

Ketamine is a dissociative anesthetic. Numbing and immobilizing, it's used for veterinary surgery, emergency field surgery, minor pediatric procedures. It's abused as a club drug for the vivid hallucinations and out-of-body experiences it induces in adults, but these psychedelic properties may have some therapeutic value. Dr. Mallory screens his guests for any history of mental illness but actively seeks people struggling with depression and anxiety for these get-togethers. Clinical trials suggest that ketamine can help where talk therapy and antidepressants have failed. The first time Alex tried the drug, the doctor warned him about "ego death," in which users watch their bodies dissipate, sometimes violently, and experience their consciousness as a pervasive, shape-shifting, and unconfined force. Dr. Mallory discovered the drug's off-label use during a period when he put a pistol in his mouth at least one night a week. These injections, he says, saved his marriage and his life.

Alex comes here for relief. Work-related stress has lately left him anxious, edgy, unable to sleep. Talk therapy is not an option, and every natural remedy he's tried has failed. Ketamine forces a perspective shift, uncomfortable at first but ultimately calming. The combination of hallucinations and paralysis reminds him that control is mostly an illusion, something Alex knows intuitively but would rather not believe.

Dr. Mallory wipes a spot on Diane's shoulder with an alcohol-soaked cotton swab while Dr. Klein administers the shot himself. Ralph asks about dosage and takes the needle in his right thigh, below the hem of his designer boxer briefs. Buckle up, Alex thinks. Finally, it's his turn.

"Ready?" Dr. Mallory asks with a friendly smile.

Alex drops his chinos and sits on the sofa. The doctor preps a mid-thigh patch of skin.

"Relax the muscle," Dr. Mallory says, pinching Alex's flesh like unripe fruit.

There's a satisfied twitch at the corner of Dr. Mallory's mouth when the needle breaks the skin, and Alex feels his muscle tremble as the doctor drives the plunger home.

"Hold that for me, please," Dr. Mallory says, nodding at the cotton ball under his thumb.

Alex stands and buckles his belt. The clock is ticking now. The other guests lie peacefully on large sheepskins and sections of sofa. Alex stretches out on the firm cushions of a beige leather sectional which, minutes later, seem to dissolve underneath him. He rides out a wave of nausea as his body leaves the sofa and begins to spin. The drug shoots through his system, numbing from the inside out. Alex turns his focus to his breathing, which creates colors against the backdrop of his eyelids— speckled, crackling neon green that deepens at the peak of every inhalation and turns to a rich and wavy blue as he exhales. The color fades like twilight, and Alex finds himself standing upright, staring at a distant point of light that grows into the head lamp of a huge steam-engine train. A wave of noise breaks over Alex: shovels clanging as men feed the fire, the hiss and heartbeat of the pistons, the shriek of wheels against the rails. His body shatters into atoms and becomes a cloud that splits in half around the train and re-forms as the final car goes flying past. The cloud retains a kind of body consciousness, but each particle has a mind of its own. A strong wind blows Alex's cloud-self across a dark and jagged landscape. The cloud descends and trails behind a figure walking toward the dark horizon. Alex recognizes the lean, long-haired young man instantly, even from behind. He tries to call out to his friend—dead now for more than twenty years—but his cloud-self has no voice, and so he follows, hovering, unable to make contact. The ground beneath him looks volcanic—black, brittle, hell with the fire burned out—but his friend is barefoot and in no apparent pain. Alex is about to overtake him when the scene before him liquefies and darkens like sugar over heat.

Two

It's late afternoon in Las Vegas, and Marvin Kowalski occupies his usual booth at the back of the Silver State Diner. Stray strands from his limp gray ponytail brush the chicken-fried steak on his plate, and a gold Rolex Daytona—worth more than his dented silver pickup parked outside—slides up and down his thin wrist as he eats. Marvin owned a string of pawnshops until his license was revoked. He waves reluctantly as Harris and Ramirez come through the door.

"Marvin, you look like a hundred bucks, as usual," Ramirez says as he slides into the booth. "This is Dave Harris from the FBI. Dave, Marvin here is the Odell Beckham of receiving stolen goods."

"Was," Marvin says. "Now I'm just a helpful citizen."

Harris shakes his hand, all business, unamused.

"Lemme guess what this is about," Marvin says.

Ramirez clicks his tongue. "Make our lives easy, Marvin. Who was underneath those helmets?"

"Sure, I got their names and addresses right here. Come on, man." Marvin swipes a slice of meat through a streak of white gravy, shoves it in his mouth, and continues talking through it. "Those boys weren't from around here and they're long gone and you know it. That crazy-ass necklace is sitting in some sultan's third wife's panty drawer right now. Which you also know, if you called in the feds."

"You see the video?" Ramirez asks.

Marvin nods and takes a sip of his spiked coffee.

"Anything stand out?"

"You're looking for the Sundance Kid and his superbike-racing friends."

"Marvin," Ramirez says, "how long have we known each other, huh? Don't embarrass me in front of Agent Harris here. Why do I feel like you're holding out on us?"

Marvin stabs a piece of carrot, chews, and swallows. "You interrupt my dinner with Special Agent So-and-So and no one thinks to mention a federal penny for my thoughts?"

"Consider it mentioned," Harris says.

"How closely are you looking at the Chinese guy?"

Harris glances at Ramirez.

"Sorry," Marvin says, "should I pretend I only know stuff from the news? Come on, guys. The developer from Shanghai, the one who bought the necklace."

"The victim?" Ramirez asks. "Li Jianrong? He's gearing up to sue everyone from Steve Wynn to Laurence Graff. He's out seven million dollars. What's in it for him?"

"Are you telling me that fucking thing wasn't insured?"

Ramirez shakes his head. "No, sir. Bought and paid for when the store got hit. His insurance would have covered it at home, but not out here. If a client wants to make a pickup like that, the piece is their responsibility. Hence the armed delivery and the armed guard in the store, both of which he paid for. Thought he had his bases covered. Not so much."

"Holy shit," Marvin says. "That I did not know."

"Why'd you ask about the Chinese guy?" Harris says.

"I heard he's dirty."

"You don't make a mint in real estate over there without a couple bodies buried in the yard," Ramirez says. "But dirty how?"

"Listen, this came through the grapevine, so take it with a grain of salt, but word is he's into more than real estate. My buddy knows a guy who takes care of the high rollers from Shanghai when they're here. Houses, girls, security, what have you. These guys all know each other. And they talk."

"Could we talk to this friend of a friend?" Ramirez asks.

"Not if he can help it. His whole book is built on keeping his mouth shut. These guys find out he's talking to the feds and he'll be pouring coffee for us next time we sit down."

"Can you talk to him?" Harris asks.

"We're talking federal helper's funding, right? Not some LVMPD bullshit petty cash?"

"If you've got the goods," Harris says.

"In that case, I'll see what I can do."

"You think he got hit because of something else he's into?"

"Who knows, right?" Marvin says. "You get into something dirty on the side and pretty soon you're in up to your ears. Seen that shit a million times."

Three

Alex comes to before the others. His limbs are numb and non-responsive, but he manages to lift his head and finds his vision marred by floaters and waves of fun-house-mirror distortion. The room rocks gently as if the house set sail while he was under. Alex feels like he was out for days, but according to the mantel clock it's been exactly forty minutes since he closed his eyes. Dr. and Mrs. Mallory sit side by side in armchairs, their heads encased in matching motorcycle helmets fitted with ear-pieces and microphones. They take a lower dose and talk each other through their trips, a form of psychedelic couples therapy that Dr. Mallory hopes to practice after he retires. Her head turns slightly toward him and his arm twitches, as if in response. Alex has often wondered what they say to each other, but has never found the opportunity to ask.

The other guests come down over the next few minutes, blinking and stretching, unsteady on their feet; the Mallorys remove their helmets. Alice busses the tray of used needles and returns from the kitchen with a platter of red grapes, French bread, and cheese while Ralph describes his first impressions of the drug to the doctor, who takes notes on a legal pad. Dr. Klein, recently divorced and always on the prowl, moves next to Diane for a hushed conversation. Alex, who can still see his dead friend walking through a barren landscape, is in no mood for small talk. He flips through an art book from the coffee table and watches the clock on the wall.

House rules state that no one drives for ninety minutes after an injection and even then departure is contingent on a motor-skill examination that Dr. Mallory administers himself. Alex returns from the bathroom and discovers that Diane has somehow managed to leave early. The doctor catches him scanning the room and assumes he's ready to go.

"Let's get you on the road," he says, leading Alex to the entryway. "Walk to me in a straight line, toe-to-toe."

Alex takes pleasure in the roadside sobriety test and return of motor function. He passes with flying colors and says his good-byes. A silver Accord is parked behind his car, and Diane leans against the driver's door, bathed in the soft glow of a streetlight with a cigarette between her fingers. She blinks rapidly as he approaches, and Alex wonders if she's fluttering her eyelashes flirtatiously or struggling to focus from the drug. He smiles at her as he fishes for his keys.

"You pass the test?" she asks.

"Yes, ma'am."

"I think I need a minute. I definitely need some air."

She looks steady and collected, but Alex knows that looks can be deceiving. He's staring at the smoke curling slowly from her cigarette when she says, "Is it bothering you?"

"Not at all."

"Do you want one?"

"I'm okay, but thank you."

"Smart. Your body is a temple."

Alex smiles. "Just a tool. How do you know the Mallorys?"

"I catered their youngest daughter's wedding. Alice and I go way back. You?"

"I got pretty banged up a few years ago and he knocked me out before they put me back together. We got to talking, became friends."

"They're one of my favorite couples. Maybe they're onto something with that motorcycle helmet thing."

"I've always wondered what they say to each other," Alex says.

"Well, you've come to the right place. I asked Alice, because I'm nosy. They describe what they see to each other and eventually the images line up. They have the same hallucinations, the same visions. They get into each other's heads."

"That sounds pretty heavy," Alex says.

"Only if you're hiding something."

"Who isn't?"

"Me," Diane says. "But I know what you mean. I saw some strange things tonight."

"Me too," Alex says. "How'd you end up here?"

"I told Alice I was feeling kind of stuck. She told me about this. What brings you here?"

"Decompression," Alex says. "How do you feel now? Unstuck?"

"I don't know what I'm feeling, to be honest with you. Sorry, this is driving me crazy—where do I know you from?"

"I don't know," Alex says.

"Do you live in Princeton?"

"New York, mostly. I have a place across the river in Bucks County."

"I swear I've seen you somewhere."

"I used to teach in Princeton on the weekends."

"At the university?"

"No, the YMCA."

"I swim there. Maybe that's it. I didn't catch your name."

"I'm Alex. Nice to meet you. Or see you. It's Diane, right?"

"It is. What did you teach at the Y?"

"Martial arts."

"Stuff to use when strangers corner you while walking to your car?"

Alex laughs and studies her face. Does he recognize her or is it the power of suggestion?

"Don't worry," she says. "I won't come any closer."

"No?"

"Because I'm going back inside. I own the catering company and the market on Witherspoon. Come in sometime."

As she crosses the lawn toward the house, he resists a strong urge to follow. Diane turns and waves to him from the doorstep, and Alex raises his right hand as she disappears inside.

Four

"Honey. Dave. David, wake up." Angela Harris kicks her husband underneath the covers. "Dave, for chrissake."

Agent Harris wakes up with a snort. "Hey, what is it?"

"Someone's calling," his wife says, covering her head with a pillow.

Harris clears his throat as he fumbles for the buzzing phone on his nightstand. 3:42 a.m. The call is from Ramirez.

"Hello?"

"Dave, it's Hector."

"Good morning."

"Same to you. Narcotics brought in this Australian kid an hour ago. Tried to buy a kilo of blow for the low, low price of twenty grand from one of our guys."

"Hang on a second," Harris says as he walks into the hall. "Twenty grand is robbery, but why'd they bring you in?"

"This young man says he knows who hit the Wynn."

"Did you tell him to take a number?"

"That's exactly what I said when they woke me up. But guess where this kid works."

"Tiffany?"

"Sin City Motorsports on I-15."

"I'm not familiar."

"It's a racetrack by the Air Force Base. He's an instructor. Teaches motorcycle racing."

"Did someone run that down?"

"He's all over their website. Kid was some kind of motocross champ back home."

"And he's saying what about the Wynn?"

"Nothing except that he wants to talk to whoever's running the investigation, whoever can cut him a deal."

"He won't talk to you?"

"Said he knows the feds took this one."

"Did he ask for a lawyer?"

"Not yet, no."

"What's your feeling?"

"He doesn't seem to give a shit about the drug charge, I can tell you that. Must have something up his sleeve."

Harris rubs his eyes and says, "I'll be right there."

By the time he gets down to the precinct, word is out, and every cop on duty is cruising by the interrogation room for a look at Craig Hollinger—a square-jawed, blue-eyed twenty-something in ripped jeans and a red Ducati tee shirt, his short blond hair slicked up into something like a shark fin. The left side of his face is scratched and swollen from a collision with the sidewalk on Freemont Street, Craig's reward for ambitiously resisting arrest.

"All yours," Ramirez says.

Harris downs the dregs of his coffee and straightens his tie before entering the room.

"Hi, Craig. I'm Agent Harris with the FBI. How are we this morning?"

"You're on the Wynn case, yeah?"

"Correct."

Craig pulls up the sleeve of his tee shirt to show off the deep gash in his shoulder, two stripes of swollen skin crisscrossed with stitches. Harris does not require further explanation. He's watched the tape a hundred times.

"That's who I am, mate," Craig says. "I'll take that lawyer now."

Five

Rain from a late-morning shower steams off the streets as Diane turns onto the road that separates Princeton's gated, Gothic campus from the quaint college town. She's a fast but conscientious driver, signaling before every turn and lane change, never on her phone. She left home at 10:35 a.m., three hours after Alex parked across the street in a green Jeep Cherokee—his other car, the one she hasn't seen—and listened to a biography of J. Edgar Hoover on CD. Her first stop was FedEx, followed by a nail salon. She's headed south now, unaware that Alex has been no more than three cars behind her all day.

After leaving the Mallorys' last night, Alex sat at the kitchen table of his house in Pennsylvania, where he opened his laptop and a bottle of red wine. He found Diane easily online. The bio on her company's website told him only that she's a New Jersey native who's worked in catering for over two decades and enjoys the ocean, classic rock, and cooking for friends. Her social media presence is mostly photos from events she's catered—elaborate raw bars, wedding cakes, a whole pig roasting on a spit. After two pages of relevant search results, Alex found himself staring at other Diane Alisons from around the country, a sorority sister from the University of Oklahoma, an elderly legal assistant from Des Moines. The dearth of information on the woman he just met raised his suspicions and meant that observation was required. He's done this before. As a former colleague pointed out, you can learn more in six hours of surveillance than six weeks of dating. He suspects Diane is who she says she is, but can't write off a chance encounter in which someone claims to recognize him.

Two miles outside town, she takes the on-ramp for US 1 South toward Hamilton and Trenton, exits south on Market Street and, to Alex's relief, passes the courthouse and the criminal justice building without touching her brakes. Two miles later, she turns into the parking lot of a Chinese restaurant. Alex pulls into the lot across the street and finds an empty spot facing the restaurant's door. A quick search on his phone reveals that Szechuan House offers takeout, which means he can't use the bathroom of the thrift store behind him in case Diane is picking up her food. They're five minutes from the courthouse, which makes Alex wonder if she's meeting someone here. And then he spots her through the window, alone at a corner table, scrolling through her phone. Alex skims the menu and a few online reviews; the restaurant is an under-the-radar critical darling, known for authentic Chengdu dishes, which explains why she came all this way for lunch. He wonders how Diane chose her profession, if catering is what she does. He's been wondering that about a lot of people lately. These days, the past two decades of his life seem to him like a long string of wrong paths and bad choices. It wasn't always like this. For years, Alex felt like the world's freest man, taking only jobs he wanted, unencumbered by a nine-to-five, content with solitude. The shift was sudden. He feels trapped inside his life in the same way he feels trapped inside his car this afternoon.

Diane's food arrives, and Alex wonders if she'd like company on these expeditions. Part of him wants to join her inside but lately he'd rather eat alone than start another rapport with half-truths and omissions. He's been putting up walls for so long that he feels unknowable. Alex reaches into the cooler at his feet and unwraps the BLT he packed for lunch. He washes the sandwich down with iced tea, pisses in the empty bottle, and settles in to wait.

Forty minutes later, Diane exits the restaurant, talking to

herself as she walks to her car. She's about to duck into the driver's seat when something across the street catches her eye. Alex freezes. Is she looking at him or beyond him? He can't be sure, and now she's coming toward him, pausing on the shoulder, waiting for an opportunity to cross. Turning his head to hide his face, Alex throws the car into reverse. Seconds later, Diane walks through his empty parking spot and disappears into the thrift store. He wonders, as he circles the block, if she shops here for aesthetic or financial reasons. Alex guesses that her income, like his, is sporadic. Is she struggling? He's been there, but not recently. Alex has spent the past decade in a position that few people can relate to: flush with cash but unable to deploy or even discuss it. There's money offshore and in the walls of his home, bricks of crisp bills bagged and boxed and buried in the yard. How could he explain that to someone like Diane, who exits the thrift shop with a stack of green glass plates in her hands.

She heads back the way she came and, two miles from Princeton, takes the exit for Cold Soil Road.

"There we go," Alex says as she turns onto Wargo Lane.

The road leads to a farm he visits every weekend in summer to collect his share of vegetables from the CSA. This, he tells himself, is where they've seen each other. When Diane turns down the dirt road to the farm stand, Alex keeps going.

Half a mile down the road, he doubles back. He won't approach her, not today. He'll collect his rainbow chard and plum tomatoes, which he had planned to do tomorrow. Alex parks as far as possible from her Accord, unlocks his glove box, and removes a CSA membership badge from underneath a loaded Glock 19.

He's bagging flat-leaf parsley when he hears his name. Diane stands behind him, head cocked, basket resting on her hip. Short denim cutoffs show her long tan legs and her forehead shines with sweat.

"Twice in two days?" she says. "Are you following me?"

"That's right," Alex says.

Her smile tells him that she sees some meaning in this second encounter. This is why Alex puts no stock in coincidence: It's either meaningless happenstance or part of someone's well-laid plan.

Diane points at the badge pinned to his tee shirt and says, "I thought the green ones were for weekend pickup?"

"I was in the neighborhood."

"So the rules don't apply to you?"

He balks at this, unsure if she's actually offended.

"Don't worry," she says. "I'm not a narc."

"Good to know. What should I do with all these leeks?"

"Cold soup with potatoes, frittatas. Anything you can do with onions, you can do with those."

"Another question for you," Alex says, surprising himself. "What are you doing tomorrow night?"

"I'm working all weekend. Are you asking me out?"

"I am."

"How's next week?"

"I'm out of town," he says. "Back Friday."

"When I'll be working again." She checks her phone. "What are you doing now?"

"Right now?"

"This afternoon. After you put that basket in your car."

"I hadn't gotten that far."

"Well, I'm free then if you'd like to do something."

"I'm free too, actually. What should we do?"

"Do you like wine?"

"I love wine," Alex says.

"There's a winery down the road that makes a decent Riesling, if you can believe that."

"I can't believe that, to be honest. But I don't mind being wrong."

"That's good, I like that in a man. You're completely wrong, by the way. Do you want to follow me?"

"Sure," Alex says. "I can do that."

In a renovated barn a few miles from the farm, Diane introduces him to the winemaker at Unionville Vineyards, a prematurely balding twentysomething whose face lit up like a struck match when she came through the door.

"Tim," Diane says, "my friend Alex has some doubts about the wines made in the Garden State. Can we show him the light?"

"We can try," Tim says. "I've got some white on ice back there. How does that sound?"

"Perfect," Diane says. "Can we take it to go and I'll give him the tour?"

Diane smiles knowingly at Alex as Tim ducks behind the bar and emerges with two glasses and a recorked bottle. He shakes his head when Alex reaches for his wallet.

"You're a sweetheart, Timmy," Diane says. "I'll bring the glasses back this time, I swear."

A rocky path runs up a low hill covered in vines, and Diane steals glances at Alex as they walk side by side. Flat chest, flat stomach, slim hips, no ass to speak of, intricately muscled calves and forearms. The backs of his large, strong hands face forward when he walks in a way that strikes Diane as faintly apelike. His grass-stained khaki shorts and worn gray tee shirt make her wonder what occupation allows him to dress for yard work two weekdays in a row.

In a clearing on the hilltop, a bench offers an unobstructed view of Hopewell Valley—a carpet of farmland, meandering developments, and woods. The distant rattle of a decelerating truck mixes with the hum of insects circulating in the plants. Diane uncorks the bottle with her teeth and fills their glasses.

"Cheers," she says.

Their eyes meet as their glasses touch. Alex swirls and smells the Riesling, swishes some around his mouth. His nerves are humming. This was not part of the plan.

"Wow," he says. "Not bad. Glad we didn't bet on that."

"I won't gloat."

"You can gloat."

"Not my style. You said you love wine. What do you drink when you're picking?"

Does he admit an obsession with cult French producers to a woman who shops at Trenton thrift stores and just introduced him to a drinkable New Jersey Riesling? Yes, Alex thinks. Don't hide unless you have to.

"I'm a big Burgundy fan," he says.

"My favorite region outside of Champagne. I have this fantasy where I move there and apprentice with some chain-smoking, leathery old-timer."

"I worked a harvest at Domaine Leflaive a while back."

"You're kidding. When was this?"

"Three, four years ago."

"What was that like?"

"I'd hang on to your fantasy. I washed a lot of bins and pulled a lot of weeds. It's not like you're tweaking blends with the winemaker."

"What were you doing in Burgundy?"

"I had some work in Europe. Went to the winery to decompress."

"Most people would just drink."

"I've tried that," Alex says. "It works until it doesn't."

Diane raises her glass to this. They're talking fast and drinking faster. The wine is going straight to his head, tilting his thoughts and tightening his skin. The light seems brighter than it did when they arrived, as if someone just turned up a dimmer on the sun.

"I went to this Szechuan place in Trenton for lunch," she says. "There's good Chinese food in central Jersey, in case you didn't know that either."

"I've read that," Alex says. "Is that your pre-day-drinking ritual?"

"I don't do a lot of day drinking. But then I don't pick up a lot of men at weird drug parties. You're a great influence so far."

"We can hit a yoga class after this. Catch a service at the Baptist church."

"Are you religious?"

"No."

"Married?"

Alex shakes his head. "I was, once. You?"

"Never married. One kid, though."

"Same here."

"Interesting. And where is he or she?"

"In Bogotá with her mother."

"How long were you together?"

"Two years. We were dating and along came Paola. Best thing that's happened to me by a mile, but not something we planned. Me and her mom decided to give it a go after we found out, which we both knew was a bad idea."

"I love the name Paola. How often do you see her?"

"Every few months. She visits, I go there. We go somewhere together every year."

"I make my son go somewhere with me every summer. Is that a single-parent thing? Mandatory parent-child family vacations?"

"I'll ask my single-parent support group. Your son lives here?"

"In Princeton, but not with me. Graduated from Rutgers, works for a wealth management firm in town. Very bright, extremely ambitious. No idea where he gets it. His dad was entrepreneurial, in a way. But never in the picture." She pauses with her glass halfway to her mouth, laughs softly, shakes her head. "Did we just discuss our failed relationships and unplanned children?"

"I try to save the small talk for the second date."

"Okay, but I feel like I'm asking all the questions. What do you want to know?"

He wants to know everything about her, but 20 Questions is a dangerous game for him. Alex searches for something he can answer easily and honestly if she turns it back on him.

"Are you from New Jersey?"

"Born and raised. Long Beach Island, mostly. Cape May, Spring Lake, Summit. I've lived all over. You?"

"Born in Miami," Alex says, omitting his childhood in Atlantic City in case it leads to a search for mutual acquaintances. "I've been in New York for about ten years."

"Why the house in Bucks County?"

"My mom's in a home not far from there. I bought the place for her, but she took a turn before she could move in."

"Sorry to hear that. Should we try to solve the mystery?"

"What mystery?"

"Where we've seen each other. I don't think it was the Y. Or the farm."

He's more eager than she is to solve the mystery, but less eager to dig into his past, and so he lies to Diane for the first time and says, "I like the mystery, to be honest. It'll come to us."

"Okay," she says.

They sit there in the sunshine, taking in the view. Alex waits for the silence to become a burden, but the feeling never comes. Her phone buzzes with a text.

"Jesus," she says. "I almost forgot: I have to be in Princeton in an hour for a dinner party. I told the host I'd show up early and help out."

"Let's do this again sometime. We could even make a plan."

"Or you could come to dinner with me. Only if you want to. Be honest. You can say no."

He should say no, but her request for candor disarms him, and he does not want this to end.

"That sounds great," he says. "You sure it's okay?"

"I'm sure," she says, placing a call, "but let's ask anyway. You'll like these people. They're just boring enough to be— Hey,

Lindsay? It's me. Listen, can I bring someone tonight? Someone I met recently. Yes, very. At a thing at someone's house. Alex. What does he— Hang on a second." Diane lowers the phone. "What do you do for a living?"

"Events," Alex says, staring at her in disbelief. "Event production, mostly."

"That would not have been my first guess. Linds, did you catch that? Yeah, he's right here. Any— What?" She laughs. "That's good, I hadn't thought of that. Alex, are you a serial killer?"

"Only on weekends."

"Right, so we'll kick him out before midnight. Age? Lindsay says a five-year range is fine."

"I'm forty-one," he says.

"He's forty-one. Yes, agreed, a good age for a man. Wait, I have a question: What's your full name?"

Fuck, he thinks. Here goes. "Alex Duran Cassidy."

"Okay, Alex Duran Cassidy, forty-one, employed, not a serial killer—you're officially invited. Linds, if you think of anything else, just text me. He's very forthcoming. What can we bring? Bullshit. Fine, fine. See you soon." Diane hangs up. "Lindsay told me not to bring anything but we should grab some wine, and not from here. Her husband is an unenlightened snob, like you were."

"Poor guy," Alex says. "We'll get wine on the way. It's on me this time."

"I need to stop at home and change," she says. "I'm gonna politely suggest you do the same."

Alex has three days' worth of clothes in the go-bag in his trunk, which he decides not to mention to Diane. The dark jeans and white button-down in his duffel will do just fine. They agree to meet up in an hour at a wine shop, her favorite and also his. And then he's following her car again, squinting against the afternoon sun, almost certainly over the legal blood-alcohol limit, worried about the loaded handgun in the glove box of his car, running through their conversation on the hilltop and marveling that it only briefly touched on work. She's driving faster than he would if he were leading. But he's not, and he trusts her somehow, so he follows.

Six

Sierra Pacific Mortgage owns 327 Kirkland Avenue, where Craig claims he dropped Rider 1 after the Wynn job. The dilapidated ranch-style home has been vacant since the lender foreclosed eighteen months ago, and the two detectives Ramirez dispatched after Craig's early-morning confession found no signs of forced entry. A Sierra Pacific branch manager referred Harris to Silver State Realty, assuring him that no one from the mortgage company has set foot on the property, and that the listing agent, Heather Richards, has the only other set of keys. Harris had another special agent do some digging on her. She's thirty-six and bottle blond, a single mother with excellent credit and no criminal record besides a six-year-old DUI.

At 2:45 p.m. the receptionist at Silver State Realty informs Harris that Ms. Richards just stepped out for coffee. When Ramirez asks if she's expected back, the young man suggests they try a nearby Starbucks with a look that says he knows law enforcement when he sees it.

Heather exits the coffee shop in a white blouse and gray skirt as Harris and Ramirez round the corner. She stops abruptly when the two men block her path, tottering slightly on stiletto heels.

"Ms. Richards?" Ramirez says. "Detective Ramirez, LVMPD, and thi—"

"Oh my God," she says, raising one hand to her mouth while a large iced coffee lists dangerously in the other. "This is about the place on Kirkland, isn't it?"

"What makes you say that?" Harris asks after glancing at Ramirez.

"Listen, I don't know that guy and I have no idea what he was doing there, okay? I took his money, but that's it, I swear. I'll tell you everything I know. Please don't tell me it was kids."

"Kids?" Ramirez asks.

"In the video," Heather says. "They shot a video there, right? It wasn't children, was it?"

"We need to have a longer conversation," Ramirez says. "And not here on the sidewalk."

"Okay. Do I need a lawyer?"

"Did you break the law?" Harris asks.

"No. I mean, I'm not supposed to let people use a house to shoot a porno, obviously. My boss will fucking kill me if he finds out. I could lose my license and I cannot, *cannot* lose my license."

"Then come with us," Harris says. "Or we can all go have a conversation with your boss. Your call."

At the FBI field office on Lake Meade Boulevard, Harris offers Heather the chair across from his while Ramirez perches on a corner of the desk. Harris instructs her to start from the beginning, which she does after a long quaff of coffee.

"This guy calls me up about a month ago and asks about the Kirkland house. Said his name was Richard, Richard . . . something—I have it written down somewhere. First call I've had about the place. We agreed to meet there the next morning. I got there a few minutes early to make sure it was still standing, look around. He showed up right on time."

"Describe him for me," Harris says.

"Big guy, muscular, about your height. Bald under a baseball cap. Thick beard, brown with some gray in it," she says, echoing Craig's description of the man who booked him for the Wynn job. "And a gray suit, expensive looking. Never took off his sunglasses. Said he was some kind of investor, looking for investment properties, something like that."

"Did you see what kind of car he drove?" Harris asks.

"He didn't drive. I was waiting by the mailbox and he turned the corner and came walking down the block. I remember thinking that was weird. We went in, looked around. The place is empty, obviously. Not much to see. He asked a bunch of questions."

"Like?"

"How old were the appliances, any pest problems, did the garage doors work. He was really interested in the garage. He asked about the neighbors and I was like, What neighbors? Four houses on that block are vacant, nobody's around. He said everything looked great and could he come back with a colleague."

"And did he?"

Heather shakes her head. "We were about to leave when he said his friend was looking for a house just like this, and would I be interested in renting it out for an afternoon."

"For a video shoot."

"Yeah. The way he said it was like, you know, wink-wink, nudge-nudge. I told him he'd have to ask the mortgage broker about that. He asked if we could keep this between us. I knew right then I should have walked away."

Harris tents his fingers underneath his chin. "But you didn't."

"From that kind of money? I couldn't. Can't. I've got a six-year-old with hemophilia, okay? It didn't sound like he was breaking any laws."

"What happened then?"

"He took the keys and told me not to show the house until after the twenty-third. Promised to have the place professionally cleaned when they were done. Said if anything was out of place, which it wouldn't be, five grand should cover it. He had it on him. Cash."

"Did you hear from him again?"

Heather shakes her head. "I stopped by the day after to check on the place. Absolutely spotless. Reeked of bleach. I figured they were cleaning up after . . . you know, whatever."

"We need the number this guy called you from," Ramirez says.

"Good luck with that. When I called to say, hey, thanks for cleaning, I got one of those nonworking-number messages. That's when I got really worried. How bad was it?"

"Was what?" Harris asks.

"The video."

"There's no video."

"So . . . am I in trouble?"

"Probably not. We'll need a copy of those keys."

"Of course. Look, I'm sorry for . . . whatever." Then, after a pause, "I'm just glad it wasn't kiddie porn. That I couldn't live with."

"Fucking bleach," Ramirez says when Harris returns from walking Heather to the elevator. "So no prints, no DNA, no clothing fibers. I'll have the crime scene techs go over the whole place anyway."

"Why not," Harris says. "Let's waste everybody's time."

Seven

Two patrolmen stroll down Hulfish Street and nod solemnly at Alex, who stands outside the Princeton Corkscrew, waiting for Diane. As the officers round the corner, Alex spots her walking toward him in a navy floral dress, high heels, and light makeup. Two men, both accompanied by women, turn their heads to watch her pass in the space of half a block.

"Simple, classic," she says, looking Alex up and down. "Nicely done. Now pick some wine."

While Diane examines a rack of American Pinot Noirs, Alex grabs two bottles of his favorite white Burgundy and walks quickly to the register. He wants her to taste the wine but not to hear the clerk inform him that the total comes to $346.52, which Alex pays in cash.

"That was quick," Diane says from behind him. "What are we drinking?"

"Something French. I think you'll like it. Where to now?"

"It's walkable," she says. "Let's walk."

Diane threads her arm through his and describes their hosts as they navigate the crowded sidewalks, both of them still nicely buzzed, the low summer sun warming their flushed faces. Rory, the husband, edits a magazine Alex has heard of but never read. His wife, Lindsay, does PR for a chef with restaurants in New York, Las Vegas, and Macau. They bought a teardown, built a house, and moved from Brooklyn a year after their second daughter was born.

"Rory would have stayed in the city forever," Diane says,

"but Lindsay wasn't having it after she had kids, who usually get shipped off to their grandmother's when their parents entertain. Lindsay's a sweetheart but she knows exactly what she wants. Smart, funny, not above dancing on a table now and then. He's—well, you'll see."

"What does that mean?"

"If he likes you, you're the center of the universe. If not, he can't be bothered. Drives Lindsay crazy, but that's who he is. The other couple, Peter and Susan, I don't know as well. I want to say he's in marketing? She's English and makes these beautiful sunglasses, speaking of which," Diane says as she pulls a pair of round pearl-white frames from her purse. "They're a few years older than you, but you wouldn't know to look at them. I'm older than you, by the way. You know that, right?"

He knows how old she is from public records he looked up this morning, but lies to her a second time and says, "I didn't know that."

"I'm forty-six."

"Congratulations."

"Thank you. This is us on the right."

Alex has often wondered who lives at 236 Harrison, a sleek, modern cedar-sided home with large windows on a block of modest Cape Cods. Halfway up the wide slate steps, Diane catches his wrist, pulls him to her like a tango partner, and stands on her toes to kiss him on the mouth. The wine hangs awkwardly at his side as he runs his free hand up her neck and into her hair, growing instantly and uncomfortably hard under the stiff denim. Finally, she pulls away and pats him on the chest, cheeks flushed and eyes shining.

"Good show," she says. "Come on, we're late."

The muted chime of the doorbell is followed by the padding of feet. A pretty, smiling brunette with a mole at the corner of her mouth opens the double-height door and steps back into the arm of a barefoot man in chinos and an untucked white dress shirt. Behind them, sleek furniture in neutral tones is arrayed over the airy first floor of their house, bathed in natural light and accented by brightly colored children's toys tucked away in corners. Alex thinks: I should have been an editor, I have varied interests and a facility with language; can there be more to it than that? He's been having these small, silent personal crises every time he encounters a man whose life is orderly and prosperous and on the up-and-up.

"Hi, Rory," Diane says, as they embrace. "This is Alex."

"Thanks for coming," Rory says. "Always glad to—" His outstretched hand becomes a pointed finger as he squints at Alex. "Hey, I know you. I took a class from you."

"At the Y?" Diane asks.

"The Y? No, no, no," Rory says, snapping his fingers. "At Princeton Brazilian Jiu Jitsu."

"Since when do you do Jiu Jitsu?" Diane asks.

"One of my writers gave me a lesson as a Christmas gift a few years back. Way, way too intense for me. I thought Jiu Jitsu was like Tai Chi or capoeira or whatever. Someone almost snapped my arm off."

"And you teach there?" Lindsay says to Alex. "Diane said you did events."

"On weekends," Alex says. "When I'm not producing events, which, yes, is how I make a living."

Alex catches Diane staring at him as he's introduced to Peter, hale and blond with the lined eyes of a lifelong surfer, and Susan, his effusive, stylish British wife. He likes Diane even more against the backdrop of this crowd. There's something raw about her that these people—polished, processed, settled in their lives—are feeding on.

"Okay," Lindsay says, "I have three things on the stove I need to see to, but can I offer anyone a drink?"

"These gentlemen are gonna help me with the fire," Rory says.

In the yard behind the house, he lights the charcoal chimney while Peter pours a round of bourbon on the rocks.

"So, Alex," he says, "you teach martial arts for kicks?"

"I trained a lot when I was younger. Just a hobby these days. Teaching keeps it fresh."

"Diane has a thing for tough guys," Peter says. "Wasn't she seeing some kind of special agent a while back?"

Rory sips his drink and says, "I think he was a firearms instructor."

"Really," Alex says. "Interesting."

"Don't worry, friend," Rory says. "Very amicable split. He won't come gunning for you."

"Alex, what kind of events do you do?" Peter asks. "The company my agency works with is asleep at the wheel."

"The stuff I do is pretty niche, outdoorsy leadership training, extended retreats, that kind of thing. I'm out of cards, but give me yours before we leave. Rory, how long have you been at the magazine?"

His host describes the arc of his career: someone's assistant, no one's assistant, someone with their own assistant, corner office, *fin*. Peter runs a kind of corporate innovation lab tasked with getting Pepsi out of the sugar-water business, among other things. Alex listens to their tales of office politics, creative sabotage, and executive psychodrama—dispatches from another world. The sun sinks along with the whiskey in the bottle. The meat goes on the grill.

Dinner is a blur of crosstalk, silverware clatter, wine splashing into glasses. Napkins go from lily white to abstract canvases in vegetable ash, soy sauce marinade, and Côtes du Rhône.

"Holy fuck," Rory says, examining one of the bottles Alex brought. "Where did this come from?"

"Diane picked that out," Alex says.

"She shouldn't have, but thank you."

"You're a funny guy," Diane whispers to Alex. "Come help me with dessert."

At the marble kitchen island, he helps her plate the summer berries that she roasted briefly in the oven, their juices thick and

dark as blood. Alex whips a bowl of heavy cream while Diane
zests a lime into the slowly rising surface. At the table, Peter
holds forth on retail advertising.

"Listen, we sell women's jewelry to men the same way we sell
cat food to people," he says. "The person picking up the tab is
not the end consumer."

Diane steps lightly on Alex's toes and rolls her eyes. A little
thrill runs up his spine at her touch and the realization that the
two of them can be part of this world and also apart from it.
There can exist between them unspoken understandings, inside
jokes. Secrets, even. The idea gives him hope. She hands him
two plates but holds on when he grasps them by the rims and
pulls him in for a kiss—chin up, eyes wide, lips slightly parted.

Rory pours a rich vintage Champagne with dessert. And
then it's over. People push their chairs back from the table,
where everything is headed toward entropy—food cooling, ice
melting, sparkling water going flat. Alex is half-listening to war
stories from Peter's groundhog infestation when, at the head of
the table, Lindsay lights up.

"Diane, have you not seen it either? Peter, you must have
seen it."

"Seen what?" Peter asks.

"The video of those guys who rob a jewelry store on
motorcycles."

"Of course I've seen it," Peter says. "It's everywhere."

"Seriously," Lindsay says. "It has, like, a million views."

Diane turns to Alex. "Have you seen this?"

Alex hears himself say, "Yes."

He's frozen. He thinks: I walked into a setup like I walk
into my home. He sees it all in hindsight—the chance encounter, the accelerated intimacy, the invitation to a stranger's home.
He waits for the front and back door to come down in unison,
for gun barrels to shatter the windowpanes behind him. Alex
rests his hands flat on the tabletop to show that he's unarmed
and willing to go quietly. This is not the way he pictured it, but

he hasn't spent a lot of time envisioning the end. Lindsay is still going on about the video, and as the adrenaline ebbs, Alex sees that this is not a setup. It's dinner guests watching viral videos after dessert. This, he reminds himself, is something people do.

"We're watching it right now," Lindsay says. "Rory, where's your laptop?"

Her guests crowd around her with the exception of Alex, who stands back and slips his hands into his pockets. A pre-roll ad for Caesars Palace plays. The number of views is closer to two million now.

The sight of the Esplanade takes Alex straight back to Las Vegas. He feels the gun sling on his collarbone, smells the perfumed air, hears the sound of his own breath inside the helmet. He doesn't want to watch this, but can't bring himself to look away. On-screen, Craig adjusts his mirrors to monitor the corridor behind him while Roy Fletcher, their other driver, revs his engine to keep the crowd at bay. Alex's interest in the details evaporates when he sees the horror in Diane's face. He studies her profile while Lindsay narrates.

"I mean, this kid just walks right up to them and starts filming. Why?"

Because he's on the spectrum, Alex thinks. Because he loves motorcycles and motorcycles are the only thing he saw. Jeremy made all the papers and reminded Alex of himself at that age: skinny, awkward, likely friendless, slave to his compulsions. On-screen, Alex strides out of the store and turns to face his unwanted videographer. The breath that Jeremy sucks down is audible over the engines, jagged with fear.

"Oh my God," Diane says. "You're sure this is real?"

"Of course it's real," Lindsay says. "It's been on every news show. Okay, this part gives me chills."

Alex purses his lips as his gloved hand swipes at the camera. The image becomes a jumble as Jeremy is manhandled by his mother and, finally, it's over.

"How have they not caught these guys?" Peter asks.

"No idea," Lindsay says. "Rory would know. He's obsessed. He wants to do a story."

"I wish," Rory says. "The cops don't have a clue, from what I hear. Those dudes could be anywhere by now."

Alex excuses himself. Alone in the upstairs bathroom, he opens an end-to-end encrypted app and dials the man who helped him undress after the Wynn job. Three thousand miles away, a phone rings on the kitchen counter of a villa in Tulum, the beach town in Mexico's Mayan Riviera. Ben Kistler answers in a robe.

"It's me," Alex says.

"I gathered."

"That video is everywhere."

"It's good content. Exciting, authentic. People love that stuff. You sound concerned."

"You're not?"

"Has someone invented retroactive X-ray vision? You know what I see when I watch that video? Anonymous, rigorous execution. A well-oiled machine. I see no cause for concern. What makes you ask?"

"I'm at a dinner party," Alex says. "The host made everybody watch it with dessert."

"You need more interesting friends."

"I keep having this dream where I'm on the bike again. It doesn't end well."

"It ended just fine in reality."

"That kid was something else."

"Your Aussie rickshaw driver? Did I tell you he was plan C?"

"You know you didn't tell me that."

"Plan A passed. Plan B passed in the sense that he's no longer with us. That happened with three days to go."

"And you didn't think that was worth passing along?"

"You were locked in by the time this happened. I needed you to stay that way."

Alex laughs and shakes his head.

"So plan C really impressed you?" Ben asks. "His name is Craig, actually."

"He's shot, he's losing the front end. I thought it was over. 'Hang on, mate.' That's what he said right before he drifted the back wheel and jumped the median."

"'Hang on, mate.' I like that. I didn't like Craig when I met him."

"Why?"

"He's cocky," Ben says. "And young, even for twenty-two."

"Okay."

"Are you saying I shouldn't lose his number?"

"I wouldn't. I'd ride with him again."

"Noted. I'll let you get back to your YouTube club. Christian and I are going to a real party in a few minutes. He's yelling at me to get dressed."

"Have fun," Alex says.

"We will. Stay off the internet."

The table is empty when Alex comes downstairs. He joins the smoking circle on the deck but declines the joint that Peter offers him. Marijuana sends him into a tailspin of self-doubt and paranoia, and he's had his fill of both tonight.

The couples linger over goodbyes in the entryway, promising to find another date before the summer ends. Alex makes an empty promise to give Rory private lessons in Jiu Jitsu as he and Diane make their exit. Susan and Peter wave goodbye as they back down the drive.

"Where's your car?" Diane asks.

"In town, by the wine store."

"I'm on your way," she says. "Walk me home."

Eight

Alex makes no attempt at conversation as he and Diane walk arm in arm down the empty street. She smokes and leaves him to his thoughts, having seen this shyness in her son, who craves silence after time spent in crowds. Diane wonders if she was too forward in asking him to walk her home, but then Alex slips his hand into hers and smiles down at her.

"This is me," she says, stopping in front of a three-story Victorian. "Can I offer you a nightcap? Water?"

"I'll take both," Alex says.

The ground-floor apartment is hers, the kitchen perfumed by fat heirloom tomatoes ripening on a wooden butcher's block. Diane hits the lights and puts on music, a man singing in falsetto over an acoustic guitar.

"I'm craving an old-fashioned."

"That sounds great," Alex says.

She gathers ingredients with swift, practiced movements: simple syrup from the fridge, bourbon and bitters from a shelf beside the stove, two ice blocks from the freezer. Alex spots the thrift store plates on the counter and wonders if her silver-rimmed old-fashioned glasses came from the same place.

"Cheers," she says. "Did you remember Rory from your class?"

"No, but a lot of people come through that place. It's less intense than he made it sound."

"He's a storyteller. Lindsay always says you should divide by two when he's spinning a yarn. How's that drink?"

"Best I've had in this town."

"Would it kill someone to open a real cocktail bar?"

Alex stiffens at the sound of footsteps on the back porch, which Diane doesn't seem to hear.

"Are you expecting someone?"

"No," she says. "Of course not. Why?"

A crash from the back of the house is followed a muffled curse. Alex takes a step toward the magnetic knife rack by the stove, eyeing a large Chinese cleaver. Diane sets her drink on the counter, hesitant but unconcerned.

"That," she says, "is my son, who keeps his surfboards on my porch. Can I introduce you?"

"Of course," Alex says, wondering how many left turns a single day can take.

At the back door, Diane speaks her son's name into the darkness.

"Shit," he says. "You scared me. Did I wake you up?"

"I just got home. You scared me too. Come inside for a second, I want you to meet someone."

Tom Alison is still dressed for the office when he steps into the stairwell—polished wingtips, gray suit pants, white shirt open at the neck. He kisses his mother on the cheek, then runs a hand through his dark blond hair and strokes the patchy stubble on the smooth skin of his face. He's been drinking; Diane recognizes the loose smile and unfocused intensity in his eyes. Her sensitive, sarcastic, workaholic son.

"I'm meeting someone?" Tom asks. "Now?"

"We're in here," Diane says, taking his arm.

They find Alex immersed in the photos on the fridge: a portrait of Diane in her twenties with bleach-blond, teased-out hair; Tom at his first Little League game with a bat over his shoulder; Tom at his high school graduation. Alex looks up with a concerned, perplexed expression as Diane comes through the doorway, followed by her son. When Tom steps into the bright light of the kitchen, Alex's eyes go wide.

"Tom, this Alex Cassidy. Alex, my son, Tom."

"Nice to meet you," Alex says, shaking it off. "Sorry, you look just like this friend of mine."

"I get that a lot," Tom says.

"How was your night, honey?" Diane asks. "You look like you've been having fun."

"That makes three of us."

"Touché. Are you around tomorrow? Melanie invited us to brunch."

"The waves look decent tomorrow," Tom says, glancing suspiciously at Alex, who's still staring unabashedly. "Just came by to grab some boards."

"Rory was asking about you. He wants you to take his new assistant out next time you're in the city."

"When I have time to go out in the city, I'll let Rory know. Tomorrow's my first day off in months."

"Well, don't let us keep you," she says. "Thanks for stopping by."

"Good to meet you," Alex says.

Tom salutes and leaves by the back door. Alex drains half of his cocktail, palms his neck, and stares at Diane in silence as her son backs down the drive.

"What?" she asks. "Did I miss something?"

"You said Tom's dad was never in the picture. Why?"

"Why do you ask?"

"Because he died?"

"Wha— Why are you asking me that?"

"Died young? In a shooting?"

Diane flinches. "That's none of your business. Where is this coming from?"

"We met once before. Not at the Y. Or the farm. In Atlantic City."

"When was this?"

"We were kids. Dock's Oyster House. You left with my friend Clay."

Shock seems to ripple outward from the center of her face, parting her lips and widening her eyes. "Oh my God," she says.

Alex nods. A siren winds its way toward them and, having reached its destination, fades.

"You know what I remember about that night?" Diane says. "Besides meeting the father of my child? They made a good martini at that place. I thought you were from Miami."

"I was born there. We moved to Atlantic City when I was six."

"Which is how you know Clay. Did he tell you what happened, or did you figure that out when you saw my son?"

"Clay told me. And Tom looks exactly like him in those pictures."

"I know," she says, shaking her head. "It's scary, isn't it? I used to wonder if he got any of my genes."

"Clay told me you weren't keeping the baby."

"I wasn't. Then I got a call from a homicide detective in Manalapan."

"Detective Steven Rizzo," Alex says.

"You remember his name?"

"We had a lot of conversations. I remember everything about that week. How much does Tom know?"

"That he was an accident, and that Clay passed away. I told him it was a car crash, which is half-true. I think he knows."

"Knows what?"

"That I'm hiding something. That it's not a good story."

Alex considers this. He understands her reservations, but the secrecy strikes him as disservice to the memory of his friend.

"This goes without saying," Diane says, "but I will murder you if you breathe a word of this to him."

"No, of course not," Alex says, amazed at how easily she can read him.

"You and Clay were close."

He nods.

"You worked with him."

"I did."

"Were you there when it happened?"

"Just after," Alex says. "Not soon enough."

Diane studies a stain on the countertop, scrapes it with her thumbnail. "You should go," she says. "I don't think— I just need you to go."

"If that's what you want."

She nods without looking up.

"This feels like a stupid thing to say, but I had a great time with you."

"I know," she says.

Nine

The deer leaps from the roadside ditch into the road and freezes in the glare of Alex's high beams. As he waits for the startled animal to move, Alex replays the moment that Tom Alison stepped into his mother's kitchen. The kid has Clay's lean build, Clay's blue-gray eyes, Clay's tic of blinking frequently while listening. Clay told his best friend about the pregnancy and his attempts to talk the girl out of ending it. It never occurred to Alex that she'd keep the baby after Clay was gone until a young man with a shocking resemblance to his dead friend shook his hand and excused himself with talk of surfing in the morning, exactly as his father would have done.

Alex met Clay Dougherty on his first day at Texas Avenue School in Atlantic City. It was the Tuesday before Thanksgiving; cardboard Pilgrims and turkeys drawn from handprints lined the halls as the vice principal walked Alex to Mrs. Cook's first-grade class. Alex and his mother arrived in Atlantic City the week before, their battered Civic packed to the roof. They drove the 1,250 miles from Miami, stopping twice for food and gas and once to tape a garbage bag over the window Alex's father had smashed with a baseball bat as they pulled away. When Mrs. Cook asked Alex where his family had moved from, he looked down at his sneakers, which were half a size too small, and muttered something unintelligible.

"Sorry, sweetie, I didn't catch that," Mrs. Cook said. "Where did you live before this?"

"My mom told me I shouldn't talk about it," Alex said.

Mrs. Cook quickly moved on.

When it came time to pair the students up for a project, she introduced Alex to Clay Dougherty, a popular towheaded troublemaker who, she reasoned, could help the quiet newcomer make friends. Both boys loved Bruce Lee movies, Clay because his father was a boxer, and Alex because he longed to feel dangerous and fearless when confronted by bad men. Both boys came from troubled homes, but between their two families, they cobbled together a single semi-functional childhood experience. When Clay's parents fought, he packed a bag and holed up with Alex until the storm of breaking glass and shouted accusations passed. Hard nights at Alex's were more frequent. Lacey Cassidy was a cocktail waitress at the Tropicana. Seven, she decided, was old enough for her son to spend her shift alone in their apartment with the doors locked and the number of the hostess's stand on a Post-it by the phone. Lacey got off work at 4 a.m., and on a good night she was home by 4:15, but her post-shift cocktail often turned into an early morning on the town. If she wasn't home by 4:30, Alex knew not to expect her before sunrise. She almost always made it back to see him off to school, bursting into his room with minutes to spare, reeking of cigarettes and sometimes still smoking, carrying a buttered roll in a brown bag from the corner deli for his lunch. "You're awake!" she'd exclaim, as if he hadn't been awake all night, listening for her key in the lock. She'd help him dress, swaying slightly on stilettos as she picked out his clothes. Sometimes there would be a man waiting silently on the sofa. Alex avoided the living room on these mornings, but he could see the shoes these men wore from the hall: scarred steel-toed boots some days, polished loafers on others. When Lacey failed to come home or put food in the fridge, Alex rode his bike to Clay's house, where his presence had a calming effect on his friend's hot-blooded parents.

Clay's father was a small-time bookie and former Golden Gloves boxer who trained the boys on a bag in his garage. They started wrestling in middle school and took karate lessons at a strip-mall dojo when their parents could afford it. In their sophomore year at Atlantic City High School, the wrestling coach drove them to a boxing gym in Margate where a Korean blackjack dealer gave judo lessons in the mornings, and the chef at Bangkok Café taught Muay Thai on weekends. The boys showed up early and often, mopping floors and washing towels when they were short on dues. Their contrasting personalities reflected in the fighting styles they developed as their bodies lengthened and grew strong. Alex was a precision striker, strategic and methodical; Clay was a buzz saw in the ring. With his long reach and meticulous timing, Alex excelled at the throws and joint locks of judo, while Clay was an explosive, scrappy, inexhaustible wrestler. The boys constantly exposed each other's weaknesses and evolved at a rate that astonished their coaches. They trained and sparred relentlessly, through injuries, family crises, holidays, exams.

Clay's uncle was a mechanic with a sideline in burglary. He taught both skills to his nephew, who excelled at the unlawful one and enlisted his best friend as an accomplice in their junior year of high school. The boys started small—condos in Margate, lonely beach houses on Long Beach Island, yachts tied up in Ocean City. Clay's uncle strongly advised them not to shit where they ate, and for a full year, his protégés ignored the gold mine in their own backyard.

Three weeks after their high school graduation, the boys sat in the bar at Trump Plaza with Angela Rizzo, an ex-girlfriend of Clay's with a pill problem and a housekeeping job at the hotel. Alex and Clay stuck to Pepsi while Angela drank martinis and complained about her manager. When the bartender moved down the bar, Clay took a toothpick from the corner of his mouth and said, "Angie, tell Alex about the new arrivals."

"Married couple from Mexico," Angela said. "Fucking loaded. They're famous or something, they got this butler type who goes everywhere with them."

"A butler type?" Alex asked. "Or a bodyguard?"

"Doesn't matter, he sleeps on another floor. She's got diamond rings, earrings, bracelets, gold like you wouldn't believe."

"And you're sure it's real?"

Angela lit one cigarette with another. "They're in a fucking king penthouse suite, Alex. And I know fugazy jewelry when I see it."

"Do they go out at night?"

"Yeah, but if you go in then, you miss the stuff they're wearing."

Clay smiled. "Miss Rizzo has a point."

"This'll make a lot of noise any way we do it," Alex said. "We'll need to lie low for a while. We need to know it's worth it."

"The guy wears a gold chain as thick as my wrist," Angela said. "You could tie off a yacht with this thing. Different Rolex every day. Trust me, this is worth your time."

"What's in it for you?"

"Five hundred bucks or twenty percent, whichever's bigger."

"I'll take that action," Clay said. "I got a good feeling about this."

Alex scoffed. "About kicking down the door while they're inside? No way. We go in when they're gone."

"We can handle married folks in pajamas."

"Take Angela if that's your plan."

"Fine, you fucking pussy. We go in when they're gone. Angie, you'll let us know when?"

They spent Saturday afternoon and evening in Clay's basement, playing Nintendo and subsisting on Pop-Tarts and frozen pizza. Clay was in the bathroom when the phone rang sometime after 10 p.m. Alex answered.

"Gone for the night," Angela said.

"Did you knock?"

"You bet I did. You boys break a leg."

Half an hour later, Clay and Alex walked through the gilded

lobby of Trump Plaza. A poker tournament was in full swing, and no one looked twice at the two young men in sunglasses and baseball caps pulled low over their eyes. Clay and Alex cut through the casino and waited several minutes for an empty elevator. A hand shot the gap in the gleaming brass doors just before they closed, and the boys were joined by two couples with cokey energy, vodka on their breath, and cigarette smoke clinging to their suits and cocktail dresses.

"You two win big at the tourney?" a man asked, adjusting his gold-rimmed, rose-colored glasses.

"No, sir," Clay said. "Not our night."

"Then get back out there. Night's still young."

"Don't encourage that shit," his girlfriend said in a thick Brooklyn accent, slapping the man's arm with her red leather clutch. "You want them to end up like you?"

The couples got off on the twentieth floor, wishing the boys better luck next time. The car continued its climb. Clay bounced on his toes while Alex stood stock-still beside him, breathing deeply through his nose. Room 3904 was at the far end of the hall, and just before they reached it, Clay shifted his father's snub-nosed .38 revolver from the small of his back to his left hip.

"That makes it armed robbery," Alex whispered. "Adds years to the sentence."

"Sentence? Jesus, listen to you. We're not gonna need it."

Alex shook his head and turned his focus to what felt like a crackling fire in his stomach. He directed his breath there, a technique his boxing coach taught him to calm his nerves before a match. Clay pressed his ear to the door, then paused.

"What?" Alex mouthed.

"Thought I heard something."

"Make sure you didn't."

Clay made quick work of the lock, but when the door opened, every light inside the suite was on. The couple sat in white leather chairs with their backs to the windows, bound and gagged with duct tape. Two men in red Trump Plaza windbreakers spun at the sound of the door and went for the guns in their waistbands. Clay's gun was already out.

"Easy," he said. "Get your hands up. Do it now."

The men complied slowly. One had a thick mustache, five-o'clock shadow, and heavy rings on both his hands. The other, clean-shaven with shoulder-length hair in a ponytail, smiled menacingly at the boys.

"The fuck do we do now?" Clay hissed, swinging the pistol from one man to the other.

"Get their guns," Alex said. "Cover me, I'll do it."

The men glanced at each other as Alex approached. They had clocked Clay's inexperience, heard the tremor in his voice. Then the clean-shaven one muttered something under his breath. Alex, who was proficient in Spanish, had no time to explain that *Por las piernas* meant Go for the legs. He shouted Clay's name as the man with the mustache dove for a tackle. Clay fired a shot into the carpet, dropped the gun, then dropped his chest onto the man's shoulders and spun over his back like a break-dancer, sinking in a body lock as his feet hit the ground. The clean-shaven man had a hand on his pistol when Alex caught him with a high kick to the head. He stiffened and then toppled over, rigid and unconscious as he fell. His eyes opened when he hit the floor, but Alex was already on him, raining down punches that bounced the man's head off the carpet again and again. When the body beneath him went limp, Alex stood, wringing his hands. Clay had the other gunman flattened out with an arm pinned high behind his back, but still the man struggled. Alex called Clay's name and tossed a .45 automatic from the floor, which Clay caught by the slide. The man froze when he felt the muzzle in his neck. As Alex scanned the room, the woman caught his eye and nodded toward the roll of duct tape on the coffee table. After both gunmen were bound and gagged, Alex and Clay stood up and stared blankly at each other. Clay's hat and sunglasses lay on the floor. He put a hand to his face and, when it came away bloody, whipped two kicks into the ribs of the man at his feet. The couple looked on, their eyes wide and wild. Alex collected Clay's .38 and trained it on the woman.

"Who else is here?"

She nodded toward the bedroom, where the bodyguard was tied up on the bed. Beside him were two open cases packed with vacuum-sealed bricks of white powder.

"Jesus fucking Christ," Clay said. "Jackpot, baby."

Alex palmed his neck. "They must have—"

The boys spun and raised their guns as someone tapped on the door with a flashlight or nightstick. A man's voice reached them from the hallway.

"Mr. Sandoval? Security. Open up, please."

Alex tiptoed to the door and peered through the peephole.

"It's them," he whispered. "Badges and everything. Untie her. Let her go to the door."

"No way."

"They know we're not the fucking Sandovals and they'll call for backup if one of them doesn't answer. You wanna shoot out a window and jump? Untie her."

More knocking. "Mr. Sandoval? Everything okay in there?"

Alex placed the barrel of the .38 between the woman's eyes and said, "You're gonna tell them everything's okay, right?"

She nodded vigorously, then looked down at the men on the floor and jerked her head toward the bathroom. Alex dragged the gunmen out of sight while Clay saw to the woman. As soon as her mouth was uncovered, she stretched her jaw and called out, "Just a moment, please," in calm, lightly accented English, as if she had just stepped out of a bath. When Clay freed her arms, she walked to the mirror and wiped smudged lipstick from her mouth.

"I'm so sorry," she said as she opened the door. "My husband tripped in the dark and knocked over the nightstand. The noise must have been terrible. Please give my apologies to our neighbors."

"We just— Yeah, we had some complaints," a man said. "Nothing broken, right? How's your husband?"

"More embarrassed than anything. He's in the bathroom. Would you like to speak with him?"

"No, that's okay, ma'am. But please try to keep it down. It's late."

"Of course," she said, taking a folded hundred from her pocket and passing it through the door. "Again, apologies. Thanks for your concern."

She closed the door and stood listening as the guards' footsteps receded—a petite, sharp-featured woman with small hands and short dark hair swept straight back on her head, her navy silk jumpsuit cinched at the waist with a gold mesh belt. Old enough, Alex thought, to be my mother. At the sound of the elevator, she walked to the bar, poured three neat whiskeys, and passed two to the boys.

"There," she said, resuming her seat in the chair she'd been tied to, "now we can talk. Please, sit down."

Her husband grunted and twisted against the tape that bound him, but the woman paid no mind. Clay and Alex glanced at him nervously as they arranged themselves on the sofa, pistols on their knees.

"Who are you?" the woman asked.

The boys looked at each other, unsure how to answer.

"Your timing was certainly interesting." She lit a cigarette from a pack on the side table. "Given our situation, we may as well be frank. What are you here for? Jewelry?"

Alex nodded.

"I see. Obviously you got more than you bargained for. Let's discuss your options, shall we? You can take what you came for and go. I can't stop you from taking what you saw in the bedroom, but in that case, my husband and I will have to track you down. We've seen your faces. And your name, I gather, is Clay."

"We could also shoot you," Clay said, "and take everything."

The woman's laugh was condescending. "There's a third option, which I think will serve us all. How much did you expect
to make this evening? Three thousand? Five?"

"Something like that," Alex said.

"Suppose I paid in cash."

"We could live with that," Clay said.

"*Bueno.* That's what we'll do. My name is Maricel, by the
way. This is my husband, Roberto. It's Clay and—"

"Alex," Clay said.

"Alex, would you be so kind as to untie my husband? You
outnumber him and he's unarmed, as you can see. We can all
agree I pose no threat."

"The other guy stays tied up till we're gone," Alex said.

"Of course."

Alex held the .38 on Roberto, who cursed and spat when
Clay tore the tape from his mouth. Unbound, he rose slowly,
smoothed his hair, and buttoned his black silk shirt. His movements were slow and controlled, but his mouth trembled and his
eyes were full of rage. In the bathroom, Roberto straddled the
clean-shaven man where he lay on his stomach, cradling his chin
and the back of his skull, whispering in Spanish. Alex winced
as Roberto torqued the gunman's head until his neck snapped
and the man appeared to look over his own shoulder as his body
convulsed. His companion begged for his life through the tape
over his mouth. Roberto closed the door as Maricel returned
from the bedroom with two stacks of worn bills.

"Five thousand each," she said, "with our compliments. May
I ask how old you are?"

"I'm eighteen," Alex said. "So's he."

"Where did you learn to fight like that?"

"Around here."

"What were you afraid of?" She smiled when Alex shrugged
and shifted in his seat. "You're more frightened of that question
than you were of those men. I must say, you seemed strangely
calm until now."

Alex shrugged again. He hadn't felt calm, even if he'd looked it. His father, the reason Alex and his mother fled Miami, was a tall Italian restaurateur with a deep sadistic streak and a love of white linen suits and cocaine. He beat his girlfriend and son, but was especially cruel to Alex, whose fear he could sense. When Alex acted scared, he got hit, and the more afraid he seemed, the worse the beatings got. Alex learned to fake calm when his heart was racing, and eventually to exude calm in the face of violence.

Roberto emerged from the bathroom and shut the door gently behind him.

"Are you looking for work?" Maricel asked.

"What?" Clay said through a laugh.

"We're about to begin operating through a small airport not far from here. We'll need some hands there in the coming weeks. If you're interested, of course. Our thanks come with no strings attached, no expectations."

"You're offering us jobs?"

"I need drivers who can handle themselves but not attract attention. Handsome young gringos would be ideal."

"Drivers?" Alex asked. "What happens at the airport?"

"Planes land. An exchange is made. The planes take off again. After that, a car needs to be driven to New York or Atlantic City, depending on the day. For each trip I can offer fifteen hundred dollars."

"Two grand per trip," Clay said. "Splits up easier. I'm not a math guy."

Maricel smiled and called to her husband, who was securing the cases in the bedroom. *"Roberto, dos mil por viaje?"*

Roberto nodded.

"Very well," she said. She crossed the room and wrote in pencil on the hotel notepad. "Someone at this number will expect your call tomorrow. The first planes land next week. And now we have a long evening ahead of us, so I'll say good night."

Clay replaced his hat and sunglasses while they waited for the elevator.

"Hold still," Alex said as he wiped blood from the swollen gash above Clay's eye, which looked like an open mouth now.

As the elevator descended, Alex replayed Maricel's question about fear. She had seen straight through him, which led Alex to believe that the job she offered was the inevitable path, if not the right one. Accepting felt to him like walking through a door and then watching both the door and the wall that held it disappear. He was in another, larger room now. There was nowhere else to go. The money was insane, incomprehensible to him. The cars at the airport would be full of drugs, which bothered him in principle. Drugs had turned his father into a paranoid, abusive tyrant and almost killed his mother more than once. Maybe they owed him this.

They stepped out of the elevator and onto a casino floor in full Saturday-night swing. As they walked toward the exit, someone grabbed Alex by the elbow. He spun around, fists clenched, and found himself facing the man who stopped the elevator on their way up to the room.

"What did I tell you?" he called to his friends, pointing at the boys. "Couldn't resist. Back for more."

Ten

Diane finishes her drink and makes another after Alex leaves. She remembers him now, a shy and quiet teenager on the day they met, with bad skin and hair that hung over his eyes. Almost unrecognizable twenty-four years later. She can't process his connection to Tom's father, not now, not yet. She wonders how she managed to find this kind of man not once but twice.

She had no plans to visit Atlantic City on the summer Saturday that she met Clay and, briefly, Alex. That morning, Diane rode with a friend to the beach town of Margate, where they worked a small afternoon wedding in a manicured backyard. The groom was in his sixties, the bride not far behind. Diane stood behind the bar, admiring the quietly assured tone of the proceedings: no tearful, overeager vows, no earnest speeches about how perfect these two were for each other. The reception wrapped up early, and the caterers were drinking leftover Champagne when someone suggested they drive to A.C. for martinis at Dock's Oyster House. Diane initially begged off, but two glasses later found herself in the back seat of a station wagon headed north on Ventnor Avenue.

Dock's was cool and dark, a welcome respite from the July heat. The bar was crowded and the half-dozen caterers gathered around three stools by a mound of ice studded with shellfish. Standing next to Diane was a blue-eyed boy with long blond hair and gold rings in his ears. His left eye was bloodshot and blackened, with a thick bandage on the brow above it. He smiled when he caught Diane staring at the injury, revealing absurdly

straight and white teeth, which got her every time. Diane felt
something catch in her throat when their eyes met but quickly
looked away.

The caterers ordered oysters, but by the time the platter
made its way to Diane, all the lemons had been used. As she
waved down a bartender, the boy with the black eye plucked the
lime wedge from his vodka soda and squeezed it over the shell
in her hand. Diane laughed and thanked him.

"Service here is garbage," he said.

"Good to know."

"You're not from around here."

"That's right," she said, "I'm not. What happened to your
eye?"

"Had a disagreement with some metal. Does it make me
look tough?"

"No," she said, "it makes you look disagreeable."

His name was Clay. He introduced the tall boy beside him,
who seemed content to nurse his drink while Clay talked to
Diane. Both boys looked underage but seemed to know the bartenders. The barroom shrank around them as patrons poured in.
Diane introduced her coworkers to Clay, who bought a round
and then another, chatting effortlessly with everyone, turning
to her now and then with a sly smile, as if they shared a secret.

"I think we lost our friends," she said an hour later when she
and Clay took a break from making out against the back wall of
the bar, his elbows resting on her shoulders.

"Good," Clay said. "Let's get out of here."

Outside on the sidewalk, they winced at the late-afternoon
light, laughing and shielding their eyes. Clay took her hand and
led her toward the water. The salt air on the crowded boardwalk
was laced with sugar from the funnel cake and cotton candy
carts, the sand below dotted with brightly colored umbrellas.
Seagulls wailed and dove for food.

"How old are you?" Diane asked. "Should you be drinking
in bars?"

"Let's just say I'm old enough."

"What really happened to your eye?"

"If I told you, you'd tell me I was full of shit. Or take off running."

"Try me."

"Can't risk it. Does it still look disagreeable?"

"It's growing on me, to be honest."

"Are you hungry?" Clay asked. "How do you feel about Italian?"

They stopped at a liquor store and bought a bottle of red wine from a man behind thick Plexiglas who asked after Clay's uncle.

"Where are you taking me?" Diane asked as they walked down a quiet residential street.

He pointed to the block ahead of them where limousines idled in front of a white clapboard home. Drivers smoked and talked on the sidewalk while Frank Sinatra played on a car stereo. Clay led Diane around the house, through an unmarked door, and down a staircase lined with signed photos of boxers, movie stars, and local politicians. The sounds of a crowded restaurant filtered through thick curtains at the bottom of the stairs. In the basement dining room, tables were tightly packed under a low drop ceiling and covered in platters of antipasto and pasta, heaping side dishes, bottles of wine. The crowd was older, filled with tanned, substantial men in French-cuff shirts and women with elaborate hair and heavy jewelry. Everyone seemed to be laughing at once.

"Mr. Dougherty," the hostess said to Clay. "How many times do I have to ask you to call beforehand? Follow me."

Their waitress recited a slew of Italian dishes in place of menus. Clay and Diane shared a mound of calamari and a butterflied veal chop drowned in red sauce and melted provolone. The wine seemed to evaporate. The chef, gruff and lumbering, stopped by to say hello and left half a bottle of Chardonnay on their table.

"To free refills," Clay said, raising his glass.

They ricocheted around the city after dinner, hand in hand, arm in arm, from an Irish bar to a basement nightclub to a speakeasy casino on a yacht tied up in a marina, ignoring everyone except the bartenders who served them drinks that Diane tasted in her mouth and in his. Their last stop was the Tropicana, a blur of ringing slots and flashing lights and cocktails floating past on crowded trays. They played roulette with a thick roll of bills from Clay's pocket until Diane, up four hundred dollars after a breathtaking run, put everything on black and lost it all. She stood there, flushed and frozen, as the dealer raked in all their chips.

"Oh my God," she whispered, "I'm so sorry."

"For what?" Clay asked. "Blackjack? Craps?"

"Are you out of your mind?"

"Or we can go upstairs."

The room—when had he booked a room?—overlooked the ocean, a slab of dark, textured glass under a quarter moon. She fell asleep against him in the bathtub, and he carried her to bed wrapped in a towel.

She woke up to knocking and enough room service to feed them for a week. After breakfast, they collapsed back into bed. Neither of them had a condom, but Clay promised to be careful.

Three weeks later she was late.

Her first instinct was to take care of it without a word to Clay, but she told him over the phone and against her better judgment. Clay shocked her by insisting that she keep the baby. He pledged support, as much or as little as she wanted. He was making money, he said, and was about to make much more. Diane refused. The money, she said, didn't matter. She wasn't ready, and they barely knew each other. Clay was irate. She agreed to meet him for lunch in Margate, and they argued afterward in the street outside the restaurant. He told her it wasn't her decision to make, not alone. "Fuck you," she said. "Watch me." Clay raised his hand, but Diane stood her ground.

"Go ahead," she said. "You think I haven't been hit before?" Clay turned away, ashamed.

Two days later, he stopped calling. On the third day, her calls to him went unreturned. Good, Diane thought, show me who you really are, make this easier. On the fifth day, her phone rang. The man on the line was not Clay but a detective from the Manalapan Township Police Department who spoke Clay's name and asked Diane how she knew him, how this number—her number—written on the torn corner of a menu, came to be inside Clay's wallet.

"Why?" she asked. "Is something wrong?"

Eleven

Ramirez conducts meetings with informants in the conference rooms of a vacant office park. Craig is out on bail. After seventy-two hours in a cell, he agreed to forgo an attorney and cooperate in full. No charges would be filed, Harris told him, provided his information was solid and led to arrests. At the arraignment, a judge ordered Craig to surrender his passport, stay inside the city limits, and meet regularly with Harris and Ramirez, who sit across from him over lunch from In-N-Out Burger, which fills the warm room with the smell of grease.

"How's the arm?" Ramirez asks.

"Good as new, mate. Thanks for asking."

"Let's go through this one more time," Harris says. "You first heard about the Graff job when?"

"Roy took me for a beer a few weeks back. Said he had some work I might be interested in."

"And Roy is who?"

"Roy Fletcher, my boss at the track."

"And Roy was on the other bike, correct?"

Craig nods and fills his mouth with French fries drenched in ketchup.

The LVMPD has been surveilling Roy since Craig's arrest. He's the general manager of Sin City Motorsports and lives in a three-bedroom house in Henderson with his wife, five-year-old twin daughters, and two Rottweilers. He gets to work between 8 and 8:15 a.m., leaves at 5 p.m. on the dot, and drives straight home to walk the dogs and push the kids on a swing set behind the house. No priors, no known criminal associates, no splashy recent purchases. According to Craig, Roy has an alibi for the Wynn job, two friends willing to swear he was hiking with them in Red Rock on the afternoon in question. Roy is forty-four and much smarter than Craig.

"Why would Roy mention a job like that to an upstanding young man like you?" Ramirez asks. "What would lead him to believe you might be interested?"

"I had a bit of trouble back home that I guess Roy caught wind of."

"Be more specific," Harris says.

"Drove on a bank job back in Adelaide. Record's sealed, though. I was underage."

"How'd that work out for you?"

"The driving? Worked out fine. Somebody talked afterward."

"Story of your life," Ramirez says. "How many other jobs did you drive on back home?"

"Just the one."

"I'm sure," Harris says. "Back to Vegas. How did Roy describe the job?"

"He said a crew was after stones. Big score, serious people. Our bit was to make sure they got in and out."

"And you said what?"

"For fifty grand? I said yes, please."

Ramirez scoffs. "Fifty grand? To drive?"

"You get what you pay for, mate."

"Did Roy say who was booking you?" Harris asks.

"Didn't give a name."

"But you met him." Harris flips back through his notes. "The gay guy, in your words."

"Right."

"And you know he was gay because?"

"We met him at a gay bar. And he grabbed my cock."

"Did you file a workplace-harassment claim?" Ramirez asks. "First thing you should do when this is over."

"Do you remember the name of the gay bar?" Harris asks.

Craig shakes his head. "It had those swinging doors, the ones you see in Westerns. And a sign on the wall about 'the lifestyle.'"

"The Badlands Saloon," Ramirez says.

"Yeah, that's the one."

"We've had dealings with the Badlands in the past," Ramirez says to Harris. "Nice folks. Plenty of cameras."

"So, you and Roy popped down to the Badlands," Harris says, "to meet the guy who's booking you. What happened then?"

"Breakfast meeting," Craig says. "Just after eight. Bar was empty, just us and the bartender."

"Was this guy already there?"

"Yeah, at a table in the back. Big boy, all muscle, tats all over his arms. Bald head, beard. Asked if I wanted a soda when I shook his hand. Crack about my age, I guess."

"Did he say who you'd be working with?" Harris asks.

"Nah, mate. He wouldn't. He was pretty clear on that—said we wouldn't get their names or see their faces, shouldn't speak to them unless they spoke to us. Roy warned me about all this beforehand."

"So Roy had worked with them before?"

"Wouldn't give me a straight answer."

Roy ducked all Craig's questions, telling him that everything would be explained at the Badlands, which it was, over two hours and in exhaustive detail. The bald man, Craig says, was responsible for shooting out the traffic cameras.

"And why did this guy grab your cock?" Harris asks.

"I asked too many questions. We were outside in the parking lot showing him the bikes we put together. Roy asked about the weight of the boys on back so we could get the suspensions dialed in. I asked if they spoke English."

"Why would you ask that?"

"I figured this was that eastern European crew from Montenegro, Serbia, whatever. Wanted to make sure we could understand them if things went pear-shaped."

"Pear-shaped?" Ramirez asks.

"You know, funny. Fucked up."

"What happened then?"

"He got my whole package in his hand, mate. Like he was about to rip it off. 'Are you enjoying this as much as I am?' Asked why I was asking. I said I was curious. 'Curiosity killed the cat, young man.' Told Roy to watch my mouth. Then he patted me on the cheek and that was that."

"And that was the last time you saw him?" Harris asks.

"Until just after the job."

"Walk me through that day again."

Craig spent the morning on the bikes, then rode with Roy to a warehouse in North Las Vegas where they found their gear laid out for them and the other riders suited up and stretching by the U-Haul. The tall one, Craig says, did a microphone check once he and Roy put on their intercoms and helmets.

"What did he say?" Harris asks.

"'Raise your hand if you can hear me.'"

"And that's the only time you heard him talk?"

"Nah. He spoke to me on the job. Gave me a bit of hell, actually."

"When was this?"

"Just before they came out of the store. The kid was filming right in front of me and I asked if I should get him to fuck off."

"What did he say to you?" Harris asks.

"Can't remember."

Ramirez says, "Try harder."

Craig extracts something from his molar with a finger. He came in hot and cocky this morning, wearing the promise of immunity like a new three-piece suit. He looks younger now, shaken by the memory.

"He told me if I laid a finger on the kid, he'd shoot me himself," Craig says. "Real calm, like he was reading me the weather. American for sure."

"What about the other guy?" Ramirez asks. "Did he say anything?"

"Not sure it was a guy," Craig says.

Ramirez laughs. "Why, did she grab your cock too?"

"Just a hunch, mate. Anyway, the taller one, the one I had on back—that's who you want."

"What makes you say that?" Harris asks.

"If anything went wrong we were meant to follow him, take his orders. The bald guy made him sound like some kind of guru. Also, they gave him to me, not Roy."

"What does that mean?"

"I'm better on a bike."

"Is that a fact?" Ramirez asks.

"If Roy says different, he's lying. But he won't."

"Okay," Harris says, "so Roy takes his guy or girl back to the warehouse and you drop the tall one off on Kirkland. What happened then?"

"Roy and I met up at his mate's garage and stripped the bikes. We'd sold the parts online the week before, anything we couldn't burn already had a buyer. Some stuff was still warm when we packed it up."

"Whose idea was that?" Ramirez asks.

"Take a wild guess, mate."

"And no word from them since?"

Craig shakes his head.

"So what makes you think they'll contact you again?" Harris asks.

"You see the spot I got us out of on the Strip?"

"When you almost ran down two officers?" Ramirez says. "Yeah, we saw that."

"Tell those boys I'm sorry about that. Had to improvise a bit."

"And you think this guy will put you on another job because of that?"

"He knows what good work looks like," Craig says. "He'll call. You'll see."

"You better hope so," Harris says. "Because unless we get something off the cameras at Badlands, you've given us exactly shit."

Twelve

On an overcast and humid Sunday morning, Alex leaves his country house in gym shorts and a rash guard with a small black duffel in his hand. Halfway to his car, he pauses to retie his sneaker and toss a stick into the grass. The bag is filled with rubber knives and dummy pistols, teaching aids for his Close Quarters Combat class at Princeton Brazilian Jiu Jitsu, and the drive takes him past the home where he and Diane had dinner. The next morning, Alex sent her a text that he's reread a dozen times: *Wanted to say again I had a great time with you and will give you as much space as you need but am here if you want to talk.* Eight days and still no reply. He wonders what she'll tell her friends when they ask about the tall event producer she was seeing. He's sure he'll never hear from her again.

The martial arts school, in a strip mall by the train station, feels like a sauna when Alex pushes through the doors, the air thick with the smell of sweat-soaked spandex. A retired firefighter holds pads for a local MMA standout while a dozen grapplers drill on the mats, practicing chokes and locks and sweeps. Alex shakes a few hands and sits down to stretch. He's in butterfly position with his back to the door when another instructor launches into the school's welcome spiel. Alex looks over his shoulder and finds Tom and Diane Alison signing waivers.

"Hey," he says, approaching with an awkward wave. "Mitch, I'll take this one. Good to see you. What brings you in?"

"I hate the gym," Diane says, "and Tom has a coworker who

raves about this place. Saw you on the schedule and thought we'd stop by."

He's reeling. The armed-assailant defense he planned to teach ends with the would-be attacker on the ground with a pistol to their temple: not a sequence Alex is eager to demonstrate in front of Diane, given her reaction to the video. He asks Mitch to run the warm-up while he hits the men's room, where he stares at his reflection and wonders what she's doing here, what this could mean. Alex skipped his morning coffee but feels the rush of an espresso on an empty stomach now.

He emerges to find his students seated in a circle, armed with dummy pistols from his bag. Mitch yields the floor.

"Okay," Alex says. "I want to try something a little different today, so you can put the guns away for now." Groans and laughter from the crowd. "Mitch, can I borrow you? So, let's say Mitch has decided to get in my face. He's inside striking range, but I don't want to go that route. Maybe Mitch is young and dumb, maybe we're in a bar full of his friends and I don't wanna start a brawl. What I'm gonna do is grab his right wrist with my left hand and then jam my right hand into his armpit and cup his triceps, like this. Now that I have two points of contact on the arm, I'm gonna give it a tug to bring Mitch across my body, releasing my hold on his wrist so I can step behind him. Once I'm there I want to give Mitch a nice, tight hug to pin his arms. At this point, he's basically immobilized, but more important, he's unharmed, and I'm in control of the situation. From here, I have options. If the situation escalates, I can snake my right arm around his neck and grab my own biceps, like this, for a rear-naked choke. If Mitch starts clawing at my face, all I have to do is apply the choke or tap the back of his knee with my knee, drop my weight, and take him to the ground. From there, I can do whatever I want with him. But the idea here is that it doesn't come to that. Think of the standing arm-drag as a pressure-release valve—like a preemptive strike with no striking involved.

I'm applying force here as a means to keep my options open. What I'm really after is a clean way out. Questions?"

Alex keeps an eye on Diane as he circles the room to answer questions and adjust technique. She's working with her son in a corner, her movement more fluid and assured than Tom's. Alex slowly makes his way over.

"How's it going?"

"Question," Diane says. "Let's say I grab his arm and try to get behind him and he grabs my head like this."

"He's forcing you down, right? Good question, by the way. I'd use that momentum and do a simple takedown to get him to the ground. Here, I'll show you."

"Let me see if I remember this," she says. "It's been a while."

Diane lowers her head and shoots for Tom's legs, closing the distance in a flash. Her left knee grazes the mat as she wraps her arms around his thighs and straightens up abruptly, throwing Tom to the ground, where he stares up at her, wide-eyed and breathless.

"Like that?"

"Yes," Alex says as he helps Tom to his feet. "Exactly like that. Where'd you pick that up?"

"My brothers were all-state wrestlers," Diane says. "Used to practice on me all the time."

Diane and her son arrived in separate cars, and after class wraps up, Tom announces that he has to swing by the office.

"Sorry to hear that," Alex says. "Thanks for coming."

"What's your story?" Diane asks as she lets her hair down. "Do you have time for lunch?"

She leads him to a classic chrome-box diner where they order omelets from a sullen college-age waiter who says that he'll be back with coffee.

"Were you surprised to see me?" Diane asks.

"I'm still surprised."

"I wanted to apologize for kicking you out the other night.

You think you've processed something and . . . I don't know. I didn't know what else to do."

"You don't need to apologize."

"I know. But I want to. Looking back at those pictures, I definitely need to apologize for my hair when we met."

"It was the eighties," Alex says. "Mistakes were made." He blanches at the unintended implication. "I mean, not that— Fuck."

"It's okay," she says. "They were. By all of us. He talked about you, you know. Clay did."

"I saw him that night at the Mallorys' while I was under. Just for a second. I couldn't see his face, but it was him."

"I'm not sure I'd recognize him at this point. I did the math again after you left. I saw Clay a grand total of three times in my life. Can you believe that?"

"A lot of things with him were hard to believe."

"Are his parents still alive?"

"I think his mom is. We haven't spoken since. Their call. Needed someone to blame, I guess."

"You're not still doing that, right?"

"What?"

"Dealing, trafficking, whatever it was."

"First and last gig in that line of work."

Which is technically true. Alex adjusts the angle of the sugar caddy between them, certain her next question will require him to lie. The waiter returns and fills their coffee cups.

"Let's leave all that for now," Diane says. "I was thinking we could start over, take this slow, get to know each other like normal people."

"No more day drinking and crashing dinner parties."

Diane laughs. "No more ketamine injections. I'm almost afraid to ask what you're doing for Labor Day."

"I'll be in Mexico."

"Which part?"

"Tulum. East coast, Caribbean side. I have some friends there. And a place in Akumal, just up the road."

"A friend of mine got married in Tulum last year, but I couldn't make the dates work. It's been on my list forever."

"Come down with me."

"That sounds lovely, but I always spend that weekend with my son."

"So bring him."

"I can't tell if you're serious," Diane says.

"He's Clay's son. I want to get to know him whether he knows that or not. And it sounds like he could use a break. We'll get him a hotel if he wants some privacy. We'll get you a hotel if you and I can't stand each other."

"That's very pragmatic. And kind of insane."

"Bad idea?"

"Going to Mexico with someone you barely know is the definition of a bad idea. Wait till I tell Lindsay. She thought I was crazy for bringing you to dinner."

Their food arrives, two plates of hash browns, overstuffed omelets, limp buttered toast. Diane requests hot sauce.

"I have to ask Tom," she says when the waiter walks away.

"Just let me know. The offer stands."

"So much for getting to know each other like normal people."

"I guess that's not our speed," Alex says.

Thirteen

The Badlands Saloon in North Las Vegas shares a strip mall with a popular Thai restaurant, an evangelical church, and a swingers club that has seen better days. Detective Ramirez parks near Lotus of Siam to wait for Agent Harris, who pulls into the lot ten minutes later with two iced coffees on his dash.

"Read my mind," Ramirez says, shaking his cup as they walk toward the bar. "Any word on our Chinese developer?"

"Mr. Li Jianrong of Shanghai doesn't even jaywalk. And my guys really looked."

"Maybe he's dirty in a way that's okay over there."

"Or your friend Marvin's full of shit. That's the bar?"

"Yeah. Cowboy-themed, open twenty-four hours. Pretty rowdy on the weekends. Owner helped narcotics with a bust a few years back, some kids dealing crystal in the bathrooms. Bartender I talked to said he's usually here in the morning."

Harris goes first through the blacked-out glass and swinging saloon doors beyond. The windowless room is lit by video poker screens embedded in the bar and empty except for a man drying glasses by the taps. He's burly and heavily bearded, dressed in denim cutoffs and a modestly sequined western shirt.

"What can I get you gentlemen?" he says without looking up.

"We're gonna stick to coffee for the moment," Ramirez says. "Are you Paul Servito?"

"I am."

"Hector Ramirez with the LVMPD. This is Dave Harris with the FBI. Mind if we ask you a few questions?"

"Not really."

"This is your place, correct?"

"That's right."

"Are you usually here in the morning?"

"Except when I'm not."

"Who comes in this time of day?"

"All kinds, plus the guys who clean the place. Depends on the day."

"Do people have meetings here? Talk business, that kind of thing?"

"I don't hear every conversation. You mind telling me what this is about?"

Harris points to the cameras on the wall above the bar and says, "Could we take a look at some footage?"

"Cameras weren't working."

Ramirez laughs. "We didn't say what day this would have been."

"What day was it?"

"The fourteenth of last month."

"That's when they were out."

"What if I gave you some other dates?"

"Go right ahead."

"Are you saying we should come back with a warrant?" Harris asks.

"I would never invite you back here, but do what you gotta do. While you're at it, tell your buddies down at the precinct that when someone smashes my door and spray-paints 'Go to Hell Faggots' on the wall out there, that shit should be charged as a hate crime, not some boys-will-be-boys misdemeanor vandalism bullshit. I don't give a fuck who the kid's dad is."

"Mr. Servito," Ramirez says, "I'm not familiar with that incident, but next time you have any kind of issue here, I want you to call me personally. Here's my card."

"If that happens again, I'll handle it personally, don't you worry."

"There's no way we could take a look at that footage?"

"Not without a warrant."

"Just so you know," Harris says, "if you delete anything based on the conversation we just had, you're obstructing the investigation of a serious crime."

"You boys know all about that, don't you? Now, unless you're drinking, have a nice day someplace else."

Fourteen

Tom and Diane touch down fifteen minutes early, but runway traffic keeps them in their seats for half an hour. Hot air hisses through the gaps between the jet bridge and the airplane as they disembark. Cancún International Airport is nicely chilled, its pink tiled floors slick with condensation like sweat on skin. Mother and son walk past gift shops stocked with silver jewelry and pistol-shaped tequila bottles, past American fast-food outposts, past an immigration officer who glances at their passports before he waves them through. Chaos awaits them outside the terminal—a corralled mass of tour operators, resort directors, and taxi drivers all shouting at the new arrivals. Alex is making his way toward them, a full head taller than anyone in the crowd. His flight landed two hours ago and, after picking up the rental car, he drove to a cantina near the airport for a late breakfast of tacos al pastor and two beers to calm his nerves. He kisses Diane awkwardly on the cheek and shakes Tom's hand.

"You made it," he says, smiling. "Don't drink the water."

"Thanks for having us," Diane says. "Sorry we're late."

"You're on vacation, no such thing. That white Toyota is us. Anyone want a beer for the road?"

"Absolutely," Diane says. "We'll grab drinks if you get the A/C going. Is that the bar over there?"

"Yes, ma'am. I'll take your bags. Need some pesos?"

"That's okay," Tom says. "I'll get it."

He follows his mother to the cabana bar outside the terminal, where she orders three beers and two tequila shots.

"Cheers," she says. "You okay? You're awfully quiet."

"Just tired," Tom says, raising his glass. "What do they say here? *Salud?*"

When Diane extended Alex's invitation to her son, she prefaced it by saying that she wasn't going anywhere without him. This was their weekend, she explained, and they could spend it in Southampton with Jay and Candace, or in Mexico with Alex and his friends, as crazy as that sounded.

"Let's go to Mexico," Tom said, and then paused as if calling her bluff.

She was reminded that Tom will try anything twice, a trait that she finds both admirable and alarming as his mother. Was he humoring her or did he see the same strange logic she saw in this plan? She worried that something—business, illness, the girl he had been casually seeing—would prevent him from coming, but here he is outside the airport in Cancún, his upper lip dotted with sweat just like his mother's. Tom jams a slice of lime into his Corona, upends the bottle with his thumb over the opening, and watches as the fruit floats through the golden lager, infusing it with citrus. Diane's thumb is too small to perform this trick, and she's about to ask Tom to repeat the process when he hands her his beer. She ruffles her son's hair, suddenly overcome with gratitude for his presence here.

"What's up?" he asks.

"Nothing. Thanks for coming."

"Why not, right? *Salud.*"

The white Toyota pulls up to the curb, hazards flashing.

"This was a dirt road ten years ago," Alex says as they shoot down a six-lane highway lined with sheet-metal taquerías, fruit stands, and strip mall after strip mall composed of big-box stores, gas stations, and banks. "It's much quieter where we're going."

"I know," Diane says. "I've seen every picture on the internet at this point."

The shopping centers become few and far between as they continue south, followed by the roadside stands. Long stretches of low jungle are broken by the gaudy entrances to all-inclusive resorts—soaring columns, gushing fountains, torches spitting flame. Alex takes the exit for Akumal, which empties onto a long unpaved road. Flashes of white sand and turquoise water are visible between the villas and blocks of condos to their right. To their left, the jungle runs for miles. Alex parks in front of a four-story stucco building surrounded by tall palms and prehistoric-looking plants. His apartment is on the top floor, and everyone is sweating by the time they reach the tiled landing. When Alex grasps the doorknob to unlock it, he finds the door unlocked and not quite closed. He backs up quickly, sweeping Tom and Diane around a corner behind his outstretched arm.

"Is someone here?" she asks.

"Probably the cleaners," Alex says. "Hang back a second, okay?"

He disappears into the apartment, where someone is singing over the synths of a dance music track.

"What the hell is going on?" Tom whispers.

"He's just being cautious," Diane says nervously. "I'm sure it's nothing."

They wait with matching furrowed brows until Alex reappears, looking embarrassed and relieved.

"Hey," he says, "all good. Come in."

A long hallway leads to an open kitchen that smells of chopped cilantro, palo santo, and marijuana. Standing by the refrigerator is a young woman in espadrilles and an electric-blue tee-shirt that fits her like a dress and bears the markings of a wet bikini underneath. She's younger than Tom, with an arresting elfin beauty and a mass of dirty-blond curls a few shades lighter than her healthy tan. She has Alex's eyes.

"This," Alex says, "is my daughter, Paola, who forgot to mention she'd be here this weekend."

"So did you," Paola says in a Spanish accent and surprisingly deep voice. "Since when do you come here in August?"

She has a knack for raising subjects Alex doesn't want to

discuss—the reason for the unseasonal visit, in this case—so he dodges the question and says, "Pao, this is Diane."

"I've heard all about you," Diane says as they embrace. "So glad you're here."

"Me too," Paola says. "Not that I'm here, that you are. I feel like I'm interrupting."

"Not at all."

"Paola," Alex says, "meet Tom."

She kisses both Tom's cheeks, leaving a residue of salt and sunscreen at the corners of his mouth.

"Alex," Diane says, "can you help me with the bags?"

"Fuck me," Paola says to Tom when their parents disappear down the hall. "I knew I should have called him. He's being nice because you're here. How long are you staying?"

"Three days," Tom says. "Sorry, do you live here?"

"No, no. Someday, maybe. I live in Bogotá, where my mother's from." She plucks a half-smoked joint from a painted clay ashtray and tucks it into a pack of cigarettes. "First time here?"

Tom nods and Paola leads him onto a balcony that overlooks the crescent-shaped bay, its turquoise water mottled by dark swaths of coral reef and rolling breakers.

"Just like the Jersey Shore, right?" Paola says.

"Yeah, I've seen worse. So, Alex and your mom aren't—"

"Together? No, dude. Definitely not. You seem a little shell-shocked. Was I that big of a surprise?"

"No one told me he had kids."

She has a man's laugh, deep and booming. "Kid," she says. "Just me. So I'm his little secret, huh?"

"No one tells me anything," Tom says. "How long have you been down here?"

"Three days? Four? I played a party Thursday night and the promoter asked me to stay for the weekend."

"You're a DJ?"

"Sometimes," Paola says, as Alex and Diane join them on

the balcony. She embraces her father and says, "Okay, *te amo mucho*. I'm gonna go."

"Go where?" Diane asks.

"To stay with a friend."

"Not because we're here, I hope."

"I didn't mean to crash the party. My friend has space."

"Don't be ridiculous, honey. We just met. You can't leave now."

Paola looks to Alex, who is struggling visibly and in vain to remain angry. "You should stay," he says.

"Why's that?"

"Because I'm your father and I say so."

"That's a so-so reason."

"Stay," Tom says. "Show me around."

He's intensely grateful for her presence, having failed to consider the awkwardness of third-wheeling it all weekend until he found himself in the car with Alex and his mother.

"Okay," Paola says. "You can have the second bedroom. I'll take the couch."

"Pao, do you have dinner plans?" Alex asks. "Diego and Catalina invited us to their place. Ben and Christian are here too. I'm sure they'd love to see you."

"I'm playing in Tulum tonight," she says. "Right near their house. Let's go."

Alex and Diane unpack in the master bedroom, which is separated from the living room and kitchen by a waist-high wall topped with shutters that open to the ocean view. The second bedroom overlooks the jungle and barely fits two twin beds and a nightstand. One bed is unmade, its sheets sprinkled with sand; the other is covered in piles of records and clothes.

"Sorry," Paola says, as she shows Tom inside. "I'll get this shit out of your way."

"Hey, I'll hit the couch. You're all set up in here."

"No, no—this is the guest room. You're the guest."

"I can't sleep in both beds."

"You're sure?"

"Your call. I don't mind."

"Okay, thank you. That couch is a piece of shit. Do you snore?"

"Definitely."

"Good," she says, "me too."

A few hours later they're on the balcony again, dressed for dinner and polishing off Paola's stash of cold Tecate. The sea breeze creates a cocktail of scents—floral conditioner, earthy essential oils, cigarette smoke, citrus. Tom looks from face to face as he sips his beer, taking in this new dynamic. Buzzing from it too.

They drive south with the windows down. Tulum, a sandy grid of streets split in half by Highway 307, is half an hour away by car. Diego and Catalina live south of town in a strip of jungle that runs between a long unpaved road and the beach. Diego answers the door in white jeans and a faded black tee shirt stained with paint or clay. He's sinewy and fortyish with a lean, handsome face and long black hair tied up in a high knot. His wife, Catalina, has a swimmer's muscular shoulders, buzz-cut hair, and the calmly commanding presence of a yoga teacher. The top of her left ear is swollen in a way that reminds Tom of boys on his high school wrestling team. Two large, bearded men loom behind her, their arms covered in gym-sculpted muscles and full sleeves of tattoos. Ben, in a silky black polo and cargo shorts, is polite, severe, completely bald. His partner, Christian, has an easy smile and a full head of curly dark brown hair.

"I have a surprise for you," Alex says as Paola steps into the light.

Catalina throws her arms around Paola, whispering in her ear in Spanish.

"We got real beef for the Americans," Diego says. "Grass-fed. None of this stringy Central American shit. Who's hungry?"

Diego and Catalina split their time between Mexico City and this single-story beach house with low ceilings and a large, open kitchen bookended by bedrooms. Ben and Christian spend most of their time in Las Vegas and keep a modest villa down the road. In the kitchen, Christian and the women pass one of Paola's joints as they peel onions, dice tomatoes, and char peppers on the stove. Diane is adding salt to a salsa when she catches Paola staring from across the kitchen island.

"What do you do in Bogotá, honey?"

"She's a famous DJ," Catalina says.

"On weekends," Paola says. "I work in microfinance for a bank that makes loans to cooperatives of women so they can start businesses, support themselves."

"You only loan to women?" Diane asks.

"Loan to the men, and the money goes only to the men. Loan to the women, and it goes to the family."

"These women pay the loans back as a group," Catalina says. "One falls behind, another one steps in to cover. They worship Pao. She rides around the slums on her *moto* all day and no one dreams of touching her. Drives Alex crazy."

"I bet," Diane says. "Thanks for having us. I've always wanted a beach house like this. What do you do down here?"

"I teach yoga," Catalina says. "And you?"

"This." Diane offers her the salsa to taste. "I cook for people. Catering, mostly. Paola, can your dad cook, or should someone be out there on the grill?"

"Don't worry," Catalina says. "He's good with fire."

On the deck behind the house, Alex holds his hand above the barbecue grate and then recoils. Two thick rib eyes hiss and sweat when he lays them down over the coals. Ben and Diego discuss the art scene in Mexico City while Alex works the grill.

"We could use a clean platter," Alex says to no one in particular.

"I'll grab one," Tom says. "Anybody need a drink?"

Diego asks for a shot of tequila; Ben and Alex decline.

"Jesus Christ," Ben says when Tom is out of earshot. "I'd swear that was him in that picture of you and Clay as kids."

"It's like seeing a ghost," Alex says.

"He doesn't know?" Diego asks.

Alex shakes his head.

"That ain't gonna last," Ben says.

Dinner is served on the deck. The sound of the surf filters through a wall of leaves, a backbeat for the tinny reggae coming from a speaker in the kitchen window. Steak and fish are sliced and passed around and picked at until all that's left are pools of spice-flecked liquid and a stack of bones. Diane digs the cheek meat from a fish head with her fingers and drops it into Christian's open mouth while Alex watches, astonished at how easily she's assimilated and how quickly his friends, notoriously insular and suspicious of newcomers, have taken to her. When Paola leans across the table to light Diane's cigarette, a thought announces itself so forcefully that he almost speaks it aloud: This is what I want. Alex feels a stab of something that he registers initially as loss. But it's not loss—it's fear of losing this, which seems likely unless he upends his life. Alex takes a long pull of Diane's margarita to combat the sudden tightness in his throat.

"Pao, are you playing tonight?" Diego asks.

Paola nods. "At Papaya Playa and an after party down the road."

"What time do you go on at Papaya?"

"Midnight."

Diego checks his watch which, to Tom's surprise, is a thin gold Patek Philippe. "We should get going, no?"

"We're too old for that party," Catalina says.

"Speak for yourself, *mi amor.*"

"Diego's too good-looking to go dancing by himself," Christian says. "We'll all have to go."

Ben shakes his head. "No way I'm waiting in that line."

"No one I bring has to wait," Paola assures him.

Like the jungle that surrounds it, the beach road comes alive at night. Cars roll slowly over the sandy pavement and occasional speed bumps, shaking the air with heavy bass lines as they pass. Alex and Diane walk arm in arm alongside Ben and Christian, followed by Catalina and Paola, her record bag slung over her shoulder. Tom brings up the rear with Diego, who offers him a quick bump of cocaine. A crush of bodies blocks the entrance to Papaya Playa, but the bouncer spots Paola in the crowd and waves her to the front. The club sits above the beach in a sparse grove of palm trees, some with hammocks strung between them, some with tables built around their trunks. Paola catches Tom's wrist as the group heads for the bar.

"Keep me company," she says. "But wipe your nose, *marica.*"

She leads him to the DJ booth, a long table under a palapa canopy where a dozen attractive and adventurously dressed people drink and dance behind the decks. While Paola unpacks her records, a slender boy in a black tank top and embroidered skirt approaches Tom. His incisors look like fangs and his green eyes flash as he opens his arms in greeting.

"Juan Manuel," he says. "Will you come to my celebration after this?"

"Sure," Tom says, feeling little fireworks behind his eyes from the cocaine. "I love a celebration."

"What brings you here?"

"I came with her," Tom says, pointing to Paola.

"Then you're already coming to my celebration. You're her boyfriend?"

"We met this afternoon."

"Plenty of time to become her boyfriend," Juan Manuel says. "You didn't fall in love right then? Is something wrong with you?"

A wave of applause and scattered whoops rise from the dance floor as the opening DJ unplugs his headphones and bows to the crowd. Paola comes out of his set with something tribal, full of echoic chants and drums, and ten minutes later has the whole club on its feet and up against the booth as she shifts from screaming disco anthems to hard-edged house music, transitioning so seamlessly that even with the genre flips it's hard to tell where things begin and end. Tom scans the dance floor for his mother, finds Alex's head above the fray, and catches glimpses of Diane, her hair hiding her face, her body racked by a pulsing kick drum. And then she's cutting through the crowd toward the booth, where she leans over the mixer, as close to Paola's face as possible, and mouths, "Oh my God." Paola throws her head back with laughter and reaches out with both her hands. The two women dance with their fingers intertwined over the turntables. When Diane disappears into the crowd, Paola turns to Tom for an openmouthed wink and quick pump of her fist.

Fifteen

The adults stop by the booth to say good night on their way out. They walk the beach road, loose limbed and weaving slightly, talking loudly over the ringing in their ears. Back at Diego's, Alex shuts the guest room door and turns to find Diane facing him at the foot of the bed, her face flushed and eyes glinting in the yellow lamplight. With his hands on her shoulders and his right heel just behind her left, he trips her gently in a modified version of his favorite judo throw and falls with her onto the mattress. The momentum of their collapse carries through the undressing process and slows abruptly once they're down to undergarments. He kisses her lips, her throat, the space between her breasts, her stomach, the soft insides of her thighs. The top hem of her panties is between his teeth when she pulls him up by the hair. Alex reaches for the bedside lamp.

"No," she says, catching his wrist. "Leave it on."

She takes his nipple gently in her teeth as she slides black satin underwear over her hips and down her legs. Her breathing and pulse quicken as he presses against her through the fabric of his boxers, but there's something distant in his expression, some concern behind his eyes. When she hooks her thumbs into his waistband, Alex rolls away.

"Can I talk to you for a second?"

"You're talking to me now."

"There's something you should know before—before this goes any further."

Diane laughs. "Let me guess: You're not in event production." She cushions the headboard behind her with a pillow and draws her knees up to her chest while Alex faces her, Indian-style, in the middle of the bed. "What exactly do you need to tell me."

"I do produce events," he says. "Just not the kind that usually implies."

"What kind of events are we talking?"

"Remember the video we watched at Lindsay's?"

"Don't change the subject."

Alex blinks.

"You're—wait, what? That kind of event?"

"That one in particular."

She laughs and then catches herself. "Come on. What—that was you on the bike?"

He stares at her in silence.

"Oh my God," she says. "Please tell me you're kidding."

"I'd be lying."

"What the fuck are you doing?"

"I'm leveling with you."

"No, what are you *doing*? Why are you doing that?"

"That's a longer story."

She stands and steps unsteadily into her underwear, eyeing him the way he looks at unfamiliar growling dogs. Alex prepared himself for this but still feels his heart rate ramp up as she gathers her clothes from the floor without taking her eyes off him.

"Where are you going?" he asks.

"To the airport with my son."

"It takes twenty minutes for taxis to come out here," he says, fishing his phone from the pocket of his pants. "I'll call one, but can you hear me out while you wait?"

"No promises."

She continues dressing while he orders a car, thanks the dispatcher, and hangs up.

"Ten minutes," Alex says. "Slow night."

"I'll give you five."

"Sit down?"

"No thanks."

He sits at the foot of the bed and looks up at her while she stands, arms crossed, by the door.

"I'm sorry to lay this on you, but I wanted to be honest."

"There's no medal for that when you're robbing fucking jewelry stores, Alex. And you thought—what? 'Well, she used to fuck my low-life criminal accomplice in her twenties, so maybe she won't mind that this is how I make a living'?"

"How I used to make a living."

"Used to? Fuck you. That 'event' was last month."

"That's it for me. I'm done."

"My friend's husband told her he was done cheating when she caught him getting head from their yoga teacher," Diane says. "I didn't think anyone could top that horseshit, but congratulations. Why should I believe you're quitting?"

"Long time coming. I wanted to be sure before I told you. To come to you clean, so to speak."

"And naked."

"Right."

"If I look up 'armed robbery' on YouTube, how many other videos of you will I find?"

"Three," Alex says. "Maybe four."

"How many times have you been caught?"

"I haven't."

"How long have you been doing this?"

"A little over twenty years."

"How is that possible?"

Alex shrugs. "No one's lucky forever."

"Some people are unlucky all their lives." Diane sets her bag down and leans against the door. "Ben works with you, doesn't he?"

"What makes you say that?"

"The way he looks at you, like you're his favorite son or

something. At first I thought he wanted to fuck you, but it's deeper than that. Answer me."

She knows the answer. Alex is impressed by her intuition and also by her willingness to leverage it. This, he realizes, is a test. He'll need to betray the confidence of his best friend and longtime partner if he wants to buy some time with her and so, with the feeling he gets while looking down from a high balcony, he says, "Ben works with me, yes."

"And that was Diego on the other bike."

"Diego? No, Diego is a sculptor. That was Catalina."

"You're kidding me."

"Because she's a woman?"

"Fuck off. I completely bought her yoga-teacher line."

"She does teach yoga. She's good at it. She's good at a lot of things."

Diane sits on the bed beside him. "How'd you two meet?"

"Paola's mother is her second cousin. One day María calls me up and says this crazy relative of hers is robbing banks with her boyfriend and some sketchy crew from Medellín. 'If she's gonna do this shit, she might as well do it with you.' I said I'd give her a try."

"And?"

"I haven't worked without her since."

"And won't ever again."

"Not if I can help it."

Diane lifts his right hand from his knee and turns it over to examine the palm. "How you make a living is your business, but I can't see you if you keep doing what you're doing. That's black and white for me. And I knew you were lying about your job, which means I know when you're lying. You're really done with that?"

Alex nods.

"You have nice hands, by the way. Do something nice with them."

He laughs. In his recurring nightmare, he and Craig fly off

the bike and skid across the intersection. Alex puts out a hand to stop himself and watches in horror as the pavement shreds his glove and grinds his skin, bone, and ligaments to pulp, leaving nothing but a bloody stump. He picks himself up, surrounded by police now, unable to raise his rifle or draw the pistol from the holster on his thigh—and then he wakes up. He's always been protective of his hands, each one a bank of muscle memory accumulated through countless hours of striking, grappling, climbing, knife drills, target practice. Useless knowledge now. Lay down your weapons, Alex thinks. Swords into plowshares. His phone is vibrating on the nightstand.

"That's your cab," he says.

"Can you cancel it?"

"Are you sure?"

"For now. Mostly because I don't want to terrify my son by dragging him onto an airplane in the middle of the night. We'll stay down here this weekend. After that, we'll see."

Alex apologizes to the driver, who hangs up on him.

"There's one more thing," he says. "I have a meeting tonight."

"Tonight? It's one thirty."

"This morning, technically. I have to go soon, but I won't be long."

"Taking meetings is a funny way of getting out."

"The meeting is the only thing I'm taking," Alex says. "Catalina set it up a while back, and you don't stand people up down here."

"Where do you have meetings at this hour?"

"At a brothel, actually."

"Charming. What's it about?"

"I don't know. And it doesn't matter. Whatever it is, I'm passing. Shouldn't take more than an hour."

"That's why we're staying here, isn't it? You barely drank tonight."

"Let's have a drink when I get back."

"There's no chance in hell I'll be awake when you get back."

"Guess I'll have to celebrate retirement alone."

"Can you really do that?" Diane asks. "Just walk away from that kind of work?"

"I work for myself. Why not?"

"I don't know," Diane says. "You tell me."

Sixteen

Paola plays her last track at Papaya Playa just before 2 a.m. After
a shot of tequila in the booth and another at the bar, she and
Tom climb into the bed of a pickup filled with speakers, mixers,
and most of the VIP section from the club. They head south on
the beach road, warm wind coming in waves as the driver accel-
erates between speed bumps. Paola taps Tom's knee and points
up to a sky filled with more stars than he's seen in months. The
truck turns into the driveway of a stone-clad villa where Juan
Manuel's celebration is getting under way. The ground floor is
a loft-like space under a beamed ceiling hung with hammock
chairs. The speakers get a standing ovation as they come through
the door.

Tom follows Paola as she works the room, greeting old
friends and new acquaintances with the same animated warmth.
The house belongs to a commercial crab fisherman named Carl
who works four months a year on the freezing waters off Alaska
and returns to Tulum to thaw out, throw parties, and burn
through his earnings. He apologizes to Paola for the setup delay
and thanks her for playing.

"It's fine, honey," Paola says. "I love the late shift."

The crowd seems to double every fifteen minutes. Lukewarm
beers and lit cigarettes float from hand to hand in the living
room, which became a packed dance floor as soon as Paola got
behind the decks. She's playing harder and darker now, filling
the room with chugging dance-hall reggae and sleek, percussive
techno. Tom is missing most of his peripheral vision after a key

bump of what looked like cocaine turned out to be ketamine. He's dancing with the yoga instructor from a nearby hotel— a wiry, smiling, dreadlocked woman who introduced herself by removing Tom's tee shirt and using it to wipe sweat from her face and arms. She invites him to the bathroom, but Tom begs off and goes in search of provisions for Paola, who throws her arms around him when he ducks under the makeshift booth with two cigarettes and tequila in a coffee mug.

"*Ay, mi amor,*" she says. "You read my mind."

"What is this?" Tom asks, squinting at the screen of the CDJ she's playing from.

"You like it? This is me, I made this. Get back out there, *marica.* Your girlfriend's looking for you."

He heads for the exit instead. Overflow from the dance floor spills out the back door and collects under a cloud of smoke in a small clearing behind the house. Tom is headed for the narrow beach path when a man emerges from the darkness, his bald head gleaming under the outdoor lights. With his dark eyes, barrel chest, and black goatee he looks bullish even before Tom spots the thick steel ring in his septum. Juan Manuel rushes to greet the heavily tattooed newcomer, and their embrace ends with a low-key, palm-to-palm exchange. Tom plucks a cigarette from behind his ear and makes a show of searching for a lighter when the stranger catches him staring.

"Here," the man says, striking a match as he approaches. "You're American. What's your name?"

"That obvious, huh? I'm Tom."

"Rafael. What brings you here?"

"Paola, the girl playing music," Tom says, wondering why this feels like an interrogation.

"Ah, *sí.* Juan Manuel's friend. Enjoying yourself?"

"I am." He's also coming off the ketamine and fading fast. "I'd love to buy a little something from you."

Rafael nods and produces a small matchbox from the pocket of his shorts.

"Put that away," he says when Tom pulls out a wad of pesos. "It's a gift."

"Thank you. Can I buy some for Paola?"

"Juan Manuel has some for her already. She's one step ahead of you."

"More than one," Tom says. "Can I get you a drink?"

"I have some business in Playa del Carmen, but we'll see each other later."

"Great," Tom says. "Hey, thanks again."

When Rafael disappears down the beach path, Tom slides the matchbox open and finds two clear capsules filled with fine brown crystals. He touches one to his tongue and winces at the acrid residue. The pill goes down easily in a mouthful of warm beer.

Seventeen

Just after 3 a.m., Alex leaves Diane tangled in the sheets and slips out the back door of the house. Ben and Catalina wait in the glow of a bare red bulb that the local Centro Ecológico mandates for outdoor fixtures. White lights are a leading cause of death for hatchling sea turtles who mistake them for the full moon that guides them toward the water when they emerge from eggs buried in the sand.

"I'll drive," Ben says.

They shut their doors softly and take the road to town. Alex rides up front. He's lived a sheltered life, professionally speaking. Under the terms of their unspoken agreement, Ben fields the offers and, on the rare occasions that Alex accepts, provides logistical and financial support while Alex researches and preps with help from Catalina. Tonight's meeting request included all of them. After weeks of cajoling, Catalina convinced Alex to fly down.

"How's our time?" he asks.

"We're fine." Ben pats him affectionately on the thigh. "We've been taking meetings without you for years now. Relax."

They pass a game of pickup soccer played by streetlight on an empty lot and hot dog carts as bright as fireworks. A pack of tourists stumbles out of one bar and toward another, and Alex scans the group for Tom and Paola. Having seen the underbelly of this town, he worries about his daughter being out at night.

They're northbound on the highway when Catalina says, "I like her."

"Diane? So do I."

"Where does she think you are right now?"

"On the way to a whorehouse."

"To do what?"

"Talk shop."

Catalina sticks her head between the seats. "You told her?"

"Yeah. Just now."

Her laugh is triumphant. "I knew it. Ben, what did I say?"

"You said, 'I bet Alex tells Diane,'" Ben says.

"I should have bet you," Catalina says. Then to Alex, "What inspired that?"

"Better now than later," Alex says.

"Later? You just met this woman."

"Technically, we've known each other longer than I've known you."

"Puta madre," Catalina says and sits back hard against the seat.

They pass a rusted red pickup with three small children in the bed and, two miles later, an army transport truck with soldiers as cargo, listless men with rifles held between their knees.

"Refresh my memory," Alex says. "Who brought this to you?"

"Santos," Catalina says. "I don't think anybody knows his last name."

"And Santos is who?"

"He owns Palm Trees, the whorehouse. Has his hands in all kinds of things."

"And you know Santos how?"

"We move things through him. The narcos have a poker game and sometimes they ask Santos to bring merchandise so they can shop while they play—watches, jewelry for their girls."

"They pay retail for the shit we bring them," Ben says, "sometimes more. Always trying to outdo each other."

"Fucking gold mine," Catalina says. "Santos said someone at the game was asking for me. Something big that has to be done right. No misses, real money. But they wanted to meet everyone."

"Who made the ask to Santos?"

"Some captain from Cancún. Asking for a friend, he said."

"You're ready to go again?" Alex asks. "You told me you could use a break."

"I always feel that right before we go. It passes. You don't feel that?"

"Not usually. I feel it now."

"What does that mean?" Ben asks.

"I'm not looking for the next thing," Alex says.

"Not looking?" Catalina sticks her head between the seats again. "Are you kidding? For good?"

"Maybe."

"Maybe out or maybe kidding?"

"What's the difference?"

"Is this her talking?"

"This is me talking," Alex says. "You're talking to me."

"Whatever. We go, we listen, we talk after that. Okay?"

"Okay," Alex says. "We're going. How's our time?"

"Shut up about our time," Ben says as he takes the exit for Playa del Carmen, a sleepy fishing village transformed over a decade into a sprawling city packed with nightclubs, beach clubs, souvenir shops, and pharmacies peddling generic drugs and off-brand sunscreen. A street fair has just ended on the outskirts of town, carnival rides flashing but unmoving, vendors packing up and breaking down their stalls. Ben stops on a quiet block across from a stately five-story apartment block, its entrance marked by a red light that serves no ecological purpose.

"Welcome to Palm Trees," Catalina says as Ben distributes pistols from the center console.

"Are they here yet?" Alex asks after chambering a round.

"I doubt it," Catalina says. "Should we wait to get a look?"

Normally Alex would insist on waiting, but all he wants is for this to be over.

"Let's be early," he says.

Reggaeton blares from a passing car as the crew steps into

the street. Ben rings a bell on the ironwork gate, which buzzes in response and opens into an arched entryway where a female cashier sits behind a desk, flanked by large men in black suits. Catalina confers with the woman, who nods solemnly and makes a phone call. A group of men in dress shirts, very drunk and British, talk loudly in the interior courtyard beyond. The upper floors are lined with landings connected to the courtyard by a series of staircases. At the sound of a bell, a dozen women exit the rooms above and, after a brief pause at the railings, descend in unison.

"This way," the cashier says as she starts up the stairs.

The women smile seductively as they parade past the crew. Heavy makeup, lacy bodysuits, clear plastic platform heels and six-inch spikes, wave after wave of perfume. The Brits clap and whistle as the procession surrounds them. Five floors above, the cashier knocks softly and opens the last door on the hall. The windowless room is lit by red wall sconces and a large flat-screen TV. Two young boys sit Indian-style on the floor, lost in a video game, oblivious to the young woman in the bed beside them. She's naked underneath a thin white sheet, wide-eyed, higher than a Georgia pine. Santos sits behind a desk made from thick plate glass and sawhorses, shaving cocaine from a half-wrapped kilo with a six-inch razor blade. He's wiry and sunken-chested under a white tank top, the comb marks in his slicked-back hair like grooves in a record. Beside him, a stocky man in a Miami Heat jersey spoons coke onto an electronic scale. The powder has the flaky shine of mica and the pink cast of a conch shell under the red lights.

"*Buenas,*" Catalina says.

"*Qué onda,*" Santos says. "*Siéntate.*"

"*Dónde están?*"

"*Me dijeron que vendrían a las dos y media. No sé dónde están.*" He looks Alex up and down, smiling with half his mouth. "*Tu amigo famoso, no? Santos. Mucho gusto.*"

Alex stares back and says nothing. On the wall behind Santos hangs a large painting in which Elvis, wearing only a white leather jacket, fucks Marilyn Monroe surrounded by fluffy clouds and a choir of angels. On a whiteboard beside the painting are three rows of names that Alex can't make out. Is his eyesight finally going? He needs to see an ophthalmologist; he'll make an appointment as soon as he gets home. Santos rips through two large lines and offers a steel straw to his guests. Alex and Ben decline. Catalina is bent over the table when the knocking starts.

Two men enter before anyone can answer. The first, in black denim shorts and a sleeveless white tee shirt, has a shaved head and thick black goatee. Tribal tattoos cover his calves and forearms, and the steel ring in his septum reminds Alex of a *National Geographic* feature on Pacific Islanders. The second man wears a tan leather blazer, stone-washed jeans, and alligator cowboy boots. Their right hands rest on the pistols in their waistbands as they scan the room. Alex looks to Catalina, who looks to Santos. Santos looks afraid.

"Vale," the tattooed man says, loud enough to be heard through the door.

In walks a slim, calm man in a white tee shirt and navy chinos. A mass of dreadlocks is bound behind his head with baling twine, and his clear, dark skin glows in the red light. On his feet are the hemp-soled espadrilles that Paola wears. Alex senses Catalina's shock, but everything he needs to know about the stranger is written on the faces of the boys by the TV, who stand up as if the floor has just caught fire. Boots jerks his head toward the door and the boys fall over each other in their hurry to leave. The younger one pauses in the doorway and goes back for the girl, hissing in her ear as he wraps the sheet around her body and drags her out into the hall.

"Tú también," the stranger says to Santos, who nods apologetically and leaves without a word of protest.

The man in the Miami jersey follows and shuts the door behind them as the dreadlocked stranger moves behind the desk and rests his fists on the glass.

"Welcome to the Costa Maya," he says to Alex and only Alex. "My name is Alejandro."

"Nice to meet you," Alex says, thinking: What are the odds that this man has my name in Spanish? He tells himself to knock it off, that coincidence is meaningless.

"Thank you for coming," Alejandro says. He speaks slowly but his accent is faint. Normally Ben would do the talking, but Alejandro doesn't seem to notice him. He glances at Catalina and turns back to Alex. "It was the two of you who made the calls, correct?"

"What calls?" Alex asks. "You called us. That's why we're here."

"Not this call. The calls to the police."

"Police?"

"In Las Vegas, before the jewelry was taken."

Alex can't imagine how this man knows about the Graff job or the 911 calls, which went unmentioned at the press conference devoted to the robbery. He tries to mask his shock, but Alejandro sees the shadow pass, he's sure of it.

"Is that what you want to talk about?" he asks.

"No," Alejandro says. He yawns unapologetically with his whole face, like a tiger, and Alex recognizes the sheathed feline capacity for violence. "That's not what brings us here tonight. We would like to speak with someone who has become difficult to reach. The job is to bring us this man."

"That's not what we do."

"It's not what you've done in the past, no."

"So why come to me? Sounds like something your boys here could handle."

"This will be more difficult, more technical than our people are used to. And it's important that the job is done with minimal violence—your specialty, not ours."

"Who are you looking for?" Ben asks.

"A producer of fentanyl, the synthetic opioid that's fifty times—"

"I know what fentanyl is," Alex says.

"Fentanyl is the future. This man is an excellent producer but a problematic vendor at the moment, which is why we need to speak with him."

"Good luck with that," Alex says.

"You know the man I'm speaking of?"

"I know the people who protect people like him from people like you."

"And?"

"They're ready for you. More than ready."

"Are they ready for you? We understand that this will not be inexpensive. The first million is available for transfer now, tonight, to cover your expenses. Another five will be sent when the work is done."

Catalina shifts in her seat as if trying to accommodate the weight of Alejandro's offer.

"I'm sorry," Alex says. "but I can't help you."

Catalina says, "Alex, we should—"

"Let's talk about Miami for a moment," Alejandro says. "About Gustavo Sabagal. You know Gustavo, no?"

"I've heard the name."

"I'm sure you have. You also heard he had some nice things in his safe last November."

"A lot of people know Gustavo," Ben says. "A lot of people know he has nice things lying around."

"But only three people arrived by Jet Ski to his home on Star Island in the night and relieved him of these things. Gustavo is a friend. He's very upset about what happened."

"I can't help you with that either," Alex says.

"No, but I can be of help to you. In addition to the payment, I can offer to erase your debt."

"I don't have any debts."

"Gustavo thinks differently."

"All due respect," Alex says, "but I don't give a shit what Gustavo thinks."

"It's more complicated—"

"No," Alex says, "it's not. If you told me I could wipe that debt by shaking hands, I'd still tell you to get fucked because that debt doesn't exist. Don't tell me you're here to collect." Catalina clears her throat, but Alex is having none of it. "Is that what this is? Is that why you brought the Mayan drugstore cowboy and his special-needs friend? Are you shaking me down?"

"Rafael, tiene un humor de perros, no?" Alejandro says, which gets a laugh from the tattooed soldier. Then to Alex, "I come to you with an offer, nothing more."

"No, you came at me talking about money I don't owe. Who the fuck are you supposed to be?"

Catalina sits up and says, "Alex—"

"A messenger," Alejandro says. "Let me tell you who I represent. Do you know who controls this coast?"

"Sure," Alex says.

"Then you understand the source of this request. It comes directly from this man."

"You expect me to believe that?"

While Alejandro inspects the fingernails of his left hand, Alex looks to Catalina, who shuts her eyes and nods her head. This is what she has been trying to say.

"You want me to believe he asked for me by name."

"By reputation," Alejandro says.

"That's impossible."

"Not at all. Like you, he cares a great deal about details. Who does a thing, how that thing is done. He saw the video from Las Vegas and said to me: 'These are the right people. Find them.' And where do we find you? In this town, my home. Strange, no? My employer thinks this is a sign."

"I don't believe in signs," Alex says.

"Qué pena. Let me tell you something I believe in: this job, this task. That's my belief tonight."

"We'll talk it over," Alex says. "I can't give you an answer now."

Alejandro smiles. "Take your time. Your friend will know how to reach to me."

Rafael closes the door behind them. After five seconds of expectant silence, Santos bursts into the room demanding answers.

"Not a fucking word to him," Alex says. "Let's go."

They exit Palm Trees in time to see three Suburbans roll down the street toward the highway. The crew walks in silence to Ben's car and sits in silence once the doors are closed. Alex is the first to speak.

"Who was that?"

"Alejandro Ixto," Catalina says.

"Who the fuck is he?"

"He runs the coast for the cartel. Everything from Cancún to Belize."

"You believe what he said about where this is coming from?"

Catalina nods.

"And you had no idea what we were walking into."

"How could I? No one knew, not even Santos. These people don't like anyone to know who they are, where they are, what they're doing. They're paranoid, more paranoid than you."

"How did he know about Vegas?"

"We moved a few pieces through that card game," Ben says. "They must have recognized the wares."

Alex scoffs. "You think they spotted stuff from Graff? What are they, the fucking Gemological Association of Cancún?"

"If you have a better explanation," Ben says, "I'm all ears."

"What about Miami? How did he know that was us?"

"Miami had a lot of moving parts," Ben says. "I don't know who talked, but I can guess."

"You don't sound worried," Alex says.

"Oh, I'm worried. I hate everything about this but the money."

"Exactly."

"That being said, it's lot of money."

"More than a lot," Catalina says. "Alex, you want out? Do this first. Put some icing on that cake you've been baking."

"You let me worry about that," Alex says.

"Let me tell you what I'm worried about: You don't say no to these people. Me and Ben live here, remember?"

"I don't take orders," Alex says. "We don't. Remember? Not from these people, not from anyone. I'm not sticking my neck out so you can keep your fucking beach house."

"The calls to the police weren't on the news," Ben says. "Nobody reported them. Not the papers, not the TV stations. No mentions at the press conference. How did he know about that?"

Catalina laughs disgustedly. "Because they don't have dirty cops in Vegas, Mr. Former Las Vegas Detective? Give me a fucking break. Alex, who are you texting?"

"Someone who can answer my questions."

"Maricel?" Ben asks.

Alex nods.

"She's retired."

"Right. But she'll know what's going on here."

"That seems like a last resort to me," Ben says.

"It's a second opinion."

Ben shrugs and starts the car.

Eighteen

Tom comes to in a chaise lounge on the beach behind the house. The air is still and the sky is pale blue striped with pink above a dark-water horizon. Scenes from last night come back to him like things blown in on the wind: a massage circle in the master bedroom, a slideshow of faces from the dance floor and, in the clearest image, Paola holding him by the hips and shaking with laughter as he tries and fails to match her rhythm. Did they kiss? He can't be sure. She's coming down the beach path toward him, calling out his name.

"Hey," he says. "Over here."

She's carrying two coconuts, their oblong green husks hacked open at one end.

"I looked everywhere for you," she says. "Drink this."

The cool, sweet liquid has the faint metallic aftertaste of blood.

"Jesus," Tom says, coughing. "I needed that."

"I know. Lie down, *marica*. Make some room."

She stretches out beside him with her head on his chest. Strands of her hair find their way into his mouth and the gold moon on her necklace digs into his ribs, but her body is soft and warm, and a quick cost-benefit analysis of these sensations leaves him disinclined to move. More memories from last night: a swig of tequila in the clearing, a swim in the ocean. Tom pats his pockets. The matchbox is gone, along with the second pill.

"You split it with me," Paola says. "Remember?"

"I don't, but you're welcome. That was fun."

"Was? It's just getting started. We should sleep before it gets too hot."

Rafael, who rejoined the party sometime before dawn, is coming down the path toward them at a jog. He slaps Tom's shoulder as he passes.

"Give us a hand," he says.

A dozen fishermen have come down to the water to launch their boats and haul in nets. Tom and Rafael flip a pair of dinghies that passed the night upside down in the sand. Carl attaches outboard motors to the sterns and the three men push the boats into the shallows. Fishermen jump aboard and tear through the shore break, their bodies backlit against the brightening sky. Carl wades into the water and shouts for Tom, who sloshes after him to help haul in a net. They drag the load ashore, where fishermen sort through the writhing catch, tossing the smaller fish into the surf and the larger ones farther up the beach where they continue flopping, powdery white sand sticking to their scales and eyes. The boats come roaring back, and the fishermen gut and fillet their catch while seagulls circle overhead. Tom staggers back up the beach and collapses next to Paola in the sand.

"Nice work," she says. "Not as useless as you look."

"I need that nap now."

"Take it."

"*Tu novio está cansado?*" Rafael says as he approaches.

"*No es mi novio, caballero, pero él está bien.*"

"We have an errand to run now, my friend," Rafael says to Tom. "Sleep later. Come with me."

Nineteen

Birdsong wakes Diane. Sensing Alex in the bed, she reaches blindly behind her and finds knit cotton instead of bare skin. He's still in yesterday's khakis and black tee shirt, staring at the ceiling with his hands behind his head.

"Hey," he says. "Good morning."

"What time is it?"

"I don't know. Early."

"You just got back?"

"I've been back for a while. I went for a walk."

"On the beach?"

He nods.

"Are you up for another?"

In a black sarong and bathing suit, she follows him through the sleeping house, past the sink full of dishes. They step lightly across the back deck and onto the sand. The light from the low sun is hazy and blinding, less clear but somehow more intense than at midday. The beach is slowly coming back to life. Men rake and bag the seaweed at the water's edge; joggers appear and recede. A hundred yards ahead, a low daybed sits between a hotel and the water, shielded by a palapa roof and four thin, gauzy sheets of fabric hung like walls. A woman sleeps on her side with a little boy in the cove formed by her body, his feet flush against his mother's thighs as if he's about to push off into water. Her hand rests on his rib cage, over his lungs and heart.

"Is it that safe here?" Diane asks.

"No," Alex says, "it's not."

"Tell that to our kids."

"What time did they get back?"

"They didn't. Sounds like I'm the only one who checked on them this morning."

"Shit," Alex says. "Did you hear from them?"

"They're fine. Tom texted me at four a.m. They're at some party down the road. 'Spending the night.'"

"But they're okay?"

"They're fine. My son has had a lot of practice getting in and out of trouble."

"What does that mean?"

"He got arrested for selling drugs in high school, if you can believe that. I mean, you can probably believe that, given what you know about his lineage. Kind of settled the nature-versus-nurture argument for me."

"That's surprising. Him doing that, I mean."

"I sent him to a fancy boarding school, which was a mistake in retrospect. He was trying to keep up. Are you going to tell me about this meeting?"

"The meeting was fine."

"So tell me about it."

"Someone offered us a job. I passed. I'm passing."

"What kind of job?"

"Something I don't do."

"Which is?"

"Find a person and deliver them."

"They call that kidnapping. And you don't do that?"

"No, I don't."

"You've never done that."

"No."

"What does something like that pay?"

"Six million, with expenses."

"Come on. Pesos?"

"No, not pesos. It's on the high end, to be honest. Very high."

"Six million? Jesus, I'm in the wrong business."

"Me too. Anything else you want to know?"

"Yes, actually. Sit with me for a minute. I want to know what happened."

"I just told you."

"I don't mean this morning. I want to know what happened to him. To Clay."

Alex scoops up a fistful of sand and lets it fall through his fingers. "It's not a good story."

"Well, I'm a big girl. If it's too hard for you, that's fine. But if you're protecting me, don't bother. I've had two decades to imagine all kinds of awful shit. Whatever the truth is, I promise it'll come as a relief."

"You know what he was doing, right? What we were doing back then?"

"Not really, no."

"Some assholes bought the Ocean County Airport at a bankruptcy auction in the early eighties. Doctors, lawyers—regular guys. It was a real estate play. The plan was to tear up the runway and put in a development, golf course, country club. One of these guys had a friend in Miami who had family in Colombia. This friend heard about the airport and had the bright idea to run coke through it while they waited for the property value to increase. The guys who bought the airport knew the cops, knew the local politicians, were the local politicians for all I know. They had a sit-down with everyone they needed to buy off. The pitch was beautiful: We'll bring in drugs that will never hit the streets here, never cause a single crime or affect the pristine quality of life, and all you have to do is look the other way, tell us if the feds get wise, sit back, and get rich. You remember the eighties. Demand was infinite."

"How did you and Clay get mixed up in this?"

"Remember the black eye he had when you met? Did he tell you where he got it?"

"He said he had a disagreement with some metal."

Alex laughs. "That sounds like him. Two days before we ran into you at Dock's, we broke into a hotel room at Trump Plaza. The couple staying there had a lot of flashy jewelry with them. I'd asked Clay's idiot ex-girlfriend to knock and make sure they were out. They didn't answer because they were tied up and gagged inside. Two guys with guns got there before us. Clay was packing, but it took these boys about ten seconds to figure out that we had no idea what we were doing. They jumped us. We got into it. It shouldn't have worked out. Somehow it did."

"Somehow? How?"

"Clay was useless with a pistol, but empty-handed he was very good. All we did back then was train and spar. When it turned into a scrap, our odds got better. Come to find out the people whose asses we saved were in the import business, in town from Mexico to check out this local airport they'd been offered as a distribution point. The wife offered us jobs."

"After you tried to rob them? Doing what?"

"Driving, moving product. They had planes landing twice a day. The door was wide open."

"You're telling me this started right after I met you."

Alex nods. "We worked out of this shitty little airport hangar. Planes would pull in, unload, take off again. Clay and I would drive a car to New York, Philly, Atlantic City, even Boston. This one afternoon, I couldn't make the run. My mom was finally going into treatment; I had to help her get her shit together. We called our contact. He said Clay could do it on his own." Alex pauses as two women in sports bras and yoga pants jog past. "He never made it. Someone called to ask me where he was, why he hadn't shown up yet. I took my mom's car and hit the highway. Traffic was backed up for miles. I rode the shoulder until I hit this wall of cops. Clay's car was wrapped around a tree off 95. Someone ran him off the road and shot him. Took the drugs."

Diane hugs her knees to her chest. "Who knew he was alone that day?"

"I only told the people we were working for, but that doesn't mean it didn't travel."

"And who were you working for?"

"The couple we tried to rob."

"It couldn't have been them?"

"It was their load. Clay and I were making money for them hand over fist. Not to mention that we saved their lives."

"What happened then?"

"We had a number to call if anything went wrong, this lawyer in New York. He put me on a plane to Mexico. Maricel took me in for a few weeks."

"Maricel?"

"The wife. She and her husband moved stuff from Colombia into the States back then, before the Mexican cartels took over. The husband's dead now. She and I are still close."

"Did she get you into what you're doing now?"

"Sort of. Her husband threw a party at their house while I was there. He was always throwing parties, but this one was for his birthday and he pulled out all the stops. White tiger cubs pissing on the Persian rugs, bowls of cocaine everywhere, orgy in the living room. Went on for days. At some point, someone mentioned I was out of work. Someone else said I should talk to Ben, this ex-cop from Vegas who put crews together. This guy was joking—everybody laughed when he suggested it. I cornered him later on and said I wanted in. I was scared shitless. Didn't know what else to do."

"Do you know the difference between a reason and an excuse?"

"I didn't say it was my finest hour."

"And you're still close with this woman?"

"We're having lunch today."

"What on earth for?"

"To make sure my 'no' on this job goes down easy. I think she knows the people who are asking. She's been looking out for me since I was a kid."

"And she knew Clay?"

"She hired us. I wouldn't say she knew him."

"But she met him."

"Once."

"It's strange for me to think that other people knew him. None of my friends did, none of my family. Except for Tom, it was like he never existed."

"You didn't try to find his family when he died?"

"When I heard what happened—and let me tell you, this has haunted me for years—a part of me felt like I dodged a bullet. I didn't want that in my life or near my kid. I was flat broke, but that kind of money? No thank you. Pass."

"Right," Alex says. "I get it."

"I don't think you did before," Diane says. "But you do now, don't you?"

Twenty

Tom and Rafael receive a hero's welcome when they return with bottled water, bags of ice, cold beer, and gas for the generator. In the kitchen, a group of Italians are adding magic mushrooms to mango smoothies from the juice bar down the road. The crowd is swelling after hours of decline, and the dance floor is a mix of fresh-faced new arrivals and jittery veterans in sunglasses and various states of undress. Juan Manuel has been behind the decks since sunrise, and Tom high-fives him as he slips out of the house and into blinding sunlight. Two fishermen have joined the party; one strums ranchera songs on guitar while the other cooks mahi-mahi over a small fire in the clearing. Paola, in borrowed aviators and a bright yellow bikini, calls for Tom to join her in a hammock chair. As he puts an arm around her, Paola sticks her nose into his armpit.

"You stink almost as bad as I do."

"Almost," he says. "Not quite."

Rafael emerges from the house with a tray of shots and sliced limes. Tom raises his glass and throws back what he assumes is tequila until every muscle in his face contracts at the chalky, medicinal taste of MDMA dissolved in water.

"Jesus Christ," he says. "Really? Again?"

"What did you think that was?" Paola asks.

"In the shot glass? I thought it was a shot."

"Be careful with him," Rafael says to Paola.

"It's not him I'm worried about," Paola says.

Rafael's half smile causes Tom's guts to contract. The feeling fades, the awful taste subsides. Tom shuts his eyes and lets a medley of birdsong, techno, and bilingual conversation wash over him. He wakes up to Paola whispering urgently in his ear.

"Hey, get up, *marica*. Let's go in the water."

Tom opens his eyes and understands her hurry. The sun feels like it's fifty feet above them, and everything in sight seems to be on the verge of combustion, popping and flaring, throwing off sparks. The rush of the drug has the force of a free fall. Tom and Paola stand and stumble down the beach path and across the sand, stopping at the water's edge, where he strips down to his boxer briefs and follows her into the shallows. His senses have been rewired: The sea feels like a cool breeze on his lower body while the hot air sits against his face and shoulders like a bath. Paola dives down and surfaces in front of him, sweeping her hair back as she emerges. The water around her glitters like shattered glass and her face glows with an intensity that Tom experiences as a low hum.

"Where does Rafael get this shit?" he asks.

"I meant to tell you this before, but be careful with Rafael."

Before Tom can ask why, she dives down again and turns sideways to swim between his legs. He senses that Paola knows a lot of things he doesn't.

"What's wrong with Rafael?" Tom asks when she surfaces again. "He seems okay to me."

"Because you're high."

"I'm so fucking high."

"It's nice, right?"

"Yeah. It's nice to meet you."

"It's funny that we just met yesterday."

"And that our parents met last month."

"They met before that," Paola says.

"What are you talking about?"

"Nothing, never mind. Does your mom have a type?"

"Before this? Mostly losers."

"Before and after."

Tom laughs. "I meant Alex seems okay to me. You don't get along?"

"No, we do."

"But you're not close."

"We are, in a way. We understand each other. But he wasn't around for a long time when I was growing up."

"Why not?"

"My mom didn't want him there. It's a long story. Were you close with your dad?"

"I never knew him."

"Not at all?"

"They were never together and he died before I was born. Car crash. Never met him, never even saw a picture."

"What does your mom say about him?"

"We don't really talk about it. Even when I was little I could tell she didn't want to. They met at a restaurant, had a one-night stand. What's she gonna tell me? That he snores? That he tips well?"

"You never wondered?"

"Not really."

"Are you lying to me or to yourself?"

Tom laughs. "You read minds now?"

"It's in your face. You're high as shit and you can't admit you want to know more? If you can't admit that to me—hey, no problem. We just met. But admit that to yourself."

"Okay," he says. "I can admit that. I still don't think it matters."

"No, you're right about that. It won't change anything. At some point you have to figure out who you want to be no matter who they are. Or were. And the knowledge doesn't always help, believe me. Hey, I can't stand out here. Can you carry me?"

"Of course."

As she wraps her arms around his neck and hooks her heels into his thighs, his vision blurs with some fresh neurochemical release and he shudders with pleasure.

"Are you cold?" she asks.

"Cold? Not at all."

"Ah," she says, "I see. I lied before, I like the way you smell."

He loves the way she smells right now, like red wine vinegar and metal. His high school girlfriend once told him that an appreciation of another person's body odor indicates a deep biological compatibility, but Tom decides to keep that to himself. They drift as a unit, his feet grazing the sandy bottom, his sense of time obliterated. The sun feels like a broiler now. Just before she lets go, Paola whispers, *"Me derrites."*

"What?"

But she's underwater again, swimming toward shore. On the sand, Tom shakes out his pants and checks his phone, which shows two texts and three missed calls from his mother.

"Let's get out of here," Paola says, wringing out her hair. "I'll come back for my records. I can't do another comedown in that house. Are they back in Akumal?"

Tom nods.

"We'll find a ride. This way."

They cut through Carl's neighbor's yard and find the beach road empty in both directions.

"What now?" Tom asks.

"Be patient, *marica*," Paola says. "Have faith."

"What does '*marica*' mean?"

Paola laughs and runs a hand through his hair. "It means sissy," she says. "Faggot, actually. But in a nice way."

Twenty-One

The northbound side of Highway 307 looks like a three-lane parking lot. Newspaper vendors, window washers, and children selling bags of chicharrones wander the maze of idling cars, their bodies blurred and shimmering through heat waves and exhaust. A fat man in a "No Fear" shirt sprays water onto Alex's windshield, but Alex waves him off. He's edgy, irritated. Maricel does not like to be kept waiting.

Her Mediterranean-style mansion sits on three acres of secluded coastline, between a five-star resort and a rock formation that looks like an oil tanker run aground. Maricel and her husband were regulars at the resort's restaurant and fell in love with the site while strolling down the beach one evening after dinner, trailed by bodyguards. The lot that Maricel envisioned was made up of beachfront owned by the resort and jungle held in trust by a national preserve. The resort's VP of real estate laughed when Maricel asked whom she might speak to about purchasing the land. Her builders broke ground six months later.

Her husband never saw the house completed. Roberto Sandoval was a gregarious, impatient man who never left a restaurant without coffee, dessert, one last drink, and one more for the road. When he passed away at seventy-one, the tabloids joked that colon cancer was an unnatural cause of death for a man who fed America's coke habit with an avalanche of product in the '70s and '80s. Roberto died a very wealthy man.

He was a lanky, handsome twenty-one-year-old when he spotted Maricel at the packed bar of an Acapulco nightclub. Alex heard the story of their first date from her and, later, from him. Maricel was struggling to flag down a bartender when Roberto, who never suffered for attention, sent her a glass of Champagne. After asking where the drink came from, she approached the young man in polished Chelsea boots, white jeans, and a loud print shirt unbuttoned to his sternum. He had six inches on her but was unnerved by her unblinking stare.

"This is nice," she said, "but I came to get drinks for my girlfriends, not to drink with you."

The bartender was in the middle of an order when Roberto summoned him and sent a bottle to the table of young women in the corner. He turned to Maricel. "Your friends have drinks now," he said. "You can drink with me."

She was on Christmas break from Wellesley College, the all-women school outside Boston where she studied English literature with the understanding that she would move back to Acapulco and marry her high school boyfriend after graduation. She laughed when Roberto said he worked in real estate. They'd attended the same Catholic high school until Roberto was expelled for selling drugs, a youthful indiscretion that quickly became a career. He sensed that she was attracted to him in spite of his notoriety, which was not usually the case, and could not have said what drew him to her given his weakness for tall American blondes like the one whose bed he had just left. Years later, Maricel chalked up his attraction to an instinct for self-preservation. Roberto's appetites were exceeded only by his ambitions, and without her tempering influence and good counsel, he would never have survived to die of natural causes.

His initial pitch to her was simple.

"I have to drive to Manzanillo in an hour," he said. "I want you to come with me."

"Well," she said, "you can't have everything you want."

"Do you believe that?"

She had, until that moment. For years, Maricel had been prone to spells of depression that lasted weeks and sometimes months before they burned off like a fog. Each bout left her lower than it found her, and she sometimes wondered if life amounted to the gradual relinquishment of happiness, a war lost inch by inch. Roberto's question shook something loose in her. The life her affluent but undistinguished parents had mapped out for her was not the one that she was meant to live. She saw her interest in literature for what it was: escapism, an excuse to explore alternate realities with academic rigor, to live in books instead of Acapulco or Wellesley, Massachusetts. There was no need for that now. The young man in front of her was a portal to another world.

"Does your car have a radio?" she asked. "I'll come if I can choose the music."

Her parents threatened to disown her when she broke off a tacit engagement to run with a mid-level trafficker. Maricel, they reasoned, would come crawling back, disgusted and defeated, once she'd seen the dark side of the disco glamour—the other women, the unspeakable violence. But their bookish, Boston-educated daughter had no illusions about what lay ahead.

Roberto came up fast thanks largely to his choice of partner. She was the brains behind his blunt force, and for this he loved her in a way that he had not thought possible. Maricel was surprised by his initial attraction, but very little else. She found men mostly predictable, a considerable advantage in an all-male industry. Roberto could not discuss Pynchon with her and could barely sit through a symphony performance. What he offered, Maricel told Alex, was the gift of her fully actualized self.

She took to Alex Cassidy immediately. She met him at the airport in Puerto Vallarta after Clay was killed and told him he could stay with her for as long as he liked. She taught him about wine, pulling bottle after bottle from her cellar over long lunches and dinners. Alex never tired of the way she talked, a mix of ESL awkwardness and excessively formal diction. They were lounging by the pool one afternoon when Alex worried aloud that Roberto might get the wrong idea. Maricel laughed.

Her husband, she said, loved watching her with other men, and not just in conversation. Years later, Alex heard a rumor that she personally screened Roberto's mistresses, that these women had to pleasure Maricel before they got to him. The rumor rang true. She had joked with Alex about her dorm-room flings at Wellesley, but it was more than that. The story described an act of self-fulfillment in the guise of prudence and devotion. It was Maricel through and through.

Alex inches toward a highway checkpoint manned by masked marines and stops on a signal from an officer in aviators. He catches his reflection in the lenses and sees what the marine sees: a middle-aged gringo piloting a mid-sized rental car. The marine waves him through; traffic gradually disperses. The sight of a young woman on a motorbike reminds Alex that Paola didn't make it home last night. He feels guilty for not checking on the kids this morning. Does Diane think he's a shitty father? Alex admires the constant low-level alarm he sees in other parents, the way a child's absence triggers momentary panic like a phantom limb. It's not an instinct he possesses. He chalks it up to sporadic custody but knows deep down he wasn't cut out for parenting. Fortunately Paola can take care of herself.

Alex leaves the highway and slaloms slowly down a dirt road, dodging potholes and palm fronds felled by a recent storm. The wrought-iron gate at the head of Maricel's drive has been replaced by a slab of dark hardwood reinforced with hammered steel. Alex wonders what prompted the change as the bullet-proof barrier rolls away. The armed guard inside stands back to let him pass.

The camera above the door is aimed down at the spot where his hair has recently begun to thin. The Sandovals' longtime housekeeper receives him and says the señora will be down in a minute. Alex hears her voice before she appears on the landing above him.

"I told Ernesto two courses for lunch because I didn't know if you had plans this afternoon, but he can always add more if you're hungry. We got some wonderful yellowtail from the fisherman this morning," she says, relying on the bannister in a way that makes Alex conscious of her age and his own. "I hope the road wasn't too bad coming in. The men were supposed to clear it Thursday, but you know how these things are." She touches his forehead with the back of her hand. "You look unwell."

"Just tired," he says, bending at the waist to embrace her.

"Come, sit." She leads him to the dining room that overlooks the water through a wall of windows. "When do you fly back?"

"Monday. I'm glad we got a chance to see each other."

"*Sí, sí,*" she says, gesturing at the empty rooms around them. "You can see I'm very busy these days."

She offers him a chair on the ocean-view side of the long glass dining table. Alex takes a small velvet envelope from the pocket of his pants.

"What's this?" she asks as he slides it toward her.

"A little something for your birthday. I know I'm early."

"Very early," she says, unfastening the clasp. Maricel takes great pride in her poker face, and Alex smiles when her eyes flash. Emeralds are her favorite. Catalina had a buyer for the earrings, but Alex took them anyway. Eighteen thousand dollars strikes him as a bargain for this audience.

"Thank you," she says. "They're lovely. Where are they from?"

"You don't know?"

"How would I know something like that? Your business is your business."

Her cook, Ernesto, appears with two steaming bowls of tortilla soup, and Alex decides he'll bring up business after the first course.

"Your daughter has become a lovely young woman," Maricel says.

"You saw her?"

"She came for a cocktail when she arrived. *Qué preciosa.* But tell me about you."

"I met someone," he says. "She's down here with me."

Maricel summons Ernesto and requests Champagne. "We'll toast," she says.

"Thanks. We're having drinks at La Buena Vida in Akumal tonight. We'd love to see you." He's certain she won't show and doubts that Maricel has ever set foot in the beach bar on Half Moon Bay.

"I'm sure it will be lovely," she says. "This sounds serious, no?"

"It is. And complicated."

"How?"

"Do you remember my friend Clay?"

"I do. That was very unfortunate."

"I'm sure I told you Clay had a kid on the way. This woman is the mother. I didn't know her then, but I knew of her. We met by accident last month. Neither of us knew who the other was until I saw her son, who looks exactly like his dad."

Ernesto returns with two glasses and a sweating bottle. He pulls the cork, releasing a soft hiss and a wisp of vapor. The wine foams into the glasses—handblown, paper-thin stemware so light that Alex feels as if he's holding only liquid.

"*Salud, amor, dinero, y el tiempo para disfrutarlos,*" Maricel says.

Health, love, money, and time to enjoy them. Right, Alex thinks. That's why I'm here.

"I want to know more about your *novia,*" she says, "but I suspect you came here to discuss something else."

Alex wipes his mouth with the stiff napkin from his lap. "I had a meeting last night with Alejandro Ixto. Do you know him?"

"I know of him, like everyone here. He's made quite a name for himself. How was your meeting?"

"He's asking me to do a job for him, for his boss."

"I see. How did they find you?"

"The last thing we did was in Las Vegas. A video made it

online, I thought maybe you'd seen it. We moved some of the pieces through associates of his. I'm guessing they put two and two together."

"That certainly sounds plausible. I assume the compensation is generous."

"The money's not the problem."

"What then?"

"I want to pass."

"You understand who Alejandro represents."

"I do."

"Then forgive me, but what is your question?"

"What to do if I don't want the job."

"What you want in this case is beside the point."

"You couldn't talk to them on my behalf?"

Maricel laughs. "You flatter me. It's a new day here. You say the request comes from the top, from Alejandro's boss? The president of my country answers to this man. When you work inside a system, you're a tool of those in power. This is a contract you signed many years ago."

"I don't work inside a system. I work for myself."

"Oh please, Alex. You sound like a child. Is this really what you tell yourself? Of course you work inside a system. Even Roberto understood this. You and Alejandro share some of the same delusions in addition to a name, now that I think of it. This juvenile idea of independence. You'll make quite the team."

"So you know him."

"I know of him, as I said. Let me tell you what I know of Alejandro. For many years he ran a meditation retreat in Tulum, a center for mindfulness. He was very well regarded as a teacher. Two years ago he left to live in a Tibetan monastery and expand his practice. He planned to stay a year, but after six weeks he received a message from his mother. She had gone to Playa del Carmen to see a friend and didn't recognize the city. Men were selling drugs on Fifth Avenue in full view of the police. This never used to happen, as you know. For many years this coast was sacred ground, a place where those in power kept their families. But when the tourists discovered Tulum, the opportunity became too great. The important thing to understand about Alejandro is that he has strong Mayan ancestry on his mother's side. The development of this coast has been devastating to the Mayan people who live here today. You may laugh at this, but these people feel their ancestors every day, feel the pain of what happened to them when the Spanish came. And now, with the water full of trash and the land full of resorts, they're forced to relive history, to watch the Europeans destroy everything again. Alejandro's mother recognized a man on the street, a man she helped to raise. He ignored her when she greeted him. She realized then that he was working, selling cocaine and pills to the gringos. It was too much for her to watch her own people destroy their home for a few pesos. She wrote to her son, who flew back immediately. He felt a duty to enforce order, to protect his home by any means. He took this proposal to the top of the cartel."

"How does a meditation teacher get a meeting like that?"

"He had something unique to offer. Alejandro asked only for the necessary resources—men, equipment, information—and a secure home for his mother and his aunt. In exchange, he would provide and maintain control of this coast. What people fear most is what they cannot understand. And how could their rivals comprehend a man who risks his life with no interest in gold chains or cars or whores, who lives in the jungle with his mother and her sister? The cartel understood that the willingness of a principled man to engage in a corrupt enterprise is a singular and perhaps a vital thing."

"How's that working out for him?"

"The other cartels were gone within six months. Alejandro has friends everywhere, eyes everywhere, men and women and even children who would inform for him for nothing but are now well paid to do so. He was efficient and even fair, in his way. The rules were made clear. Those who defied them found no mercy. He streamlined distribution, cleaned up the streets."

"A mindfulness coach took the coast inside a year?"

"When you arrived at my doorstep years ago, you were like a small dog whose legs had been broken by its owner. Terrified, unsure of everything. Helpless in every sense. Two months later you walked out of a warehouse in Miami with a small fortune in cash and art, and you need me to remind you that highly motivated and capable people can accomplish extraordinary things in small amounts of time?"

"Fair enough," Alex says. "And good for him. That's one way to expand your practice."

"His life today is not what he imagined, no. I assume he sees it as a necessary sacrifice. You met with him last night?"

Alex nods, remembering the fear in the eyes of the two young boys when Alejandro entered, the frantic obedience that followed.

"What was your impression of him?"

"Focused," Alex says. "The guru thing makes sense. He seemed oddly humble to me."

"There's humility, certainly. But to think of it as weakness would be a very bad mistake."

Alex refills his glass and drinks as fear seeps from his stomach into his lungs. Ernesto reappears with two plates of cochinita pibil, a Mayan dish of pork tied up in banana leaves and buried under coals to cook. The meat reminds Alex of the handless stump from his recurring nightmare. Orange liquid specked with fat pours off the pork and pools at the edges of his plate.

"When you arrived," Maricel says, "I thought you looked unwell, but now I suspect it's something else. Are you afraid?"

"I'd say I'm concerned."

"What about?"

"They want me to deliver someone, which isn't what I do. Why come to me? I feel like something else is going on here, but I've been up all night and I still can't see it. Does this make any sense to you?"

Maricel dabs the corner of her mouth with a napkin. "I can't tell you what a relief it is not to think in these terms anymore. Those are fair questions, of course. And completely irrelevant. There are always unknowns. What makes this so different?"

"Everything feels different now."

"Are the circumstances different? Or are you? If I told you I could pick up the phone and make all this disappear, what would you do? Join this woman in civilian life?"

"Is that unheard of?"

"That was honestly your plan?"

"People change."

"Perhaps. Rarely and by degree, if at all. If these earrings come from Las Vegas, then you recently pulled off the largest job in the history of a city that men have been robbing for a century. I saw the video you mentioned, along with the rest of the world. It was very entertaining, and I don't mean that as a compliment. The video is what put you in this position. And the man I saw on my computer did not look ready to retire."

"It wasn't meant to be an ad campaign."

"It doesn't matter. I say this not to flatter but simply to remind you: There are very few people as competent as you are at this kind of work. The cartel may have other reasons for seeking you specifically, but I can assure you that it comes down mostly to this. They want the best of everything—sports cars, weapons, poppies from Afghanistan." Maricel sets down her knife and fork. "I've told you the story of the night Roberto and I met."

"You have."

"Then I've told you his response when I told him he couldn't have everything."

Alex nods.

"After all these years, it turns out I was correct: You can't have everything you want. My advice is that you do what Alejandro asks and take his money. If you'd like for me to speak to him on your behalf, I will, for whatever it's worth. Ernesto makes a lovely coconut sorbet. Can I offer you dessert?"

Twenty-Two

A red convertible pulls up in front of Alex's condo, the car that skidded to a stop minutes after Paola stepped onto the beach road and stuck out her thumb. The driver, a jowly, silver-haired man named Javier, owns a Cancún factory where images of inebriated frogs are screened onto tee shirts and shot glasses. Paola thanks him for the ride and follows Tom upstairs. In their bedroom, she turns on the air-conditioning and kicks off her shoes.

"Want some water?" Tom asks.

"God, yes. *Gracias.*"

"Be right back," he says.

He's filling a bottle in the kitchen when he spots his mother on the balcony. Tom assumes that she's smoking and hopes that she has one to spare. The comedown feels like a slow-motion free fall, and he's itching for a quick nicotine lift before sleep. Diane turns at the sound of the door. She's not smoking, and Tom sees in her face that something has changed since she waved good night at the club.

"Hi," she says. "I was getting worried."

"Where's Alex?"

"He had to see someone. He'll be back after lunch."

She embraces her son, then pulls back for a better look. His sweat reeks of tequila and his pupils are like black holes drinking in the sunlight.

"Wow," Diane says.

"We went to a party."

"I can see that. You two have more in common than I thought."

"Can we save the D.A.R.E. lecture?"

"Sure. Can you do something for me?"

On the beach below the condo, she spreads a linen sheet on the sand with help from the offshore breeze. Diane sits behind her son and wraps her arms around his waist.

"Do you like it here?" she asks.

"I love it."

"Did you and Paola have a good time?"

"Yeah, we did."

"I really like her. That music was amazing."

"She's good. She played all night."

"What was the party like?"

"Sweaty, crowded. Probably still going."

"Did you get any sleep?"

"Not really. I need to crash soon."

"I know you do. Just hang on a little longer, okay?"

He feels her shiver like he did in the water, but his mother isn't high. She's crying.

"Hey, what's the—"

"No, no, it's okay, honey. Just sit."

"I'm sitting. What's the matter?"

"There's something I need to talk to you about."

"Then talk to me."

"Baby, Alex knew your dad."

The scene before him blurs as his heart rate slows and then ramps up alarmingly.

"Tom?"

"I'm here."

"I met him when I met your dad, but only that one time. I thought he looked familiar, but I couldn't place him when we ran into each other. Alex figured it out when he saw you. I wish I had a picture of your dad to show you. You look so much alike it scares me sometimes. Clay and Alex were close. He told Alex about you, told him I was pregnant. Your dad knew you needed to be here, that I needed you."

"How did he really die?"

"What makes you ask that?"

"The way you're talking about him."

"You knew I was hiding something, didn't you?"

"Can you answer my question?"

"Yes, I can. Someone shot him. We never found out who."

Tom doesn't know what to feel or if he's capable of feeling anything besides exhaustion and unsteadiness. A man in jean shorts and large sunglasses strolls by with a calico cat on a leash and wishes them good afternoon. Tom waves in response and wonders if he's seeing things, or dreaming.

"He was dealing, wasn't he," Tom says.

"Yes."

"With Alex?"

"Right. They were young—younger than you are now. Alex has done a lot of things he shouldn't have. He knows that. He's moving past it."

"What does that mean?"

"That he's ready for a change, another kind of life. The only way he'll stay in my life—in our life—is if he makes some changes."

Tom wipes sweat from his forehead and tries to place the feeling in his chest.

"Honey, talk to me."

"Does Alex know I know?"

"That's up to you. If you think he should, I'll tell him. Or you can. Whatever you want. What else can I tell you?"

"A lot of things, but not right now. I need to go to bed."

"Okay."

They stand up in unison, and Diane stifles a gasp when Tom turns to face her. He looked bad on the balcony, but his face is drawn and dark now, as if he's aged five years since they sat down.

"I love you," she says, holding him by the shoulders. "You know that, right?"

Tom nods.

"Go get some sleep."

He takes the stairs slowly, as if feeling out a recent sprain. In the bathroom, he assesses his sunburn as he tries and fails to pee. Ignoring Alex's warning, Tom drinks straight from the tap and uses Paola's toothbrush. She's snoring softly in the bedroom with her back to the door. Tom gets into bed, but the leaden exhaustion he felt on the beach has vanished like the morning haze, and his mind is dredging up memories. His mother seemed oddly unsurprised when he was arrested for selling drugs in high school. Underneath her fury and disappointment was something that felt to Tom like resignation, which makes sense to him now. What it must have done to her to witness that behavior in him, like the onset of some congenital disease. The last thing he does before closing his eyes is find his phone and translate the phrase that Paola whispered to him in the water.

Me derrites: You're melting me.

Okay, Tom thinks, that makes two of us.

Twenty-Three

The condo is quiet when Alex returns, his arms filled with groceries. Diane sits at the kitchen table with a coffee mug between her hands.

"Hi," she says. "How was lunch?"

"Okay. Did the kids make it back?"

"They did, about an hour ago. High as kites. At least my son was. They're sleeping it off."

"Occupational hazard for my daughter, unfortunately. Is there more coffee?"

"This is tequila, and there's half a bottle left."

"Everything okay?"

"I told Tom about his dad."

"How did that go?"

"I honestly have no idea. Poor kid could barely keep his eyes open. There was never going to be a good time for that conversation, but Jesus Christ."

She shuts her eyes as Alex moves behind her chair. When he sinks his thumbs into the taut muscles of her neck, Diane feels something shift, as if she's floated through a patch of sunwarmed water in a lake. She thinks: Are we in this together now? If she envies her married friends anything, it's these moments of quiet solidarity in the face of hardship. She had closed off a part of her heart to Alex, but now those walls collapse like a magician's trick coffin.

"Do you think he wants to talk to me about it?" Alex asks.

"He'll let you know if he does. I doubt it. Not today, at least."

"Not that it makes any difference, but I'm glad he knows."

"I know you are. Can I ask you something? How did this go from the most to the least relaxing beach trip in history?"

"The hard part's over."

"Says who?"

"All we have to do tonight is get drunk at a beach bar."

"Sorry," she says, holding up her mug, "but I can't wait."

"Is it helping?"

"I think so. Grab a glass. See for yourself."

IN HER last moments of sleep, Paola dreams of a man falling out of the sky, his head and body encased in a red-hot iron suit. He smashes into a vast ocean and tumbles slowly to its floor. The water, powerless to quench the smoldering metal, begins to boil all around it. Steam rises from the surface, where it condenses into pearls that rain down to form a mountain and then an archipelago. The pearls pile higher and higher, scattering the clouds—and then she wakes up.

It's almost 5 p.m. according to the Rolex Tom left on the nightstand.

"You bougie motherfucker," Paola whispers.

He's on his side, facing her, the top sheet tangled at his ankles. Paola sits delicately on the edge of his bed. There's tension in his expression, as if he's fighting his way back to consciousness or struggling to stay asleep. And then he reaches out with his right hand, missing her hip by inches, a gesture that strikes her as both desperate and hopeful. She gently lifts his arm and stretches out beside him, close enough to feel the warmth radiating from his sunburned skin and count six grains of sand stuck to his temple. When she brushes them away, Tom wakes up and blinks wildly.

"Hi," she says. "You looked lonely."

"What time is it?"

"Just after five."

He seems relieved to see her but then something darkens his expression.

"Is your dad back?" he asks.

"I think so. I hear them in the kitchen. How did you sleep?"

"Did I sleep? It doesn't feel like it."

"Is everything okay? You look like something—"

Tom slips a hand behind her head and pulls her to him. Their kiss answers the question he asked himself at sunrise: They have not done this before. The sensation of her body both expanding and contracting as she presses against him, the way she catches the tip of his tongue between her teeth—all of it is new. Paola straddles him and then sits up to peel off her tee shirt, the only thing she wore to bed. They kiss while she works his boxers down his legs with her hands and then her feet, flicking them away with her toes once they're past his ankles. Suddenly she sits up, lifts a finger, and grabs her phone from the nightstand.

"Really?" he says.

She moves the finger to her lips as she selects some Ethiopian jazz to mask the creaking of the box spring.

"Do you have a condom?" she whispers later.

Tom shakes his head.

"You came down here without a condom?"

"For a weekend with our parents? We don't have to have sex."

"No, we do now, *marica*. Promise you won't come inside me."

"I won't."

"Swear to me."

"I swear."

She shifts her hips and suddenly he's all the way inside her. Tom and Paola freeze and lock eyes, subsisting on sips of air, twitching as she presses her hips slowly into his. He has no trouble matching her rhythm now. Minutes later, he grabs her by the waist and lifts her straight into the air. Paola wriggles free and presses her body against him as he comes.

"Jesus," Tom says, red-faced from exertion and embarrassment. "That was fast."

"Get some fucking condoms, please," she says.

They're catching their breath when the sound of glasses in the sink reaches them from the kitchen. Paola laughs softly and shakes her head.

"Yeah," Tom says. "Not sure I'm ready for that."

She buries her face in his chest. "God, we really stink now. I'm getting in the shower. You should too."

"Maybe not at the same time."

"No, no. Ladies first."

"Should we stagger our entrances?"

"Like we have something to hide? Just act natural, *marica*. You worry too much."

"I'm not dying for your dad to know we just had sex."

"You're scared of him, aren't you?"

"Is that crazy?"

"No," she says. "You're right. It's not."

IN THE kitchen, Diane skims a romance novel on the love seat while Alex stares into his laptop at the table, the tails of his powder-blue collared shirt hanging over the edge of the chair.

"Look who it is," Diane says as Tom and Paola make their entrance. "Back from the dead."

"Almost," Tom says, rubbing his eyes sheepishly and stretching.

"Good evening," Alex says. "I hear you two had some fun last night."

"Are we grounded or something?" Paola asks on her way to the fridge.

But Alex is already back on his computer, too preoccupied to notice the fresh tension between Tom and Paola, which Diane can't ignore. Her son avoids her eyes, and the space between the two of them is so charged that Diane can almost hear it hum.

"Who wants a drink?" Alex asks.

He stopped at the Super Chomak on his way back and, seeking the comforts of home to calm his nerves, bought the most expensive Champagne he could find. He feels Tom's stare from across the room as he uncorks the bottle.

"What are we celebrating?" Tom asks.

"Independence," Alex says. "Or labor, in honor of the holiday. I just want a drink."

He's relieved when Tom avoids his eyes and surprised at how unsettled he feels now that a conversation about Clay is imminent. Tom drains half a heavy pour before he catches himself—and catches Paola doing the same thing. She gives him a guilty smile and lowers her glass. Alex and Diane are also drinking quickly. The bottle is kicked in minutes.

"Okay," Alex says, "let's take a walk."

It's half a mile to La Buena Vida, the swish sand-floor beach bar under a palapa roof at the south end of Half Moon Bay. The bar itself is a large oval of dark hardwood ringed by stools and swings. Suspended from the ceiling is the skeleton of some imaginary prehistoric sea snake, its plaster vertebrae and toothy skull hung with fishing line. Diego and Catalina share a wide swing near the entrance, flanked by Ben and Christian, beers in hand. Catalina hops down to offer Tom and Diane a tour, but Tom begs off and orders a margarita at the far end of the bar. The breeze stiffens as the sun drops, creating tiny whirlwinds in the ashtrays. Paola slides onto the swing beside him and slips a small glass vial into the pocket of his shirt.

"From Diego," she says. "A little pick-me-up."

"*Gracias.* Come with me."

"I don't touch that shit, but go ahead, before you fall asleep."

"Don't threaten me with a good time," Tom says.

Paola points him toward the bathrooms. She's waving down the bartender when Alex takes Tom's seat.

"Thanks for showing Tom a good time," he says with no trace of irony. "Can I get you a drink?"

"You need to tell her," Paola says.

"What? Tell who?"

"Diane. And you know what. Don't feed her your bullshit. She deserves better. If you're gonna lie, just let her go."

"I'm not lying to her."

"You told her what you do?"

Alex nods.

"And she was okay with that?"

"'Okay' is not how I'd describe it. She heard me out and she's still here. There's something else I told her, which I wanted to tell you in private. I'm done, Pao. Out for good."

"Don't lie to me."

"You think I'd lie about that?"

Alex stumbles off his barstool when she throws her arms around him.

"What are you gonna do now?" she asks with her head against his chest.

"Survive," Alex says.

"That's good. That's very good. I'm buying you a drink."

Tom exits the men's room with two heaping key bumps of cocaine searing the frayed edges of his consciousness. He has seven things to say to Paola, but Alex is in his seat. Just then Catalina whistles sharply and nods toward the entrance of the bar where a large white SUV is idling in the road. Alex stands and clears the untucked shirttails from his hip just far enough for Tom to spot the pistol in his waistband. Tom freezes as a hulking man steps down from the driver's seat and opens the rear door for a petite silver-haired woman with a brightly colored scarf around her shoulders. The driver scans the crowd as he walks her slowly up the stairs. Alex looks surprised, but the gun is out of sight now. He hurries to greet the woman and relieve her escort as Diane comes in from the beach and finds her son alone at the bar.

"Are you okay?" she asks.

"Who's Alex's new friend?"

"No idea. Did you get enough sleep? You don't seem tired."

"I'm going back to bed as soon as possible."

"I bet you are. Are you sure that's a good idea?"

"What are you talking about?"

"Don't play dumb with me."

"I'm not. Just wondering which bad idea we're talking about—yours or mine."

"Very funny. Listen, I'm not telling you what to do, just asking you to think before you do it."

"That's your advice? Think before you act? Let's back up for a second. How did we get here in the first place?"

"Keep your voice down."

"Whose idea was that, Diane? Who decided we should spend Labor Day in Mexico with your ex-con boyfriend or whatever Alex is? I came because you asked me to. Last I heard, it was us and his amigos. Did you tell me Alex had a daughter? Did you even know?"

"Of course I knew."

"Well, thanks for sharing. While we're talking, can you tell me why Alex has a gun on him right now? And why his new friend has a bodyguard?" Tom lights a cigarette from Paola's pack. "No? So, here we are. Am I helping? Probably not. I have no fucking idea what I'm doing, to be honest with you. But don't put this shit on me. This is your show. I'm along for the ride."

She expected an outburst after what she told him on the beach. She braced for it. But Diane assumed he'd lash out over nothing, allowing her to identify the root cause of his anger, forgive him, and move on. This is not nothing. He's right: She never should have brought him here. She insisted on his presence because the idea of a long weekend with Alex made her nervous. And she knew that Tom, given the option, would choose Mexico over Long Island. She turns to face him, to attempt an explanation and apology, but Alex lays a hand on her shoulder before she can begin.

"Sorry," he says, "can I borrow you for a second? There's someone I want you to meet."

"Okay," Diane says. "Who?"

"Maricel," Alex says, wondering at the chill in her voice as he points to the elderly woman seated beside Paola at the bar's only table, stroking the girl's hair. "I told you about her this morning."

Because she spotted Maricel on the arm of her driver, Diane expects physical and mental frailty, but finds herself instantly unsettled by the piercing eyes that track her approach. Maricel smiles, which does nothing to soften her gaze.

"Don't get up," Diane says as Paola excuses herself. "It's lovely to meet you."

"And you as well," Maricel says. "Please, sit down. Alex, you can bring us drinks? Blanco tequila with two ice cubes, please."

"I'll have the same," Diane says.

"Your first time here?" Maricel asks as Alex walks away. "How are you finding it?"

"It's a special place."

"It is. My husband used to say it changes everyone who visits."

"I can see that. I've had a few shifts so far."

"Were you surprised by them?"

"No, come to think of it," Diane says thoughtfully. "I wasn't."

"When I think back to the biggest surprises of my life, I often realize they were things that I suspected all along."

"I was just talking to my son about that."

"He's a very handsome boy."

"He gets it from his dad. But I don't need to tell you that, do I?"

"No," Maricel says. "I'm sorry for your loss. For your son's loss."

"Thank you. It was a long time ago."

"Yes. Another lifetime. And things have turned out well for you, I gather."

"I'm happy with my life, I guess."

"Because you understand that change is constant, that nothing is certain."

"That sounds right."

"It is. You seem concerned, if you don't mind my saying so. Is something on your mind?"

"I'm worried about dragging my son into the past. I'm not sure that's something he needs."

"Perhaps you need to accept that your role as a mother is different now, that your son's role in your life has also changed. I say this to you as a woman who posed a constant danger to her children from the moment they were born. We choose our paths and do what we can to protect those around us. You take your responsibility seriously, as you should. And I assume your son came willingly."

"But without all the facts."

"And what if he had had them? My guess is he would still be here."

"We'll never know, though, will we?"

"You've earned the right to pursue the things you want. Just be sure to choose them wisely."

Alex returns with their drinks.

Maricel takes a sip and says, "Unfortunately, I have to be going. Alex, will you walk me to my car?"

He helps her down the front steps and to the open door of the armored SUV.

"Thanks for coming," he says.

"Thank you for the invitation. She seems like a perfect match for you. *Felicitaciones.* I spoke to the people you asked me to speak to, by the way."

"And?"

"They understand your position."

"Does that mean I'm in the clear?"

"It's as good a sign as you're likely to get."

"Thank you for doing that."

"It was nothing. Good night."

Her driver helps her in and shuts the door. Alex watches the taillights fade as the car rolls slowly toward the highway, rising and falling over the speed bumps as if rocking on waves. He has the feeling that he gets on subways when the doors close and he stands there, braced for movement, while the train stays in the station. Is this what the end looks like for him?

Twenty-Four

Just after sunrise, Tom gently disentangles himself from Paola's arms and legs and pauses at the window between her bed and his. A haze of evaporating rainfall hangs over the jungle, but the sky is clear, shot through with early-morning light. Tomorrow he flies home. Back to New Jersey, to financial markets and portfolio reviews, to his unmade bed. Beside him, Paola rolls onto her stomach, filling the space where he slept. He has no idea if or when he'll see her after this. When a friend from work texted him to ask how things were going, Tom confessed that he was sleeping with his mother's boyfriend's daughter and his friend shot back: *so ur on a double date with ur mom lol.* And while his mom obviously caught on, Alex is either oblivious or putting on a show. He made Tom uneasy before yesterday's revelation, before he and Paola became more than friends. Tom has a sudden urge to wake Paola and pepper her with questions. Did she know what Diane told him on the beach? Why is Alex armed? And what the fuck is going on between them? He leaves for the airport in twenty-four hours and, given the frequent left turns of this long weekend, wonders what today will bring. His sheets are cool and dry compared to hers, and he's finally nodding off again when someone knocks.

"Rise and shine," Alex says through the door.

"No, no, no," Paola says, pulling a pillow over her head.

"Yes," Alex says. "Up and at 'em. We're going to the beach. Be ready in ten."

"Come back to bed," Paola whispers.

Tom wags a finger. "You heard your dad," he says.

The kitchen smells of freshly brewed coffee and the bacon in the breakfast tacos on the table. Tom fills two mugs while Paola makes a plate for them to share.

"Seriously?" Paola says, pointing to the neon green "Señor Frog's" fanny pack around her father's waist. "You already look like a *turista* gringo."

"Someone left it here," Alex says. "I'm embracing the look. Ready to go?"

They're loading the car when a trim, tan retired couple rolls past on rusty beach bikes, all smiles underneath their matching visors.

"Beautiful day!" the man calls out.

"Sure is," Alex says.

In his flip-flops, swim trunks, and La Buena Vida tee shirt, he looks every bit the gringo tourist, right down to the fanny pack which, as Diane discovered while he showered, contains a semiauto pistol and spare magazine.

Paola plays feathery techno from her iPhone while Alex drives south under a cloudless sky. Halfway to Tulum, he leaves the highway and turns left down a long, unmarked dirt track. The guard inside the guardhouse is asleep when they pull up, his chin on his chest. Alex taps the horn, and the man jumps down from his stool with a friendly grin to lift the salt-stained rope that blocks their path. Xcacel is a nature preserve and well-kept secret, a horseshoe bay hemmed in by jungle. No cars in the parking lot, no one on the beach. The tide is high, and Alex drops their beach bag by the water's edge while Diane wades into the surf to pee. The red-and-white umbrella is up and open when she returns. Alex lies on his back in its shade, his head propped up by a folded beach towel, the fanny pack beside his hand. Tom and Paola loll in the shallows, their quiet conversation masked by crashing waves.

Alex lifts his head and says, "It's nice, the way they get along."

Really? Diane thinks. How can he not see it? How can he be this blind when it comes to his own daughter? She has a sudden urge to rub it in his face, but there's another matter to discuss.

"Did you pick that gun up at the whorehouse?" she asks.

"It's a loaner," Alex says. "It's not coming back with us." He sits up and removes his sunglasses. "All this stuff stays here. I mean that."

She crawls on top of Alex, forcing him back down to kiss his neck, his mouth, his forehead. As Diane rolls off him, she spots the guard standing in the parking lot above them, talking on a cell phone. Tom and Paola come jogging up the beach and collapse in the sand. They share a cigarette and earbuds as they dry off in the sun.

"You're right," Diane whispers to Alex. "It is nice how they get along."

Just before noon, Paola announces that she's taking Tom to the cenote.

"The what?" Tom asks.

"This limestone sinkhole," Paola says, "filled with freshwater. Looks like a big blue eye in the ground. It's in the jungle, over there. Not far."

"Go for it," Alex says. "We'll pack up and go to lunch when you get back. I made us a reservation at this great seafood place down the road."

"Perfect," Paola says. "We'll be right back."

THE PATH to the cenote is barely wider than a footprint, with rotting two-by-fours laid over the muddy stretches. Paola leads the way, reaching back to brush Tom's fingertips as mosquitoes whine around their heads. The path ends at a clearing with a rocky depression at its center. Paola leads Tom out onto a limestone ledge six feet above the water.

"Can you dive?" Tom asks.

She responds by diving. Tom follows, and they surface seconds later, gasping from the cold. Paola pulls him to her and they kiss, kicking hard to keep their heads above water.

"Come down with me," she says.

They take deep breaths and descend, fingers intertwined, exhalations intermingling in a stream of bubbles. The light fades as they fall and finally they lose sight of each other, let go, and kick back to the surface. Tom wipes the water from his eyes and sees that Paola is staring at something over his head. He turns. Rafael stands on the ledge above them with three men Tom has never seen.

"Hey," Tom says. "What's up?"

DIANE LIES on her stomach in the shade of the umbrella, drifting in and out of consciousness to the soft buzz of the surf and the caress of the sea breeze. She starts when Alex sits up beside her and turns toward the place where Tom and Paola disappeared.

"What's taking them?" he asks.

"Come on." Diane rolls over, smiles up at him. "Do you not see it or not want to see it?"

"What?"

"They're only using one bed in that room."

"They're—what?"

"Can I ask you something? How does a man who robs jewelry stores on motorcycles not know what his daughter's doing right under his nose?"

"I thought they were just being friendly."

"Extremely friendly. Do you want to get them or should I?"

"I'll go," Alex says.

"Okay. Make a lot of noise. Let them know you're coming."

Diane smiles as she takes down the umbrella, imagining Alex's excessively loud and hesitant hike. Ten minutes later, he emerges from the jungle, looking up and down the beach with a hand shielding his eyes.

"They're not there," he says, arriving at a jog.

Diane drops the beach bag. "What do you mean 'not there'?"

"Not at the cenote."

"Did you look?"

"Did— Yes, of course I looked. I looked all over."

"Okay," she says slowly. "Where could they have gone?"

"There's a path that leads out to the road, but they weren't on it. They hitchhiked from Tulum yesterday. Maybe they walked out and caught a ride?"

"Why would they do that?"

"I don't know," Alex says. "Just thinking out loud. Maybe we should go back to the condo."

"You think that's where they went? What if they show up here and we're gone?"

"We can leave word with the guard."

"This is crazy," Diane says. "Why would they leave without telling us? What got into them?"

"I don't know. I'm sure there's an explanation."

Alex calls the restaurant as they cross the sand and parking lot, but no one has shown up for their reservation. Every surface in the car is scorching hot. The guardhouse is empty now, the rope coiled on a post.

"Try Tom's phone again," Alex says as they head north on the highway.

"I just did. It's off. I think he left it at the house. You don't think something happened to them, do you?"

"Like what?"

"I don't know. You told me yesterday it isn't safe."

"I said it's not safe enough to sleep outside. It's not safe enough to do that anywhere."

The young family in unit 3 is piling into their minivan when Alex and Diane pull up to the condo in Akumal. Alex ignores the father's greeting as they jog across the lot toward the stairs, which they take two at a time. On the landing, Alex tries the knob and finds the door unlocked. He lets out a deep sigh and shuts his eyes.

"They're here," he says. "Paola's the only one with keys."

"Okay, thank God," Diane says as she follows Alex down the hall. "What the hell were they thinking? I'm gonna murder Tom when—"

Alex stops so suddenly that Diane slams into him. He stumbles into the kitchen, extending his arms to block her path.

"Go back," he hisses, one hand hovering above the fanny pack. "Now."

Alejandro sits at the kitchen table, rolling a lime from the fruit bowl between his palms. Rafael and his cowboy-booted companion from Palm Trees stand behind him with flat expressions and submachine guns in their hands.

"Let her go, Alejandro," Alex says. "Diane, wait for me in the car."

"This won't take long," Alejandro says. "No need for her to leave us."

"What do you want?"

"You know what I want, and I can't wait for an answer now."

Diane is looking frantically around the room.

"You won't find them here," Alejandro says. "Your children are with me now."

"With— Why are— Alex, why is he saying that? What's he saying?"

"Explain it to her, Alex," Alejandro says. "No? I'll try: We made him a generous offer in exchange for his services, which he refused. He no longer has that luxury. Your children will be returned to you when the work is done. For now, they are my guests."

"No," Diane says. "No, please. You can't take them."

"Can't? I did. It's done." Alejandro stands and sets a burner phone down on the table. "This is for you," he says to Alex. "In it is the number that you'll use to reach me. I'll have more information about the job in the next forty-eight hours. This inconvenience with her son and your daughter means we can no longer offer you a fee, but what could be better than a long, happy life with your children?"

"Take me," Diane says. "Take me, please. I'll do anything you want, he'll do the job. Just let them go, I'm begging you, just take—"

"Señora," Alejandro says, "unfortunately I have to ask that you stay here."

"What if this doesn't go your way?" Alex asks.

"If it goes very badly, then what happens here won't concern you. Nothing will. If you miss him, you try again. And again, if necessary. You have four days to put your team together. Have you been to Spain?"

"Yes."

"Good. Marbella is where we see each other next."

Alejandro and his entourage are halfway across the kitchen when Diane lunges for the fanny pack, grasping at the gun inside, fumbling with the zipper. Rafael and his partner exchange amused glances before they train their guns on Alex, who grabs Diane's wrists and twists an arm behind her back.

"Not afraid to fight," Alejandro says approvingly. "Maybe you can use her."

They leave the door to the apartment open, and someone laughs loudly as they take the stairs down to the street. Taking Diane by the shoulders, Alex sits her on the love seat and crouches at her feet.

"Diane, listen to me, we're getting on the first flight out of here to deal with this. I'll get them back, I swear to you. I just need you—"

The slap stops him mid-sentence, turns his head. He endures two more with his eyes closed, but grabs her by the wrists when she starts whaling on him with her fists.

"Listen," he says. "We need to get—"

"No," she says, the color rising in her cheeks. "Oh, no. *I'll* tell *you* what happens now: You get those kids back. That's the only thing that happens now. Get them back or die trying. Even better: Get them back and then die."

"Okay," Alex says.

She sends him sprawling with a hard shove, stands, and walks unsteadily onto the balcony. In the bedroom, Alex packs her suitcase and then his, rolling clothes for maximum efficiency, arranging toiletries as tightly as a game of Tetris. As he wheels their bags into the hall, Alex spots Paola's records and Tom's boat shoes on the floor between their beds. The cramped bedroom smells of damp towels and essential oils. They'll need their passports to get home, and Alex finds them side by side in the top drawer of the nightstand. Paola looks like she's trying not to laugh in her picture, but it's her printed birth date that sends a surge of adrenaline through Alex. He feels it shoot down his veins and soak into the marrow of his bones like whiskey filtered through charcoal, blurring and refocusing his vision. He's primed now, fingers tingling, itching for a fight.

He tries Maricel's cell phone three times before he sends a text and calls the house. When a housekeeper informs him that the señora is sleeping, Alex instructs the girl to wake her boss immediately, which she does.

"Yes?" Maricel says.

"They took the kids."

"I beg your pardon?"

"Alejandro Ixto. He took Paola and Tom at Xcacel an hour ago. There was nothing I could do."

"I see."

"You see?"

"I understand that there was nothing you could do. I hope you know that there was nothing I could do. This is a terrible thing, Alex."

"Where would he take them?"

"I wouldn't tell you if I knew the answer, which of course I don't. Going after them in this way will solve nothing. I assume Alejandro gave you some instructions."

"I have four days to put a crew together for this job, which is in fucking Spain now."

"Is that enough time?"

"Of course not."

"Is there anything that I can do to help?"

"You can tell them this is insanity, that I can't work like this. I thought you said they understood?"

"They did say that. Something must have changed since then."

"Something? Seems to me like fucking everything has changed."

"Alex, this is what I tried to tell you over lunch: When they ask something, they're not really asking. Be thankful Alejandro is involved. The people he works with are not to be trusted, but if he says the children will be returned to you, they will."

"This is a fucking nightmare."

"No, there's no logic to a nightmare. This is a transaction. An unfortunate transaction, but a transaction nonetheless. Do your part. Expect that he'll do his. If I can be helpful in any way, I'm entirely at your disposal."

"Yeah. Thanks."

"Good luck."

He finds Diane on the balcony staring at the lit tip of her cigarette.

"We're packed," Alex says. "I'll call the airline from the car."

"I'm coming with you."

"Of course you're coming with me."

"To Spain."

"I can't take you to Spain," he says. "I'm sorry. Not an option."

"Either you take me to Spain or I go to the FBI."

"I understand why you're saying that. Believe me, I do. But I swear to you if I thought the FBI had a better shot at this, I'd turn myself in now. They can't help us, Diane. And if these people find out you're talking to the feds, the line goes dead. Period. We'll never hear from them again."

"Then you better take me to Spain or shoot me right now, because if you don't do one of those things, I'm turning on my phone as soon as we touch down and calling the FBI with you sitting next to me. This is my son we're talking about. My only son. The only thing that matters to me. I'll do whatever it takes to get him back—with you, or with them. Your call."

Twenty-Five

The Suburban slows for a sharp turn and then coasts to a stop. The engine dies, the front doors open and close. Alone in the car now, Tom hears approaching voices. His body jerks as the door beside him opens. A hand grasps Tom's bound hands and guides him onto sandy ground. Rafael's men smashed his forehead on the roof as they stuffed him, blindfolded, into the car, but this light touch is somehow more alarming, one final kindness, the run-up to an execution in Tom's mind. A breeze cools the patches of sweat on his shirt—a sea breeze, from the smell of it. Late-afternoon light leaks in at the edges of his blindfold.

Voices surround him now, speaking Spanish too fast for Tom to understand. A man laughs beside him, another snorts and spits. Tom wonders how long his legs, liquefied by fear, will hold him. A hand grips his biceps and pulls him through hard sunlight and dappled shade and into an enclosed space—cooler, darker, echo-y.

"*Cuidado,*" someone says as Tom stumbles on a stair. The staircase ends in a larger, brighter space. Someone pulls his blindfold. Paola stands before him, flanked by teenagers with automatic weapons. The shorter one is Paola's height and heavyset, with a broad, dark face and neatly parted hair. His companion, sinewy and heavily tattooed with acne scars like constellations on his cheekbones, turns to Tom.

"*Caballero, hablas español?*"

Tom shakes his head.

"*Tú sí, pero . . . ,*" he says to Paola, who stares back at him in silence.

"Pao," Tom says, "talk to him."

"Fuck him," Paola says. "*Chinga tu madre, pendejo.*"

The boy smiles and pats her cheek with a hand that has "rich" tattooed in script across its fingers. Paola doesn't move.

"*Te traeremos comida cada día. Si intentas escapar, sabes lo que pasa,*" he says, touching his gun.

The boys leave and lock the door behind them. Paola tears away the rope that binds Tom's hands and they embrace, their breathing fast and shallow.

Tom whispers, "Where are we?"

"I don't know," she says. "Let's see."

Their prison is the second-story guest suite of a compound buried in the jungle, an unfinished apartment that sits above some other room. A mattress wrapped in plastic leans against the wall beside a ladder and two ceiling fans in boxes. Plywood covers all the windows, and the smell of paint is dizzying.

"We drove south and east," Paola says. "I think we're somewhere in the biosphere. You're not supposed to build here."

"What the fuck just happened?" Tom asks. "Why would Rafael do that?"

"Rafael works for the cartel. Remember when I told you to be careful with him? This is why."

"Listen," Tom says, "I have some money, not a ton—two, three hundred grand—that I can transfer now, today, if someone gives me a computer. If they need more, my boss is good for it, but I need to get in touch with him. Can you tell them that?"

Paola's laugh is deep and bitter. "Keep your money. That won't save us. You don't know what this is."

"What is it?"

"This is Alex, your mom's new boyfriend. I knew something was happening. I felt it. *Pendejo de mierda.*"

"What are you talking about?"

"You don't know about him, do you?"

"I know he worked with my dad."

Paola nods.

"You knew that?"

"Alex told me at the bar last night," Paola says. "Alex is a thief, *marica*."

"A what?"

"*Un ladrón*. He steals things. There was a video a few weeks ago, people taking jewelry in Las Vegas, motorcycles—"

"Are you fucking kidding me? My boss sent that around."

"That was Alex and Catalina. Ben too. That's what they do."

"What does that have to do with us?"

"He took something from these people or they want something from him, I don't know which it is."

"Are they going to kill us?"

Paola shrugs. "Girls like me? Brown girls? We die all the time. The newspapers don't write about it because the cartel comes after them and then more people die. You? You're safer. Kill a white boy with a Rolex and you have a bigger problem."

"So what do we do?"

"Do? We do nothing, *marica*. We stay here and breathe."

Twenty-Six

Agent Harris is halfway through a round of golf at the Mirage when his phone lights up with a call from Ramirez. Harris excuses himself and walks down to the edge of a placid water hazard, putter in one hand, phone in the other. His next-door neighbor, a special agent turned corporate security consultant, calls out that this better be a big break if he's holding them up.

"Merry Christmas, friend," Ramirez says.

"Excuse me?"

"Happy birthday too."

"Yeah?"

"Yessir. Craig's fixing bikes in the garage this morning when his phone rings. It's the guy who booked him for the Wynn calling from—before you ask—some Mexican burner phone. Guess who's on another job."

Harris looks over his shoulder to ensure his partners in the round are safely out of earshot.

"You're kidding me," he says. "In Mexico?"

"Not quite. Good news and bad news on that front. They're not coming back to Vegas, but we have a logistical shitshow on our hands. This guy wants Craig on a plane to Málaga tomorrow."

"Africa? For chrissake."

"No, sir. Málaga's in Spain."

Twenty-Seven

Flight 642 from Newark to Málaga is overbooked. At the gate, small children run circles around the crowded benches, flustered parents in pursuit. Outside on the runway, late-afternoon light glints off the 757 which looks, to Diane, like a bullet with wings. Just before she and Alex left the house, Diane pointed to his duffel bag and said, "That's all you're bringing?" Having seen him at work, she expected a military footlocker packed with body armor and assault weapons. What she meant was: How are you going to get my son back with sneakers and tee shirts and natural deodorant? "Everything we need is there," he told her. "Trust me."

They've barely spoken since, and haven't touched each other since just before sunrise when Diane initiated six minutes of rough, half-conscious sex that Alex experienced as an assault. He was dreaming of a lake that curved upward at the horizon and filled the sky, and then Diane was on top of him, forcing blood into the head of his half-hard cock by tugging at the base like she was trying to uproot it. His mind was clouded with sleep and alarm, but his body was willing. She fucked him as hard as she could, smashing her hips into his, achieving what felt like terminal velocity with each downstroke. She pressed her palms against his sternum as she came so that her convulsions felt to him like chest compressions. When Alex placed his hands on her hips, Diane ripped them away. She caught her breath with her head bowed and her hair covering her face, collapsed, and turned her back to him. Alex lay awake as daylight filtered slowly through the blinds and filled the room.

A voice on the intercom announces boarding for the premium cabin.

"That's us," Alex says.

She's never flown first-class before. Their seats, a small island in the center of the cabin, are angled away from each other, the headrests close enough for quiet conversation. They stow their bags and sit in silence while the in-flight safety video plays. "Illuminated lights will guide you toward the exit," says a handsome actor in a pilot's uniform. "Oxygen will be flowing to the mask." Alex winces at a line addressed to "Those of you traveling with children," and turns to find Diane's fists clenched tightly in her lap.

The plane takes off and flies east, speeding up the sunset. A flight attendant walks the aisle with warm mixed nuts and sparkling water.

"They're feeding them, right?" Diane asks.

"Of course they are."

"How do you know that?"

"I just know."

"I don't believe you."

"Thank you," Alex says to a second flight attendant as he takes two short flutes from her cocktail tray.

"I'm not drinking fucking Champagne," Diane says.

"It'll help you sleep."

She considers this and downs the whole glass like a shot.

"Listen," Alex whispers, "and I wouldn't say this unless I believed it: No one is going hurt them. They're not at the Four Seasons, but they're safe."

A flight attendant clears their untouched dinner trays an hour later. Alex and Diane recline their seats and stare up at the illuminated seat belt signs and hissing air vents while their fellow passengers tune out with eye masks, Ambien, noise-canceling headphones, and red wine. She can't sleep and senses he can't either.

She whispers, "When you said you've never done this kind of job, you were lying to me, right?"

"I wasn't lying."

"But you know how to do it."

He nods confidently. "Do you want a sleeping pill? You should get some sleep."

"What happens when we land?"

"A lot of things."

"And you'll explain them to me so I don't feel like I'm in the dark the whole time?"

"Of course."

Diane lies back and shuts her eyes, but the engine noise feels like it's coming from inside her head. She's cold without a blanket, too warm with one on. She sits up and taps Alex on the shoulder.

"What's your secret?" she whispers. "Why are you so good at this?"

He's never thought of it like that: one succinct explanation for his past success. That isn't how it works. Alex has no secret, nothing he returns to or relies on besides instinct and obsessive preparation, but he can't tell Diane they're flying blind here. She wants to hear some whispered recipe for flawless victory, which means he'll have to make one up. He's concocting a response when something occurs to him.

"Everybody asks the same questions when they're looking at a job," he says. "'What's their weakness? Where are they vulnerable?' Those are the wrong questions. I don't give a shit what anybody's weakness is." He turns his head and whispers in her ear. "I'm interested in one thing: What's your strength? What's the source of all your confidence? And when I take that away from you, what do you have left?"

"What was their strength in Las Vegas?"

"Insulation. A casino on one side, a thousand tons of concrete on the other. It's the perfect spot for that kind of business. If you're not on the street, you're not worried about what comes in off it."

"So you brought the street to them."

"We—yes. That's exactly what we did."

"These people, the ones in Spain, what's their strength? What are they hiding behind?"

"I don't know yet," Alex says. "I'll know it when I see it."

The captain comes over the intercom to announce that they're expecting turbulence and ask that everyone please take their seats. Diane buckles her seatbelt with a bitter smile.

"It's funny," she says. "I always hoped someone would come along and fly me first-class to Europe. Careful what you wish for."

Twenty-Eight

A drug-sniffing dog has taken a shine to Craig Hollinger inside police headquarters at McCarran International Airport.

"Good boy," Craig says, scratching the black Lab behind its ears. "Gonna catch some bad guys, yeah?"

"Craig, I know you can't read, but leave the dog alone," Ramirez says. "Says right there on his collar not to touch him. Follow the fucking rules for once. Come over here."

Craig gives the dog an apologetic shrug and joins Harris and Ramirez at a table by the water cooler. He's on standby for the job in Spain. The bald man gave him the name of a hotel in Marbella, forty minutes by car from the Málaga–Costa del Sol Airport. Craig's orders are to check in, charge the phone he'll find at the front desk, and wait for the call. Marbella's Guardia Civil is holding two rooms in the hotel across the street. Weeks of red tape and procedural bureaucracy were eliminated when Raúl Fuentes, the Interpol liaison assigned to the case, sent the comandante of Marbella the video from Vegas and explained that he had three days to stop this crew from hitting his hometown. Fuentes is coordinating the efforts of the FBI, LVMPD, and Spanish agencies. Harris is flying over shortly after Craig to join a task force assembled to prevent an undetermined crime.

"You have the name of the hotel, right?" Harris asks.

"Got it all written down," Craig says.

"Good. Go straight there when you clear customs, get that phone charged. Do not leave the room for any reason. You live on room service till you hear from them. We need details and we need them fast. I want to know who they are, where they are, what the fuck they're looking at over there. You'll help us ascertain all that before anybody from this crew so much as shoplifts. If we have any reason to suspect that you're not giving this one hundred and ten percent, I'll give your assistance agreement to my grandkids to color on. Have a nice flight, son."

Twenty-Nine

Diane wakes up to an announcement of the flight's final descent. Her neck is stiff, her eyes swollen with sleep. Coffee, water, Advil—nothing helps. She glimpses ocean and then arid mountains through the window as the plane turns slowly toward the runway. Behind her, a group of Texans in the first row of economy is having beer for breakfast and joking loudly about staying drunk all week.

"Where are we?" Diane asks Alex. "What is this place?"

"The Costa del Sol. Vacationland. Runs from here down to Gibraltar. They called it the Costa del Crime in the eighties. Brits with legal troubles would buy villas, get bad plastic surgery, drink themselves to death by their pools. All kinds of stuff flows through here into Europe."

"Lovely," she says. "You should run for office."

When Diane reaches for the water bottle at his feet, Alex catches her wrist and says, "My throat's a little sore."

"You're not coming down with something, are you?"

"I don't think so, but why risk it."

Alex wheels her suitcase through the crowded terminal with his duffel perched on top. They go through customs as a couple.

"And the purpose of your visit?" asks the agent, a young man about Tom's age with black hair gelled up into spikes.

"Pleasure," Alex says. "Vacation."

The thought of enjoying their time here makes Diane nauseous, but she manages a weak smile when the agent meets her eyes.

A taxi drives them to the edge of town and drops them at a small cantina fronted by red plastic tables where reedy old men sip beer from small glasses. The bar inside is stacked with dark liqueurs Diane has never seen before, and a leg of cured ham sits on what looks like a torture device: a steel clamp grips the ankle-bone and thick screws penetrate the thigh meat. Catalina leans casually on the bar in white jeans and a tie-dyed tank top, look-ing like she's about to join the table of young Spanish women in the corner. Ben sits beside her in khaki cargo shorts and a tee shirt cut from navy moisture-wicking mesh. Diane is grateful for his imposing, all-American presence, having underestimated the disorienting effects of jet lag, a new country, and unfamiliar liquor.

"*Bienvenida*," Ben says, opening his arms. "Let's get this done and go the fuck home."

She wants to throw herself against the town house of his body and weep into his chest with relief. Catalina greets her with a cool double kiss while Ben wraps Alex in a hug.

"Is Craig here?" Alex asks.

"Craig had a passport issue," Ben says. "He lands tomorrow."

"Who's Craig?" Diane asks.

Catalina shifts uncomfortably at the question. She doesn't want Diane here; Alex warned her about this.

"Craig," Ben says, "is a young and not particularly charm-ing Australian man who's hell on wheels. Speaking of which, we should hit the road. We have lunch in half an hour with our friend here."

Alex cocks an eyebrow. "Lunch?"

"Yes, lunch. Me and him go back a ways. I leaned on him a little for Marseille. Remember what didn't show up at the last minute? This is who came through. Good Rolodex, great Guar-dia Civil connections. He runs a full-service, ask-and-you-shall-receive operation, and he wants to meet us—you, specifically."

"Last time you told me that," Alex says, "we wound up here. Does our friend know what this is about?"

"Didn't ask. I'm sure he thinks it's stones again."

"Let him think that."

"Done. For what we're paying, lunch is the least he can do."

They drive southwest in a silver SUV, out of the city and into the mountains that surround it on three sides, past blocky white apartment complexes that cover the lower ridges like patches of dead skin on the dry brown land. The road narrows to a single lane as they ascend and ends at a steel-slat gate that rolls shakily away as they draw near. A gardener plants his shovel in the ground and eyes the car as it rolls up the drive onto a bluff that overlooks the city and the sea beyond it. Ben parks in front of a modest pale pink villa that sits below a grove of olive trees. Two dogs explode inside, their barking angry and undomesticated. Diane puts a hand on Alex's arm as he starts toward the house.

"Why are we here?" she whispers. "What didn't show up in Marseille?"

"Sorry," he says. "Guns."

The dogs claw at the double doors so hard it sounds as if they're chewing through them. A woman, sixtyish and sun-creased with a silver-streaked chestnut bob, cracks the door and pokes her head out.

"They're actually quite friendly," she says, holding the animals at bay. "Just hold still for a moment while they get to know you."

There is nothing friendly about the muscled German shepherd mixes who shoot past her, tails and ears erect, black eyes burning in their long dark faces. The dogs circle the stock-still newcomers, nosing hands and crotches with inquisitive growls until, satisfied, they trot back to their mistress as a unit. The woman, in a yellow housedress and white apron, stands in the doorway, beckoning to her guests.

"Fernando called to say he's running late. Please, come in. I'm Isabella."

The entryway feels like a hothouse, filled with tall plants and the heavy smell of mulch. The rooms beyond are sparsely furnished with antiques and threadbare Persian carpets on terrazzo floors. Diane slows to take in a row of photographs: two young girls in the ocean, Isabella in a ball gown on a spiral staircase, the family underneath the Eiffel Tower. The last shot is black and white: a young man, square-jawed and broad-shouldered, kneels beside a fallen water buffalo, one hand on a horn, the other on his rifle.

"Ah," Isabella says. "Here he is."

The dogs race to the door, and Fernando curses them affectionately as he enters. He's still broad-shouldered, with a thick hard-looking gut below his barrel chest and skin that matches the worn oil-stained leather on the shotgun case in his hand.

"Fernando runs the shooting program at his club," Isabella says, eyeing his mesh shooting vest and sweat-stained safari shirt. "He takes it very seriously."

"It's very serious," Fernando says, smiling at his wife. "Sorry if I kept you waiting."

"We just pulled in," Ben says. "You're looking well."

"I'm still here," Fernando says. "That's well enough."

In the kitchen, a countertop monitor shows camera feeds from the road, the driveway, and the hill behind the house. Fernando pours Diane a glass of cold, cloudy white wine that reignites her appetite. At a long table in the dining room, Isabella portions two steaming sea bass into fat white chunks while Diane stares at their chalky, lifeless eyes and open mouths. During the meal, she catches Fernando glancing furtively at Alex, who eats with surgical precision, striving for some ideal ratio of fish to roasted fennel with each bite, which Diane finds infuriating. She also shares Fernando's fascination. She wants to understand why drug cartels will stop at nothing to recruit this man. She hopes their confidence is not misplaced.

"Are you looking for more hands?" Fernando asks.

"Possibly," Ben says. "We'll know more this afternoon. Did you have someone in mind?"

"We have an interesting group here: young toreros, bull-fighters from the academy in Ronda who finished their training just before the crisis hit. An exceptional class, the best I've seen in years, but when it came time for their debuts, the bullrings were bankrupt and the pay was slashed to almost nothing. They start training very young, these boys, and by the time they finish they're grown men with few skills besides taking care of animals. And killing them, of course. They're underemployed at the moment."

Alex, Ben, and Catalina have stopped eating.

"How many of them are there?" Alex asks.

"Three or four that I can recommend, boys I sponsored personally at the academy. They're tremendous athletes, but it's more than that. They've been playing for high stakes their whole lives, which changes your relationship to fear and risk. They've done the kind of work you do before."

"Where are they?" Ben asks.

"Just outside Marbella."

"How soon can we meet them?"

"Do you have plans after dinner?"

"We do now," Catalina says.

After lunch they follow Fernando's white Land Cruiser up a long dirt track that ends at a row of caves cut into the mountainside, their mouths covered by overhead steel doors. The gardener is waiting for them with a slim, thirtyish North African man who flicks away his cigarette to greet Fernando with a long embrace.

"This is my friend Omar," Fernando says.

He's strikingly handsome, with bright green eyes and a nose like a knife blade above a full, feminine mouth. His white dress shirt is open to his sternum, and he wears a woodsy aftershave that Diane has now encountered twice: once on a blind date who took her out for sushi in Philadelphia, and a second time on a Moroccan gunrunner in the hills outside Málaga, Spain.

"Listos?" Fernando asks.

The gardener looks both ways before he lifts the last door on the row and waves the crew into a narrow chamber lined with racks of bottles, the wine inside them black as oil under the fluorescent lights. The steel door rumbles down behind them. A dozen firearms are laid out on a sorting table in the center of the room. Alex and Catalina circle slowly, ejecting and replacing magazines, passing pieces back and forth. Diane wonders if they enjoy picking out heavy, dependable hardware in the same way she enjoys shopping a farmers' market when everything is fresh and fragrant, when the meal is still a series of perfect outcomes in her mind. Unsure what to do with herself, she joins Ben by the door. At the table, Alex checks the chamber of a silver semi-auto pistol, puts the far wall in his sites, and pulls the trigger; Diane flinches as the click of the firing pin echoes off the rock.

"Let's have a smoke," Ben says to her.

They duck under the door and emerge into the piercing light and dry heat of afternoon.

"Stupid question," Ben says, "but how's your mind?"

"I can't stop thinking about them. What they're doing, what they're thinking. How scared they must be."

"I'm sure Alex told you this, but hurting those kids is a non-option. They're just collateral. Alejandro knows that. Do you?"

"You obviously don't have children."

"I do, actually. Two of them. I was married to a woman in my twenties, if you can believe that."

"What are their names?"

"Robert and Lily."

"What would you tell Robert and Lily if someone ripped them off a beach at gunpoint on your family vacation?"

"After I got them back, I would tell them I was sorry, that I would always do everything in my power to protect them. Which I would. Which you would. Which is why we're here."

"Sorry? 'Hey, honey, sorry a cartel locked you up over Labor Day in Mexico. Pass the salt.' Sure, Ben. That'll fix it." Diane takes a drag and shakes her head as she exhales. "Jesus, listen to me. *I'm* sorry. You didn't do this. Why am I taking it out on you?"

"Because you're terrified, which is understandable. Speaking of which, there's something you should know about Alex that I'm not sure he can explain because I don't know how well he understands it. He seems obnoxiously calm, right?"

"It's driving me crazy."

"Let me assure you: He's not calm. His external reaction to stress is the opposite of what you see in most people. Put the screws to him, and he relaxes, at least on the surface. I've never seen anything like it. What's happening on the inside is another story. And I've never seen him this calm on a rush job, which means it's probably hell inside his head right now. Does that make sense?"

"Not really. Can I ask you something? How long does this usually take? The planning, preparation."

"Months. Years, even. But we hit the Wynn on three weeks' notice."

"And now you have three days."

"Four, technically."

"I don't care how good Alex is. That's insane."

"It's not ideal. Can it be done? Of course it can."

"What if something happens to him?"

"The rest of us will see this through."

"You won't vanish on me?"

"Vanish? No. I'll deal with Alejandro Ixto if it comes to that."

"He's here, isn't he," Diane says softly.

Ben checks his watch and nods.

"When do we see him?"

"After this."

Thirty

Diane fights sleep as Ben drives southwest toward Marbella, a port city with a reputation as a party town, its marina lined with yachts owned by plutocratic Middle Easterners and Europeans who flock here in summer to overspend on bottle service and designer clothes. Diane scrolled through photo after photo of the city while she and Alex waited on the runway in Cancún, unsettled by how peaceful and pretty it looked. Alejandro is somewhere in the tangle of narrow streets dotted with sidewalk café tables. She has fantasized endlessly about killing him—with a screaming drill bit to the temple, with bleach poured past a dental clamp and down his throat—but part of her is strangely excited to see him, worried he won't show. He's her only link to Tom, which has created an uncomfortable intimacy between them in her mind. She feels the same way about Alex to a lesser degree, bitter and resentful but also afraid to let him out of her sight, bound to him by helplessness and fear.

Ben drops them in the circular drive of a white apartment tower and drives off to find parking while Diane follows Alex and Catalina through the empty marble lobby and stands between them as the elevator climbs. The striped silver wallpaper and white leather sectional in the three-bedroom apartment remind Diane of condos at the Jersey Shore. Alex leads her to the master bedroom, where she lies facedown on the bed.

"Can I get you anything?" he asks.

She's already asleep. Alex slips her shoes off and closes the door quietly behind him. Ben and Catalina sit in silence at the kitchen table.

"She's out?" Ben asks.

Alex nods.

"He'll be here in two hours."

"I know."

"Do I need to tell you to be calm and civil, no matter what he says?"

"You don't."

"If you want to go after him when this is done, I'm right behind you. But today we're working toward a common goal."

"I get it."

"Does she?" Catalina asks.

"Cat, relax," Ben says as he checks his phone. "Craig's flight is on time. He'll be here first thing tomorrow."

"Okay," Alex says. "I'm going out for a minute."

"Diane needs cigarettes. And alcohol, I'm guessing. I'd get both if I were you."

A ruffled sheet of clouds has mapped itself over the town, softening the heat. Alex follows the smell of salt water and diesel down to the marina, where a blacktop promenade runs between the aft decks of moored yachts and a row of cafés, restaurants, and shops. Thin Nigerian men hawk counterfeit bags and watches on the pavement in front of luxury boutiques while eastern European escorts vie for the attention of day-drunk Russians watching Spain play Germany in soccer at the bar of an Italian restaurant. Alex ducks into a slim café and orders an espresso, glad to be out of the apartment. This job feels like the freight train that he saw on ketamine: unstoppable, undefined, hurtling toward him in darkness. It's all happening too fast. He's used to researching and planning until the idea of a job is so fully formed that execution feels like an afterthought. He has the will to act this time, but not the information he requires. The uncertainty is like an acid bath on his nerves and the soreness in his throat, which he noticed just before takeoff, is getting worse by the hour. Where's my fucking coffee, Alex thinks as he watches the bartender chatting idly with another customer. The languor of the people here is maddening. He loathes the vacationers padding down the promenade, thinking only of their next meal, tee times, the progress of their tans. The bartender arrives with his espresso, and Alex comes out of his trance. Be here, he tells himself. Be present. Stop drifting backward into a lake of regret and forward into a fog of uncertainty and fear. It's been decades since his life felt like a nightmare that he couldn't wake from. He's less helpless now, or at least that's what he tells himself as he downs the scalding coffee and leaves two euros on the bar.

Thirty-One

Diane is up and about when Alex returns with white wine, two packs of Marlboro Lights, and a stack of legal pads. She smiles uncomfortably when he offers her the bottle, but pours herself a lukewarm glass and rejoins Ben and Catalina in front of the TV. When Ben settles on a dubbed episode of *Law & Order: SVU,* Diane turns to him and stares, but the irony of watching a police procedural while planning a kidnapping is apparently lost on him. She's refilling her glass when a knock at the door stiffens her spine. Standing in the hallway is the man who took her son—the same clothes, the same calm, probing expression, and what looks like the same disposable cell phone in his hand. He nods to Alex and goes straight for Diane, ignoring Ben, who stands up from the couch to block his path. Alejandro offers her the phone.

"Who's— Oh my God," she says, "give me that. Hello?"

"Mom, it's me," Tom says.

Diane moves to the window and holds a hand to her mouth. "Honey, are you there? Are you okay? Is everything okay?"

"Hey, yeah, I'm fine. We're both—yeah, we're okay."

"Paola's with you?"

"She's right here."

"They're feeding you, right?" Diane asks, eyes closed, crying silently.

"Yup. Fast food, twice a day."

"And they're not hurting you?"

"They're not."

"Promise me you're not just saying that," she says, opening and narrowing her eyes, searching for clues in his voice.

"No one's hurting anyone. Where are you?"

"Spain. Alex is— Everyone is doing everything they can, okay? He needs to do something for these people and then you're coming back to me. It's all— Honey? Tom? Hello?"

The line is dead.

"Thank you?" she says to Alejandro as she wipes the wet face of the phone on her jeans.

"You're welcome. Where do we talk?"

They gather around the coffee table, where Ben opens his laptop and Alex rests a legal pad on his knee.

"What are we looking at?" Ben asks.

"Lunch," Alejandro says.

"Beg your pardon?"

"A lunch meeting. The day after tomorrow a boat called *Sweetest Dreams* will arrive at the marina here. A large shipment of fentanyl is hidden in the hull. The seller, Li Jianrong, arrives on the boat with his prod—"

"Whoa, whoa, wait a minute," Alex says. "Li Jianrong?"

"Correct."

Alex, Ben, and Catalina search each other's faces.

"What are you doing?" Alex says to Alejandro. "What the fuck is this?"

"This is why you're here."

"Who's Li Jianrong?" Diane asks.

"The owner of the necklace in Las Vegas," Ben says. Then to Alejandro, "Don't tell me that's who we're gunning for."

"How much do you know about him?" Alejandro asks.

"Born in Guangzhou," Alex says reflexively. "Made his money in chemicals and real estate, splits his time between Shanghai and Pangkor Island in Malaysia. Fifty-two next month. Recently remarried."

"He has a large chemical business," Alejandro says, "part of which is making high-quality fentanyl, which he agreed to sell exclusively to us. It's still legal to produce in China, and quickly becoming an important product for us in the States. A large shipment from this man, two hundred million dollars' worth, was on its way to us when a disagreement caused a delay. We need this shipment to complete its journey. So yes, the man you robbed is the man I need you to deliver."

"You need to tell me how that's possible," Alex says.

"As you said to me at Palm Trees, I can't help you with that. You're not in a position to ask questions now."

"What can you tell us?" Ben asks.

"The seller, you already know. The buyer is Dimitri Sokolov, a Russian. These two men plan to have lunch at a restaurant on the water while the money changes hands at the Marbella Club Hotel, where the Russians are staying. The money will be driven to the docks and delivered to another boat, provided by the Russians, on which Li plans to depart. The product is yours, if you want it, but it shouldn't leave here in the hands of either party. The money, around fifteen million U.S., is also yours, if you can get to it. What I need from you is Li. And I need him alive."

Alex scoffs. "Fuck up a shipment, grab a mountain of cash, and rip someone out of a restaurant in broad daylight? You said you had *a* job for us. That's three jobs."

"The restaurant is outdoors and their lunch begins at noon, so daylight is the only option. The money and the product are secondary to the man."

"How heavy does he travel?" Catalina asks.

"He'll have at least two men with him at lunch, more men on the boat. He uses a mix of Chinese and American security when he's abroad, well trained, ex-military. The reservation is for six, so expect at least two Russians with Dimitri. The restaurant is called Belvedere, like the vodka."

Alex saw it on his walk, one of three restaurants at the

south end of the promenade, tourist traps with tables on the water.

"What's our window?" Alex asks. "How long is he here?"

"He arrives on one boat, eats lunch, leaves on another. An hour, maybe less."

"And you know all this how?"

"From someone close to him."

"How do we know your source isn't fucking you?"

"He's proven himself many times."

"Once we get him for you," Ben says, "then what?"

"Turn him over to me, preferably in a vehicle. Then the work is done. I assume you know what he looks like. I have photos of Dimitri I can share with you. The Russians check in to their hotel tomorrow around two p.m. if you'd like to get eyes on them. We know less about Li's itinerary, but his boat should arrive in time for lunch, and the Russians will lead you to him. Other questions?"

"I've got one," Diane says. "When do I get my son back, you piece of shit?"

THEY RECONVENE around the kitchen table when he's gone.

"Tell me one of you knows what the fuck is going on here," Alex says.

Ben throws up his hands. "They just happen to be looking for this asshole we ripped off in Vegas? That's a hell of a coincidence. Did they bring him to our attention, or is it the other way around?"

"I don't see how either of those things is possible," Alex says. "Did we know Li was into fentanyl?"

Ben shakes his head. "The guy who tipped me off works for the courier, the company that shipped the necklace from Paris to Vegas. Based in San Diego. Doesn't know Alejandro or his people, didn't know anything besides the transit details."

"Who tipped him off?" Alex asks.

"He wouldn't say."

"What if it was the same person who tipped Alejandro off about Li's travel plans?" Diane asks.

"Why would this person be talking to them and to us?" Catalina says.

"I don't know," Diane says. "But what's the connection? How is this possible? Who bought his necklace from you?"

"This Mexican cell phone magnate," Ben says. "Real reclusive, strange tastes. Collects dinosaur bones, rare insects, and fine jewelry, for some reason. No link to the cartel that I know of. I can't see the connection. Maybe there isn't one."

"I can't see it either," Alex says, "which doesn't mean it isn't there. Set that aside for now. What else? Anybody, anything."

"Lots of bystanders by the water," Ben says. "No margin for error if things get heavy."

"The police here are good," Catalina says. "And everywhere."

"They've been dealing with this shit for decades," Alex says. "They know exactly what they're doing. And it sounds like Li has good people watching his back. I'm less worried about the Russians, but not by much."

"What else are you seeing?" Ben asks.

"Li's cautious," Alex says. "Barely setting foot in Spain— coming by boat, meeting by the docks, in public, in broad daylight. Steering clear of the actual transaction. Also, he has shitty taste in restaurants. I walked by that place earlier."

"What's the worst part?" Diane asks. "I mean, this is a fucking nightmare, but what worries you the most?"

"Alejandro could be lying to us," Alex says. "It's also possible that Alejandro's being lied to, which is worse. And now we need to set those possibilities aside so we can plan and execute without losing our minds. Is there anything besides the obvious that doesn't make sense now?"

"You think he had his muscle wait in the lobby?" Catalina asks.

"Alejandro?" Diane asks. "He had muscle with him when

you met in Mexico? He sure as hell had muscle when he took the kids. Is it weird that he's alone now?"

"We don't know that he's alone," Ben says. "Just that he's alone tonight."

"But why bring muscle and leave it at your hotel?" Diane asks. "How high up is he? Is he that important to the cartel?"

"They needed the coast and he gave it to them," Catalina says. "He's untouchable there. Essential."

"This may be a stupid question," Diane says, "but if he already delivered the thing they wanted from him, why is he essential?"

Catalina opens her mouth and closes it again.

"He's enforcing the peace," Ben says. "But that's not a stupid question."

"Look," Alex says, "we can sit here and second-guess ourselves all night. Let's assume everything we heard is true, which means we have Li arriving on a boat, eating at a restaurant, and leaving on another boat. I don't like the boats for this. The docks are a dead end, and they can see anything coming from a mile away."

"And if anything goes wrong," Ben says, "they can be in Africa in ninety minutes."

"That kind of money can get you in real trouble over there," Catalina says. "We're doing him a favor by ripping him off."

"We're not going after the money," Alex says.

Catalina looks at Ben, then back at Alex. "Can we take a vote?"

"If he happens to have a money order in his pocket when we grab him, great," Alex says. "But you're talking about three, four hundred pounds of cash. Unwieldy as fuck. We don't know when or where it's showing up, and Li won't be anywhere near the money until he's on the boat surrounded by people we don't want to shoot it out with. We don't have enough hands to grab everything."

Catalina frowns. "This is where you say, 'Just kidding,' right? Ben? I mean, what the fuck?"

"Listen to me," Alex says, "we wouldn't be here if we hadn't taken that fucking meeting in Mexico. Do you know where my daughter is? No? Me neither. You're doing this pro bono. End of story."

Thirty-Two

Fernando calls just after 11 p.m. to say he's ten minutes away. Ben and Diane abandon the dishes, and the crew walks to the corner, where well-dressed twentysomethings clutching gin and tonics spill out of a bar onto the sidewalk in a cloud of cigarette smoke and perfume. Diane wonders if the world is full of people Tom's age, or if she's only noticing them now that he's been taken from her. The white Land Cruiser stops across the street, and Fernando nods in greeting as they pile in. The seat belt sensors in the car have been disabled, and only Diane buckles up for the drive.

The bullfighters live in a sprawling white apartment complex outside town, a gated community where the parents of Juan Carlos, the youngest member of the group, bought a unit at the height of the recession. They gave keys to their son who was struggling, along with his friends from the academy, to find work. In the two-bedroom condo, between four and seven young men exist in a kind of Marxist Peter Pan utopia: From each according to his ability (waiting tables, selling drugs, busking, burglary), to each according to his need (painkillers, car tires, hair product, one abortion). The boys share everything from formal wear to antibiotics.

Apartment 6B sounds like a nightclub from the quiet, private street. Fernando knocks and then knocks louder. Someone kills the music just before Juan Carlos opens the front door and sweeps his long brown hair back to reveal a handsome and clean-shaven face, deeply tanned and puffy in the cheeks with baby fat or beer bloat.

"*Discúlpeme, Comandante,*" he says with a sheepish smile.

Behind him, two boys load a trash bag with beer cans and red Solo cups from the kitchen counter while three young women apply makeup in the powder room through a haze of cigarette smoke. Fernando shakes his head in mock disapproval, shadow-boxes with Juan Carlos, then grasps the boy and pulls him close. This, Alex thinks, was Fernando in his early twenties—fearless, flat broke, fancy-free. Juan Carlos nods in greeting to the crew but doesn't introduce himself.

"Come in," Fernando says.

He leads them through the apartment and out onto a narrow deck. The pool in the yard below is shared by the surrounding units, but overrun tonight by the toreros, two of whom are mock-bullfighting with a bright pink cape and horns screwed to a wooden handle. A bullfighter in a bathing suit cracks a beer bottle with his lighter and backflips into the pool with his thumb over the opening. As her eyes adjust to the darkness, Diane notices the marks on the boys in the yard—lumps of scar tissue on arms and legs, long jagged wounds like cartoon lightning. A slim, dark-skinned boy is missing a chunk of his left calf and arguing with Juan Carlos about the music coming from a small waterproof speaker. The disagreement devolves into a wrestling match that goes quickly to the ground, where Juan Carlos wriggles out of a body lock and scrambles to his feet. The boys trade hard open-handed slaps until Juan Carlos catches his friend's wrist, steps in, and slips an arm around his waist. Suddenly they're salsa dancing, spinning and dipping each other along the edge of the pool and then over it into the water. Alex laughs in disbelief.

"Is this real?" Diane asks.

"No," Alex says, "we just fell into Ben's wet dream."

"Fuckin' A," Ben says. "Are you complaining?"

"A little rough around the edges," Fernando says, "but they're good when the chips are down. Luis, who just went swimming with Juan Carlos, is another I can recommend. They work very well together."

"How long have they been living like this?" Alex asks.

"Here? Six months. But they spent years together on a farm with the bulls and the horses, training every day, caring for the animals, going slightly crazy."

"How much to put those two on hold for the next two days?"

"Nothing," Fernando says. "A hundred euros each?"

"Make it a thousand," Alex says, "with more to follow if we need them. I want them sober and rested, starting now. Can they handle that?"

Fernando nods and takes the stairs down to the yard.

"You sound like a man with a plan," Ben says to Alex.

"You should get your hearing checked."

"So we're just ingredient shopping?"

Alex nods. "Not sure what's for dinner yet," he says.

Thirty-Three

Diane opens her eyes in the blue half-light of the bedroom and stifles a scream at the sight of a figure standing by the window. She reaches out blindly, but the bed beside her is empty because it's Alex staring out at the darkened apartments across the street. Diane sits up slowly, clutching the sheet to her chest, her heart pounding under her hand.

"You can turn the light on," she says.

"You— What? No, that's okay. Go back to sleep. Sorry I woke you."

She can tell from his voice that he's just now coming back from wherever he goes when his eyes glaze over and he seems to mute the world around him.

"Talk to me," she says.

Alex glances over his shoulder to politely decline, but something in her face changes his mind.

"There's no surprising them," he says.

"What do you mean?"

"The people these guys hire for protection have spent years, decades living in an ambush. They're always ready, always expecting it. And Li's sticking his neck out here, which makes it worse."

"So don't surprise them."

"Right. We can't. Not possible."

"What, then?"

"I don't know." Alex rests his hands on the glass and scans the street. "I don't know yet."

Diane lets the sheet fall and pulls back her hair. "They're always expecting something, right? What if the thing they're expecting starts to happen?"

"Their training kicks in. They confront, engage."

"And they're good, right? So you can't touch them then."

"Casino security gets paid to make sure no one pulls the trigger. These guys get paid to take bullets. Their whole job is to engage. A shootout is not an option. I'd rather not kill a bunch of tourists and Li's useless to us if he's dead."

"Okay," she says, "but let's say something happens. Then what?"

"They neutralize the threat. Move him, make him safe."

"What happens after that?"

"They regroup."

"Do they relax? Let their guard down?"

"Not really, no."

"They must at least downshift, right? After all that adrenaline? They're human."

"What are you saying?"

"You can't surprise them, I get that. But what if you don't surprise them? What if you do exactly the thing that they're expecting?"

"And then what?"

"Did you take driver's ed?"

"Yeah, twenty years ago."

"What's that statistic they teach? Most accidents happen within a mile of your home? You're almost in the driveway, so you relax a little, let your guard down."

"Go on."

"Say there's a threat, a bad threat, and they move him to a place they think is safe."

Alex cocks an eyebrow and sits on the bed beside her.

"And then something else happens," Diane says. "Not in the safe place, but just before it. They think they're almost home and that's when something hits them."

"That's good," he says. "Get them on the run, let them see the goal line. Then we move for real."

"What's the goal line?"

"The boat they're leaving on. Before he gets there, we need to get him in a car and move him. That's where our Australian friend comes in."

"You flew this kid in from Australia?"

"From Vegas," Alex says. "He's based there. Teaches motorcycle racing. He's raced everything with wheels."

"Were you on the bike with him?"

"I was."

"And?"

"He got shot and still managed to get us out of a clusterfuck in the middle of the Strip. Two cops in front of us, a SWAT team on our asses. This kid timed a turn into oncoming traffic with six inches to spare. 'Hang on, mate.' I thought those were the last words I'd ever hear."

"Why doesn't Ben like him?"

"Thinks he's cocky. Sounds like Craig was just being a kid. Ben doesn't have a lot of patience for the younger generation."

"He seems like a good judge of character, though."

"He is, but I didn't fly Craig out here to lead team-building exercises. We need someone who can drive. This kid is as good as they come."

"Another ingredient?"

"One I always want to have on hand, even if we don't end up using it. Even if it doesn't fit into your plan. Look, I know this plan is yours, but I'm not gonna mention that, because I don't want static from Catalina. I'm not saying that's right, just easier."

"Jesus," Diane says, pushing him away, "you think I give a shit about that? All I want is my son back. Take the fucking credit."

"It's a good idea."

"Good," she says, "so make it work."

Thirty-Four

"Took my date to that Spanish restaurant in the Cosmopolitan last night," Ramirez says, when Harris calls him with an update. "A little spendy, but not bad. How's our friend Craig?"

"On ice at the hotel. Probably fluent in Spanish from watching TV."

"No word yet?"

"Not a goddamn one. I've got everyone here trying to figure out what the fuck they're looking at. Robbery squad talked to every watch and jewelry store. Nobody has the kind of inventory they'd come all this way for, but they're beefing up security, and we put extra uniforms all over the shopping district. Banks here don't keep that much cash on hand. Couple big safe-deposit box joints, which worries me, but we gave them all a heads-up. The marina's full of fuck-off yachts, every other car is a Ferrari. Could be anything—art, boats, some stash of drugs or cash that we don't know about. There's all kinds of money here, plenty of it dirty."

"Sounds like Vegas," Ramirez. "At least they have a type."

Thirty-Five

It's check-in hour at the Marbella Club Hotel and the lobby is packed with arriving guests and clusters of luggage. Ben and Alex sit by the elevators in tee shirts and tennis shorts with a racquet bag on the bench between them. Leaning against the wall to their left is Juan Carlos, who checked in to a ground-floor room this morning with Luis. Their orders are to drink club soda in the lobby bar in shifts and let Ben know when the Russians come and go. Alex takes a call from Catalina, who's outside in the arrivals area.

"Our friends are here," she says. "About to make their entrance. Forward guard in a suit, then the man."

"Okay," Alex says. Then to Ben, "Here we go."

The revolving door releases a tall, broad-shouldered man in a pale blue shirt and sharkskin suit who pushes sunglasses up onto his forehead to survey the lobby before he turns and nods. The door spins again, and in comes Dimitri Sokolov—compact, impassive, and potbellied in a green velour tracksuit and black horse-bit loafers, his thinning hair dyed a faded black. He turns toward the elevators, and Alex quickly drops his gaze.

"Feel that?" Ben asks, his eyes hidden behind sunglasses. "Don't look up."

"What?" Alex asks.

"He's looking right at you, like I'm not even here."

Alex calls up his mental picture of the man and stares back in his mind.

"Okay," Ben says, "it's over. Back to you."

The second guard has a slight hunch and heavily lined face under close-cropped gray hair. The third—doughy, baby faced, not a day over twenty—approaches the front desk with a stack of passports.

"*Estás bien?*" Alex asks Juan Carlos. "*Los ves?*"

Juan Carlos looks up from his phone and says, "*Claro que sí.*"

Giving their targets a wide berth, Ben and Alex leave by the rear entrance, which opens onto the promenade behind the hotel.

"That was something else," Ben says, "the way he looked at you."

"It was three seconds," Alex says. "Don't read into it."

"If it was nothing, I'd have said nothing."

They find Catalina at the entrance to the tennis courts where the crew gathers by a high chain-link fence and pretends to watch the children taking lessons.

Catalina pops a piece of gum. "I'm glad they brought the fat kid."

"Don't write him off," Alex says. "Good posture, light on his feet, moves well. He's definitely the translator, but I've had my ass handed to me on the mats by guys like that a hundred times. The Russians will go for the hotel or the dope when things get hot. Li and his boys will go straight for their boat, which means they'll be headed my way, with Ben right behind them. We drop Li's muscle and get him into the trunk as fast as we can. Cat, if you're there, great. If you're still doing your thing, that's fine too."

"I'll be quick," she says. "Don't want to miss that."

"Good," Alex says. "I'm heading over to the restaurant."

"We'll take a look at the docks," Ben says. "Have a nice lunch."

THE PUERTO BANÚS marina is a large rectangular basin carved into the coast and edged on three sides by a blacktop promenade. Long docks lined with yachts are affixed to the blacktop, which is shared by pedestrians and luxury cars parked along the water. The seawall, a long curved spit of rocky land, stops just short of the marina's southwest corner, like a curled finger about to tap the coast. Belvedere overlooks the narrow waterway from a patch of tiled concrete, its bar and kitchen separated from the outdoor seating by the promenade. Waiters weave around the foot traffic as they ferry trays to and from a sea of tables under a canopy of red and white umbrellas. The lunch rush has just started when Alex arrives. Juan Carlos knows the daytime host-ess, a waifish Romanian girl who provided tomorrow's reserva-tion list and seating chart, no questions asked. She shows Alex to a table near the one reserved tomorrow for his target. The menu is a grab bag of continental cuisine: pizza margherita, sal-ade niçoise, linguine alle vongole, assorted tapas. Diane is due to meet him here in twenty minutes. Alone at their table, Alex sketches on a legal pad and makes three trips to the men's room, taking a different path back to his seat each time. The sore-ness in his throat has spread to his jaw, and his temperature has been rising steadily all day. He's beginning to worry about Diane when he spots her weaving through the seated crowd toward him. She left the apartment two hours ago having decided, for one afternoon only, to use alcohol and retail therapy as numbing agents for her guilt and terror. After an Aperol spritz at a side-walk café, she bought the dress she's wearing, sleeveless white silk with a row of buttons that starts just below her breasts. A table of Italian men suspend their conversation and turn their heads in unison as she walks past. Alex rises quickly and pulls out her chair.

"Hi," he says. "You look great."

"You look ridiculous," she says. "Please never take up tennis."

"This is strictly business. The Russians showed up right on time. We've got eyes on them."

Diane nods approvingly and orders another spritz as the waiter hands them menus.

"So many Russians here," she says, scanning the specials. "And Arabs. And Brazilians."

"Welcome to the European capital of people with more money than taste."

"I'm getting the fish."

"Sounds good."

"And a bottle of white."

"I'm okay on wine," Alex says, "but go ahead."

"You seem okay, which is incomprehensible to me. This could be the last time we eat lunch together. Or the last time you eat lunch. Tomorrow you could be dead or sitting in a cell somewhere, so I'm having a drink. If you can forget where your kid is, congratulations. I don't know how to do that."

Alex blinks and sits back in his chair. He has calmly weathered half a dozen of these outbursts since Mexico, but Diane sees that she's finally crossed the line.

"You're angry," he says. "And you have every right to be. It's my fault we're here. So keep lashing out at me if you want to, if it helps. Is it helping? Why don't you channel that into something that could help us, like you did last night?"

Diane stares at him in silence. He knows how to fight with her, to patiently absorb the occasional blasts of anger without hitting back or shutting down completely. Under any other circumstances this would be an attractive quality, but today it makes her hate him even more. The waiter returns, pen in hand.

"We'll have the dover sole," Alex says. "And the prawns, and a Caesar salad, and a bottle of the Chablis."

"What did you think when you met me?" Diane asks when the waiter departs. "At the Mallorys', not back when we were kids."

"Did I tell you my mom had a drug problem?"

"No. Don't change the subject."

"She had people over at all hours when I was a kid, bartenders, waitresses, casino dealers, coke dealers. One of her party friends used to babysit me sometimes, Claire LaValle, a cocktail waitress at the Tropicana, like my mom. Me and Claire were close, weirdly close for a ten-year-old and a woman in her thirties. She used to sneak into my room while everyone was getting high in the kitchen, apologize for the noise, ask how school was going, if anything was on my mind. One night I asked her why my mom took drugs. Claire didn't know the answer to that question, so I asked if Claire took drugs, and she said yes. I asked if she was on drugs then, and she told me that she was. I wanted to—"

The waiter returns and pours a splash of wine, which Alex passes to Diane.

"Fine, thank you," she says. Then to Alex, "Go on."

"I asked Claire what it felt like. She said it was like coming home after a long trip and also like arriving in a beautiful new place you never knew existed. For years, I wondered what she meant. Or took. I tried a lot of drugs and none of them did that for me. I hadn't thought about that night in a long time. But that's the first thing I thought of when we kissed outside Lindsay's dinner party. I know that wasn't your question. I didn't know what to think at the Mallorys'."

"Save the Hallmark shit for when you get the kids back," Diane says softly. She reaches across the table, touches his forehead with one hand and hers with the other. "Jesus, you're burning up. Are you okay?"

"Nothing serious," he says. "It'll pass."

Their food arrives and Alex sketches while they eat, thinking that the two of them look like a married couple who've run out of things to say. Diane asks a waiter for directions to the bathroom, and Alex pours his wine into her glass as she walks away. He's checking the weather forecast on his phone when someone steps between him and the sun.

"Mind if I sit down?"

It takes Alex a few seconds to place the backlit face.

"Hi, Derrick," Alex says. "Be my guest."

Derrick Salant takes Diane's seat. He's as tall as Alex, heavily bearded, and more muscular than he was when they first met fifteen years ago. On their second job together, Derrick found himself facedown on the floor of a Sedona warehouse with a boot between his shoulder blades and a pistol pointed at his head, a predicament he escaped when Alex doubled back to ambush and disarm the unexpected guard. The incident scared Derrick straight. Alex hasn't seen him in over a decade, but Derrick is some kind of security contractor now, judging by the crew cut and wraparound sunglasses. A gun for hire, in Spain on business. Alex recalls that Ben mentioned Derrick in connection with a shooting at a Kabul marketplace that the military tried to sweep under the rug.

"What brings you to Marbella?" Derrick asks.

"You know me, I love the *sol*. What brings you here, Derrick?"

"Look, we don't have a lot of time here, so I'm gonna put my cards on the table: I have a plane for you, gassed up and ready to go. I don't know what you're doing here and I don't want to know, but I need you wheels-up in the next six hours. The pilot will take you anywhere within range, no questions asked."

"Why would I leave this lovely town?"

"Leaving's your best play," Derrick says.

"Can't do that, pal. My hotel's nonrefundable. And there's the rental car."

"Give me a reasonable number."

"Three."

"Three? Come on, man. That's insane."

"What's insane? You think I meant three million? I was just giving you a reasonable-sounding number. I don't want your money, Derrick."

"Alex, look—I owe you. We both know that. That's why I'm coming to you like this. You don't want to cause a scene here, not this week."

"You didn't answer my question."

"What question?"

"Why you're here."

"You know I can't get into that."

"You're working, obviously. Not the worst gig you've had recently, from what I hear. Here's some free advice: Go shopping. Get some clothes that don't scream: I do renditions for a living. You don't exactly blend."

"I don't need to blend," Derrick says. "I'm doing my job."

"What *is* your job, Derrick?"

"Keeping people safe."

"Really? I thought you gun down civilians and little kids and let a bunch of lawyers clean up after you. That's what the papers say you do for a living, soldier."

"Alex, just get on the plane, okay? Go vacation somewhere else. I'm doing you a fucking favor here."

"Do you know what I do for a living?"

"Do I— What? Yeah, of course I do. We don't—"

"What's that?"

"You— You take things that don't belong to you."

"Sure, I've done that. But what I really do is come for lazy, spineless fucking drones like you—undertrained, unimaginative motherfuckers like you, Derrick—and I embarrass them. I show the whole world what you are. I hit you where it hurts and then I hit you again and again. You think *I'm* in over my head? You don't know the half of it. I'm glad you know I'm here. I hope you see this coming. It won't change a fucking thing." Alex stands and drops his napkin on the table. "You better hope I die in a fire tonight, pal. That's about the only chance you've got. Happy hunting. Thanks for lunch."

He's halfway to the restrooms when Diane emerges, smoothing her dress against her sides.

"Let's go," Alex says, spinning her by the elbow. "This way."

"Did you get the bill? What's going on?"

"Lunch is taken care of, come with me."

He hurries her down the promenade and stops behind the nearest hotel.

"Listen to me very carefully: I need you to go inside and

order a taxi from the concierge, not the guys out front. Have the cabstand call the front desk when the car is here. When it shows up, walk directly to it and get in. I'll be right behind you, but until then, I'll be waiting right inside this door. If anyone approaches you or talks to you, walk to me as quickly as you can. Can you do that?"

"Only if you tell me what the fuck is going on."

"Someone recognized me at the restaurant and I need to be sure no one's following us now."

The concierge nods agreeably at Diane's request. Alex sees no sign of Derrick, senses no undue attention. Is it possible that his former colleague just told him the truth? That he spotted Alex, talked to his superiors, and found a spare Gulfstream to make sure nothing unexpected happens while they babysit some high-value target? Alex doesn't know what to believe. The concierge takes a call and gestures to Diane, who thanks him and heads for the taxi idling outside. Alex has the driver drop them at a hotel down the road, where Diane orders another car and waits inside while Alex surveys the street from behind the valet stand. In the second taxi, certain now that they're not being followed, Alex gives the driver an address near the apartment.

"Who recognized you?" Diane whispers.

"Someone we used to work with."

"Who just happens to be here?"

"That's what he said."

"And you believe him?"

"He's not with the Russians, and Li's crew doesn't show up till tomorrow. I don't know what he's here for, but I let him think I do. Keep this between us, okay?"

Ben and Catalina are playing gin rummy at the kitchen table when Alex and Diane come through the door.

"How was lunch?" Ben asks.

"Not bad," Alex says. "And the restaurant is better for this than I thought. Do we have wheels for tomorrow?"

"We will," Ben says. "Those kids say they can have damn near anything we want by morning."

"Good. Get Craig on the phone."

Ben makes the call and puts the phone on speaker.

"Hello?"

"Hi, Craig," Ben says. "How was the flight?"

"Slept like a log, mate."

"What kind of car do you want?"

"Cars this time?"

"Just one. What's your dream ride?"

"BMW 3 or 5, manual trans, tires broken in but not old. I'll take a turbo if that's on the menu."

"I'll see what I can do. Tomorrow at eleven a.m., walk to the Hard Rock Cafe on the southeast side of the José Saramago traffic circle. In a parking space in front of the restaurant, you'll see a car with a dark-haired kid in the passenger seat. Put your hand flat on the windshield to let him know it's you."

"Can I ask what we're after this time?"

"You can ask. Hang on a second. Someone wants to talk to you."

"Hi, Craig," Alex says. "Do you know who this is?"

"Yeah," Craig says. "I do."

"Do you have a laptop with you?"

"No."

"Go down to the front desk and get a street map and a pen. I'll wait."

In the lobby, Craig makes the request loud enough for Alex to hear and, while the clerk digs around for a map, jogs to the window and waves his arms. Across the street, Harris and a plainclothes policeman step cautiously out of a windowless white van. As they cross the road, Craig catches his reflection in the glass—a translucent image of his body that contains two law enforcement officers approaching at a run. Craig blinks. The clerk emerges from the office, map in hand. Craig leads the way up to his room, puts the call on speaker, and spreads the map out on the bed.

"Craig, you there?" Alex asks.

"Yeah," Craig says. "Hang on, mate."

"What?"

"Just getting set up here. Hang on, mate."

Alex looks from Ben to Catalina and back again. "Everything okay?"

"All good. Go ahead."

"Do you see the Puerto Banús marina?"

"Yeah."

"See the road that runs along the water? The promenade between the marina and the buildings?"

"Sure thing."

"At the south end, there's a restaurant called Belvedere. Tomorrow at one p.m., you'll park on the promenade near the restaurant, as close to Calle Tramo de Unión as possible. Trunk popped but not open, doors unlocked. You'll have three passengers, plus some cargo in the back. Once we're in the car, we need to hit the Carretera Nacional 340 as fast as possible. Avenida José Banús is the most direct route, but by tomorrow afternoon, you'll know every street between the marina and the carretera like the back of your hand. Traffic patterns, light durations, street directions, alternate routes—all of it. Is that clear?"

"Too easy, mate."

"Good. Go down there now and look around."

"All right. See you boys tomorrow, then."

Alex hangs up with a concerned look on his face.

"What?" Ben asks.

"He kept saying, 'Hang on, mate.' Like he did on the bike. Like he was trying to tell me something."

"Tell you what?" Ben asks. "That's just how he talks."

Thirty-Six

In a conference room at Guardia Civil headquarters, Harris watches as Raúl Fuentes from Interpol paces with a cell phone to his ear.

"*Sí,*" he says. "*Sí, sí, lo comprendo. No, no. Está bien. Gracias.*" He hangs up. "They won't do it. Tried everything and then some. That was our last shot."

"Perfect," Harris says. "So we're completely fucked."

They have the number Ben used to call Craig, but after two hours of heated back-and-forth with security managers and executives at Telefónica, their request for real-time location data hit a wall. The company won't release that information without an imminent threat to human life. A child kidnapped by a violent offender? Telefónica is happy to help. A suspected terrorist plotting an attack? They've cooperated in that instance many times. But the potential robbery of an unknown target doesn't clear the bar in Spain. Fuentes made a last-ditch plea to a contact at the company, who just delivered the final verdict. This leaves the task force with the name of a restaurant and the first leg of an escape route which, as Harris reminds Fuentes, is better than nothing, but not by much.

"All we can do now is throw bodies at the problem," Harris says. "We need every inch of that marina covered by tomorrow afternoon. That's our only shot."

Thirty-Seven

Catalina answers the apartment door at 10:36 a.m. and finds Omar dressed like an expensive personal trainer in silver track pants and sleeveless camo tee shirt. He sets the balance of Ben's order on the kitchen table: a duffel filled with extra magazines and ammunition and a glossy shopping bag with three Kevlar vests hidden under tissue paper. From the bottom of the bag, Omar removes a small black plastic box and hands it carefully to Catalina, whose eyes light up at the sight. Ben offers coffee, but Omar says he's late to fetch his daughter from his ex-wife's house. He's on his way out when Catalina asks if he's taking his little girl to lunch near the marina. Omar says that they have other plans.

"*Qué bueno,*" Catalina says.

The gunrunner gives a little bow of gratitude and slips out into the hall. Alex emerges from the bathroom, drying his hair with a towel. Diane catches him by the elbow as he passes her on his way to the kitchen.

"Did you use my conditioner?" she asks.

"Yeah," he says. "That okay?"

"Of course."

That he softened his hair in the shower gives her hope. You wouldn't do that, Diane thinks, if you expect to die. Or is that exactly what you'd do? Maybe he used every product within reach to prolong this morning's shower, thinking it could be his last. She's unsure if he slept last night. They sat around the cof-

fee table for hours, going over every detail, permutation, and
potential pitfall of the plan, gaming out worst-case scenarios,
guessing at unknown unknowns. Catalina seemed ready to pack
it in after a dozen verbal run-throughs, but Alex kept going
back to the beginning, questioning his partners and even himself as if he was blindfolded and the job was an object placed
into his hands, something he could understand only by touching every surface. It was after 2 a.m. when Diane got into bed
and swallowed half a Xanax to gum up the wheels of her mind.
She awoke an hour later to unfamiliar voices and stuck her head
into the hall to find Luis and Juan Carlos staring down into a
laptop over Catalina's shoulders. Diane was drifting off again
when Alex tucked her hair behind her ear and whispered that
he was going down to the marina. If he came to bed, he did so
without waking her. She was alone when her alarm went off at
6 a.m., and found Alex sitting Indian-style by the coffee table,
eyes closed, lips slightly parted, hands on his knees. He looks
so ordinary and unthreatening now—a trim, shirtless, middle-
aged man standing in a block of sunlight with a cup of coffee in
his hands. Catalina, in a sports bra, latex gloves, and wireless
headphones, unpacks the weapons and lays them on the kitchen
table like a feast. She field-strips and reassembles the guns one
by one, adding drops of oil to the actions, swaying slightly to the
music in her ears. Ben, also in gloves, loads the extra magazines.
The atmosphere is hushed and there's an undercurrent of nervous energy that reminds Diane of mornings when her brothers
would suit up for big wrestling matches, stretching silently in
the kitchen while they ate and rehydrated after weigh-ins.

The guns disappear into waistbands, racquet bags, and ankle
holsters except for a pistol and pistol-grip shotgun that Ben
stashes underneath the kitchen sink. Catalina removes a small
tube of superglue from its packaging and puts it in her handbag
along with two pistols, an expandable baton, a neoprene beer
cozy, and the black box Omar brought her. Alex stretches by

the window in a pair of navy cargo pants, hugging his knees to his chest with his eyes fixed on the ceiling fan. Ben takes a call, thanks the caller, and hangs up.

"Craig's got the car," he says. "Good to go."

Alex sits up, rocks his head from side to side, and rises slowly to his feet. As he pulls a vest from the shopping bag, Diane understands that this is finally and irrevocably happening. Ben puts on a baseball cap and sunglasses that seem to render him unreachable while Alex threads his long arms through the armholes of the vest and fastens the wide Velcro tabs over his ribs. He pulls on a white tee shirt followed by a gray polo and stretches both until the vest no longer shows. Diane wants to speak, but not to break their concentration. What if they've forgotten her? What if they walk out without a word and get gunned down in the streets, leaving her alone in this apartment, in a foreign country, in her life? Catalina takes a knee and double-knots the laces on her shoes. Diane is having trouble breathing.

"Hey," Alex says, "come with me."

He shuts the bedroom door and turns to face her, arms at his sides. "I need you to stay here until this is over, but once we know the kids are safe, you're free to go. I'll do anything you want after that—charter you a plane to pick up Tom, sell my place in Bucks County, never talk to you again."

"That's what you want?"

"Of course not. If it's up to me, we spend every day together after this. A dysfunctional family where the kids are sleeping together, I'm retired at forty-one, you're retired if you want to be. We can go anywhere—California, Nova Scotia, Kuala Lumpur. I don't give a shit, as long as you go with me. It's whatever you want after this."

"Two cats."

"What?"

"I want two cats. They don't rip up the furniture if you have two of them."

"We can have two hundred cats."

"I just want two."

"Two cats, then."

"And a sauna. Nothing fancy, just the wood-burning kind behind the house. Assuming you get the kids back. Otherwise, I'll kill you myself."

Alex almost smiles.

She wants to embrace him but the energy radiating from his body feels like static, promising a shock on contact. Diane wrings her hands, then wraps her arms gingerly around his waist and presses her cheek against the top edge of the vest.

"You're still burning up," she says. "How sick are you?"

"Pretty sick. But that won't save our friend from China."

"Alex, I'm fucking scared."

"Good," he says. "This is scary. Be ready for anything. But count on me coming back."

"Okay. Go, then. Make this stop."

Unable to face Ben and Catalina, she watches them leave from the bedroom. One of them locks the door from the outside.

Thirty-Eight

The elevator descends slowly and stops on the third floor, where Alex, Ben, and Catalina are joined by a middle-aged woman in sunglasses and a pink sweat suit. She turns her back to them as she coaxes her suspicious Pomeranian aboard with hisses and tugs on its leash. The car continues its fall to the lobby, where Catalina holds the elevator doors until the woman and her dog leave the building. Halfway across the marble floor, Alex shoulders his racquet bag, moves between Ben and Catalina, and cups the back of their necks. All three stop and stand in silence, side by side, eyes front. Then Alex drops his arms and moves past his companions, through the doors and out into the street.

THE STRENGTH of the sun makes Alex think of melanoma, black cancerous spots, his own skin cells reprogrammed to eat him alive. He pushes death from his thoughts and checks in with his surroundings—the smell of the sea, the weight of the bag on his shoulder, the group of teenage girls laughing loudly as they step out of the Starbucks in front of him. The heat is stifling even without the fever, which is holding steady at 103.2 F according to the thermometer Alex bought last night at a pharmacy near the apartment. Sweat trickles down his sides and spine and pools at the small of his back. Vegas, he thinks, was good practice for Marbella. So was Marseille two years ago, with its narrow streets and heavy summer crowds. It's all been one extended training exercise for this—his last gig, one way or the other. There's death again, worming its way into his mind. Alex flicks the thought away a second time as he walks down the promenade toward the restaurant, past the silver BMW parked near Calle Tramo de Unión with its engine quietly humming.

THE ELEVATOR opens onto the ground floor of the Marbella Club Hotel and releases the Russians, freshly shaved and showered, their dress shirts still creased from their suitcases. They cross the lobby, confer briefly by the concierge desk, and leave the hotel by the rear entrance, pausing under the awning to light their first cigarettes of the day. Luis makes a phone call as he follows them down the promenade at a distance, ignoring Ben, who sits at an outdoor café table across from Belvedere with a newspaper covering his face.

"*Caminando*," Luis says to Alex. "*Dos minutos.*"

IN THE small industrial marina south of Puerto Banús, Juan Carlos sits astride an idling Jet Ski, one sneaker in the footwell, the other anchored to a floating dock. The sea breeze pops the collar of his polo and threatens to blow the hat off his head. He turns at the sound of wheels on gravel as Catalina steps out of a taxi and crosses the parking lot toward the water. She lowers herself carefully onto the ski behind Juan Carlos, stashes her handbag between them, and places her hands on his hips.

"*Listos*," she says.

Juan Carlos nods and pulls slowly away from the dock.

THE BENCH that Alex picked out yesterday—a stone slab with an unobstructed view of Belvedere—is occupied this morning by a young couple. He's headed for a nearby lamppost when the man whispers something to the woman, who nods in agreement. And then, as if Alex willed it, the pair stands up and walks away. Alex sits, unzips the racquet bag, and places it between his feet. To slow his racing thoughts, he scans his body with his mind, starting with his head and working downward, noting spots of tension and discomfort, which are everywhere today. Twenty minutes until this kicks off, assuming Li Jianrong is punctual— twice as much time as he had to himself inside the U-Haul in Las Vegas while Craig drove them from the warehouse to the drop on Lisbon Avenue. Alex fingers the zip ties in his pocket as he runs through a visualization in which Li is hustled down the promenade, oblivious to Alex on the bench and Ben approaching from behind. Two in the heart and one in the head for each of the bodyguards, and before they hit the blacktop, Li is clubbed, bound, and stuffed headfirst into the trunk. Alex wipes sweat from his forehead and wills his fever to break.

IN THE apartment, Diane stares blankly into the refrigerator. Ketchup, olives, half a bottle of white wine, a cluster of take-out containers. She knew what she'd find here and wants none of it, but she's on autopilot, moving around their empty rental in a daze. She closes the refrigerator and sits down at the kitchen table before moving to the couch. After staring at the dead TV, she lies down and looks up at the static ceiling fan, wondering what Alex thought as he studied it earlier, what he's thinking now, whether she'll get the chance to ask those questions. Sweat from her palms soaks into the leather cushion covers. She can't take it anymore. She won't.

CATALINA AND Juan Carlos bob gently near the entrance to the Puerto Banús marina, midday sun baking their heads and shoulders, water in the footwells covering the soles of their shoes. Juan Carlos feathers the throttle to keep the incoming tide from pushing them into the rocky seawall. Two large fishing boats leave the marina and accelerate toward open water; a schooner with its sails struck motors slowly into port. Juan Carlos whistles softly as a boat approaches from the south—a long white flybridge yacht with a row of portholes along its muscular hull. The engine coughs and sputters as the captain eases off the throttle and aims for the marina's entrance. When Catalina sees the gold lettering on the stern, she pulls a cell phone from her bag and sends a text, and once the yacht is safely inside the seawall, Juan Carlos follows in its fading wake. The Jet Ski rounds the rocky corner as the *Sweetest Dreams* backs slowly into a slip at the end of the nearest dock. Two men drop rubber bumpers over the sides, then move to the aft deck and stand ready, lines in hand. When the engine dies, they jump down onto the dock and secure the boat. Li Jianrong emerges from the cabin in a pale yellow button-down and khakis, his eyes hidden behind mirrored sunglasses fitted with a neoprene neck strap. Cautious, Catalina thinks, like Alex said. But not cautious enough. Li looks left and right, then up at the cloudless sky. Catalina sends another text.

ALEX GLANCES at the phone in his hand, then casts his eyes toward the docks without turning his head as Li and two men— one Asian, one Caucasian, neither of them Derrick—file through the gate onto the promenade. Li is shorter and slighter than Alex expected from corporate head shots showing a stern man with a strong jaw, broad cheekbones, and neatly parted hair. He walks a few feet behind his guards, head down, typing on his phone, and passes close enough that Alex clocks the heavy square-cut diamond in his pinky ring. He's between 150 and 160 pounds, unremarkable except for his escort, unnoticed in the flow of foot traffic. The hostess at Belvedere shows Li and his men to their table, where the Russians stand to greet them. A waiter arrives with menus and an ashtray. As he scans the promenade, Alex spots the previous occupants of his bench leaning on a signpost near Belvedere's bar. When the man turns his head to whisper to the woman, Alex sees the earpiece headset attached to a coiled wire that runs down his neck.

"*OTRO CAPPUCCINO?*"

Ben looks up from his paper. "*No, gracias,*" he says to the server. "*La cuenta, por favor.*"

The young man drops the check and says, "You pay inside, please."

Two men and a woman stand just inside the entrance to the narrow café, blocking Ben's path to the bar. As he turns sideways to bypass them, Ben sees that the men wear identical necklaces under their shirts, the thin steel-ball chain visible above the collars. Ben stops and turns. The collar on the woman's rugby shirt covers her neck, but when she shifts her weight from one foot to the other, a holstered pistol prints against her shirttail. Three plainclothes police, badges and guns poorly concealed under their shirts, all of them staring intently at Belvedere's outdoor seating.

"*Señor?*"

Ben turns to find a bartender pointing at the check in his hand.

"*Muchas gracias,*" the young man calls out when Ben drops a fifty-euro note on the bar and turns on his heel.

WHILE JUAN CARLOS steers the Jet Ski slowly toward the *Sweetest Dreams,* Catalina takes the beer cozy from her handbag and uncaps the tube of superglue. Juan Carlos kills the engine and extends a hand as they coast toward the yacht. He holds them off by the keel while Catalina reaches gingerly into her bag, unlatches the black box, and removes one of two M14 thermite grenades, dull green cylinders the size of beer cans. She fits the grenade into the cozy, and she's coating the neoprene with superglue when the wake from a large boat bangs the nose of the ski against the yacht, producing a sharp knock and then another before Juan Carlos can react. The door to the cabin opens and two men jump down onto the dock, peering into the space between the *Sweetest Dreams* and the pilings, guns in hand. Juan Carlos puts the ski in reverse as Catalina pulls the pin with her teeth and, rising unsteadily onto her tiptoes with one hand on the boy's head, affixes the grenade to the foredeck of the boat.

"*Vamos,*" she says and sits down hard.

Juan Carlos rips backward into the basin and opens up the throttle, drowning out the shouting of the men on the dock as the grenade detonates with a burst of white-hot flame and heavy shower of sparks. A cocktail of aluminum powder and an iron oxide, burning at over 2,000°F, produces a steady flow of molten iron and liquefied fiberglass as the thermite reaction eats through the hull of the boat.

ALEX IS on his feet now, a surge of adrenaline like stinging nettles underneath his clammy skin. He scans the crowd and finds another man with an earpiece at a corner table, then another, this one two tables from his target. Alex spins at the sound of shouting from the docks, which is followed by the high-pitched buzz of a redlining engine and the pop of small-arms fire. The phone in his hand buzzes with a text from Ben: *walk away cops everywhere.*

DIANE WALKS quickly toward the marina, weaving around couples pushing strollers, tourists hung with shopping bags, and old men walking slowly arm in arm. Heads turn at the sound of an explosion on the water. Diane stumbles, backpedals, and stares up at a column of black smoke that rises above the row of shops in front of her. She collects herself, adjusts the pistol in her waistband, and sprints toward the water.

ALEX EXPECTED the grenade to get his targets on their feet, but they're not alone. All over the restaurant, men and women leave their seats like spring-loaded toys, pulling pistols and badges from underneath their shirts. Li ducks down while his guards and the Russians stand and spin, guns in hand, surrounded by plainclothes police and unsure where to aim as officers in uniform sprint toward the restaurant and the smoking yacht. A multilingual shouting match ends in gunfire, and diners seem to levitate before they run for cover, toppling tables, chairs, and potted plants like a hurricane, clawing at each other in a frenzied rush for safety. They pour toward Alex, who pulls a compact assault rifle from the racquet bag and battles the stampede toward the place where Li disappeared until two officers spot him, put him in their sights, and shout him down. He ducks and turns back, moving with the flow now, scanning wildly as he struggles to keep his footing. The officers are still shouting behind him; Li is nowhere in sight. Nowhere to go now but the car, which is still parked around the corner on the promenade. Real stones on that kid, Alex thinks. Thank Christ for Craig.

JUAN CARLOS throws the Jet Ski through the maze of the marina and drops Catalina at the ladder closest to the BMW, two docks over from the smoking yacht spilling wrapped kilos of fentanyl into the water through a gaping hole in the hull. Catalina climbs quickly but stops at the top rung and ducks down, astonished at the speed of the police response as officers in tactical gear run past her toward the restaurant. Peering over the edge of the blacktop, she sees the car but not her crew or target.

She waits until the wave of police passes and then climbs onto the promenade, one hand on the pistol in her purse.

AS HE sprints for the BMW, Ben spots Catalina coming toward him from the opposite direction.

"You see him?" Ben asks, breathing heavily, one hand on the hood, the other clutching his unzipped racquet bag.

"Li? No, not this way. You?"

"Lost him in the crowd." He flinches at a burst of gunfire from the restaurant.

"What the fuck is happening?" Catalina says. "Where's Alex?"

"Probably on the docks." Ben knocks on Craig's window and says, "Don't fucking move."

Behind them, two men with automatic rifles repeat Ben's command in shouted English and Spanish as they step out of a white van parked on Calle Tramo de Unión. A heavyset American orders Ben and Catalina to raise their hands.

"Give me a reason to take your fucking heads off," he says, "and I will. I'd love to."

HARRIS, ABANDONED by all but one Spanish officer when the shooting started, advances slowly toward the suspects, ordering them to their knees and then to the pavement, facedown, arms spread wide. Once they're on the ground, he nods for Officer Rosario to cuff them while he provides cover. As Rosario drops a knee onto the man's shoulder and catches his right wrist, Harris notes the full sleeve of tattoos, the beard, the bald head under the baseball cap—an exact match for the Las Vegas realtor's description. And judging by the woman lying next to him, Craig's hunch about a female rider was correct. Only one member of the crew is missing. Harris scans the promenade for anyone of unusual height.

———

HAVING JUST lost his police tail with a quick sprint up a side street, Alex rounds a corner onto Calle Tramo de Unión and sees Catalina lying facedown on the promenade. For a heart-stopping second, he assumes the worst. But then he spots the plainclothes officer on Ben's back and the American in a white windbreaker calling for backup with a rifle trained on Catalina. Alex flattens himself behind the open door of a white van as the Spanish cop wrenches Ben's left wrist behind his back and locks it to his right. The rest of the force is occupied with the mayhem at the restaurant and the fire on the dock, but the call is out, and Alex knows his window here is closing fast. He moves quickly around the back of the van to the sidewalk and, ducking low behind a row of parked cars, runs toward the promenade, where Catalina lies with her face turned toward the street. She spots Alex, who puts a finger to his lips and draws the pistol from his waistband. As Alex rests his elbows on the hood of a red Mercedes, a breeze ruffles the American's windbreaker, revealing the outline of a thick vest underneath. Lucky you, Alex thinks, as he takes aim at the man, who spins and buckles as rounds slam into the Kevlar on his back and the exposed meat of his biceps. The rifle leaves his hands and clatters on the asphalt. The Spanish officer is reaching for the pistol on his belt when Catalina comes off the blacktop like a striking cobra and takes him down at the knees. The gun goes off as she rips it from his hands.

HARRIS IS crawling toward his rifle when someone stands down on his ankle and then yanks him to his feet by the hair. A gun barrel grazes the back of his head as a hand digs through his pockets and extracts the cardholder that contains his badge and government ID.

"FBI, huh?" Rider 1 says. "Wonder who brought you along."

He snakes an arm around Harris's neck and spins him

toward the BMW. Through the passenger-side window, Harris locks eyes with Craig as the gun comes up between them. Craig throws the car into gear, then vanishes as gunshots whiten the glass. The window crumbles and falls away to reveal the twenty-two-year-old Australian confidential informant shot three times in the head.

"Fuck you," Harris says as he's pushed across the promenade, the pistol pressed against his temple now.

"Not this time."

"You think killing me solves your problem? Go ahead, you piece of shit. See how that goes for you."

With his toes at the edge of the asphalt, Harris stares down into the space between the promenade and a yacht called *Lucinda's Folly*, wondering if oil-slicked water is the last thing he'll see.

"Came pretty close," Rider 1 says. "Was it good for you? This is as good as it gets."

A hard kick in the ass sends Harris over the edge. He flails as he falls six feet to the water, clipping his chin on the bow deck of the yacht before he goes under, stars in his eyes from the blow.

WHEN CATALINA hears the splash, she whips three kicks into the head of the officer at her feet and spits on his unconscious body.

"Ben, come on," she says. "Let's go."

No response. As she lifts him by his cuffed hands, blood trickles and then streams from the bullet hole above his eye, an entry wound from the single round fired by the Spanish cop. Catalina lets Ben down gently and holds two fingers to his neck.

"Get in," Alex says as he unbuckles Craig and drags his body from the car. "Where's Ben?"

Catalina meets his eyes over the roof and shakes her head.

"Cat, get him in the fucking car. I'll do it. You drive."

"Alex," she says, "twelve o'clock."

Two Spanish uniforms are jogging down the promenade toward them, pistols pointed at the blacktop. Keeping his gun out of sight, Alex holds the stolen badge above the driver's-side door.

"FBI," he says. "We got one of them, he's shot pretty bad, can't wait for an ambulance, we're taking him ourselves. English? *Español?*"

As Catalina drags Ben's body into the back seat, she hears the FBI agent surface with a splash, choking on seawater as he screams for backup. The two Spanish officers stop and crane their necks toward the voice. One of them spots Craig's body on the promenade and elbows his companion just as Catalina heaves Ben's torso into the car.

"Go," she says to Alex, who ducks into the driver's seat and peels out with the back door still open and Ben's feet sticking out. The cops dive for cover as Alex makes a sharp right and fishtails up Calle Tramo de Unión.

Thirty-Nine

Six blocks north of the marina, the city of Marbella goes about its business, oblivious to the carnage by the water and the scene inside the silver BMW screaming through the streets. Having finally pulled Ben's legs into the car and closed the door, Catalina straddles his body and covers his open mouth with hers, one hand holding his nose, the other braced against the window, the back seat slick with blood. She's on her third round of chest compressions when Alex takes a turn on two wheels, throwing her against the door.

"The hospital's on Vargas Llosa," he says, banging through the gears. "Less than a mile."

"Hospital? He's fucking dead, Alex. Look at him."

"Right off the highway. We'll drop him at the door."

"Alex, listen to me. Look at him. Turn around."

He swerves into a bus lane and slams on the brakes, but keeps his hands on the wheel and his eyes on the road when the car screeches to a stop.

"How sure are you?" he asks.

"I'm sure."

"No hospital."

"No point."

"We need another car," he says, "and then we're going back to the marina. He's still here, I feel it. No way any boats made it out and we're gonna toss every one till we find him."

They drive past their rented SUV four times before Alex is convinced no one is watching.

"There's no cleaning this thing up," he says as he stops the BMW across the street.

Catalina hands him keys from her handbag and says, "Move our car to the corner. I'll take care of this one."

From the nearest intersection, Alex watches in the rental's rearview mirror as Catalina tosses her spare grenade into the back seat of the BMW and shuts the door. She's sprinting toward him when it detonates, blowing out the windows and setting off a chorus of car alarms as flames shoot out of the sedan and lick the roof. An automotive Viking funeral pyre, Alex thinks, trying to suppress the image of his best friend's body burning in the back seat of a stolen car.

"Call Diane again," he says as Catalina ducks into the passenger seat. "And then we need to ditch these phones."

"I just did. No ans— Wait, who's this?"

Alex grabs the buzzing phone. "Hello?"

"It's me," Diane says.

"Get out of the apartment now. Go down—"

"I'm not in the apartment."

"Listen to me, everything went to shit, the whole—"

"I know," she says. "I saw."

"You—what?"

"I was there. Meet me at Fernando's."

"No," Alex says. "No fucking way. We don't know Fernando didn't sell us out."

"Fernando didn't sell you out," she says.

"How can you know that?"

"Because I'm here, at Fernando's. Juan Carlos is with me. Just get here. Toss your phones before you do, he says. I'm hanging up now."

"No, wait," he says, "we're going back to the marina. We have to find him."

"No, Alex, you have to come here. I need you to trust me right now. And get off the phone."

Alex turns to Catalina with a blank look on his face. "She's at Fernando's."

"She's— What the fuck? How?"

Alex whips the car around and heads for the highway. Traffic is light on the northbound side of the Carretera Nacional, but the road seems endless. Long straights rise gradually and crest like waves, revealing longer downslopes and gentle curves that disappear at the horizon. Ambulances, fire trucks, and squad cars fly past them in the opposite lane, sirens wailing. Finally, the exit appears. Catalina pulls the pistol from her handbag and racks the slide.

"Be ready for anything," Alex says as they shoot up the narrow mountain road.

Diane stands on the gravel in front of the house, flanked by Fernando and the gardener, two nervous sentries with automatic rifles in their hands. Behind them is a dented red Renault sedan that Alex hasn't seen before. Juan Carlos steps out of the driver's seat and leans against the open door while Diane lights a cigarette by the trunk. Her hair and shirtfront are streaked with blood, and Alex recognizes the pistol in her waistband from the stash Ben left in the apartment. He's out of the car almost before it stops. As Alex stumbles toward Diane with outstretched arms, she plucks the cigarette from her lips and lifts the trunk of the Renault, revealing a wrinkled mound of yellow and khaki fabric that shifts as the sunlight hits it. Alex stands and gapes. The bridge of Li Jianrong's nose is shattered, indented in his face. Caked black blood fills the crevices in the pulped cartilage, and the left leg of his pants is dark and wet from a thigh wound. His eyes are closed but he's breathing, possibly conscious, certainly alive.

Alex says, "Where the— How did you get him?"

Diane takes a drag and glances over her shoulder at Juan Carlos. "Who cares?" she says. "He's here."

Catalina laughs and places her hands on her knees.

"Ricardo will take care of him," Fernando says. "Everyone else, inside now."

The TV in the living room is tuned to a news channel showing helicopter footage of the marina, its docks and promenade crisscrossed with police tape and swarmed with uniforms.

"If I'd known what this was," Fernando says, "I would have shot your girlfriend in the driveway. How dare you bring this to my home."

"Not part of the plan," Alex says. "I'm sorry. We'll make it worth your while."

"You will. My fee just tripled."

"Fine. Just help us, please."

"I spoke to someone at the Guardia Civil to make sure they weren't on their way here. They don't know who you are or where you are. Your driver was the problem. They flipped him in Las Vegas. He led them here."

"I took care of him," Alex says. "Ben's dead too."

Fernando lays a hand on Alex's shoulder.

"Later," Alex says. "Right now I need to get that motherfucker off your property and to our contact here while he's still alive."

"You won't get anywhere until the roadblocks come down."

"Then I need a clean phone."

Alex turns his phone on just long enough to dial Alejandro's number on a burner that Fernando provides.

"Who is this?" Alejandro asks when the line opens.

"You know who this is."

"What happened?"

Alex turns to face Diane and says, "We have him."

"Is that possible?"

"You want a picture? Him holding up a newspaper? I'd put him on but he's not real talkative right now."

"He's hurt?"

"He'll be fine."

"Then bring him to me."

"No, you come to us. We can't risk moving him, not now. My friend here will give you directions."

Alone on the pool deck, Alex sits on the edge of a chaise lounge in the shadow of the house. After a moment of silence, he pivots, grips the rim of a large terra-cotta pot, and dry-heaves into the soil. He's wiping his mouth when one of the German shepherds drops a hard red rubber ball into his lap. Alex thinks of Ben and Christian's dog, a disobedient pit bull mix named Molly that the couple rescued years ago. The shootout will be international news by now, and Alex imagines Christian learning of Ben's death from a TV anchor, a news alert on his phone. He wants more than anything to call Christian himself, but can't risk it. The shepherd noses his thigh, and Alex fakes a toss with the saliva-covered toy. The dog whips around and then, realizing she's been had, skids to a stop, her nails raking the slate. She crouches down and growls, tail going like a windshield wiper. Alex fakes another throw.

"I wouldn't do that," Fernando says as he emerges from the house. "Even I can't control her if you wind her up that way."

Alex lobs the ball into the deep end of the pool, and the shepherd dashes to the edge and stares down into the water, whining softly.

"Your contact—Alejandro is his name? He'll be here later, much later," Fernando says. "Best if everyone stays off the roads for now. Ricardo is treating the man from the trunk."

"He's a doctor?"

"He has some veterinary training. The gunshot wound is superficial. Would you like to know how he got here?"

"Diane told you?"

"She explained while Isabella examined her for injuries. She has none, fortunately. The blood is his, not hers. She followed you to the restaurant, arrived just after the explosion. When the shooting started, she watched this man escape into the crowd and followed him down one of the docks. He was shot when she cornered him, but he put up a fight, so she did that to his face.

Juan Carlos saw them from the water and managed to get there in time. They ripped a man out of that car and showed up here."

Alex laughs and shakes his head.

"I knew the boys were capable," Fernando says. "I didn't realize she was."

"That makes two of us."

"I worried when I met her. She seemed like someone mixed up in this by accident."

"That's what she is."

"What she was," Fernando says.

In the kitchen, Isabella offers Alex a neatly folded change of clothes and, anticipating his question, says, "She's resting. It's the last room on the hall."

Alex slips quietly into the childhood bedroom of Fernando's daughters and finds Diane with her back to the door in one of two twin beds. School pictures of the girls, willowy, sun-kissed brunettes with deep dimples and dark eyes, hang below a shelf crowded with soccer trophies and stuffed animals. Alex lowers himself slowly onto the empty bed. The sheets smell dusty and the mattress ends at his ankles, but he's never been so grateful for a place to lay his head.

"Does time slow down for you?" Diane asks, still facing the wall.

"Yes," he says. "Not always, and not always in the same way. But I know what you mean."

"I watched him duck and run and then I lost him. I thought maybe he wasn't going for the boat. Then everything went into slow motion. I turned around, and there he was. My body knew before I saw him somehow."

"It happens to me too."

"Why are you in that bed?"

"I don't know."

She makes room for him without turning around. "I don't feel different," she says as he fits his body against hers.

Forty

Alex wakes to find his fever broken and the sheet beneath him soaked with sweat. It's dark outside and he's alone on the thin, springy mattress. Someone opened the window while he slept and a draft animates the thin pink curtain above the bed, puffing it gently into the room, then sucking it against the opening. Just after 2 a.m. by the clock on the nightstand. Alex shuts his eyes to assess his physical and mental state, which triggers an image of Ben's lifeless body laid out on a tan leather back seat. Not now, he thinks. Grieve when it's over. Footsteps approach and stop outside the bedroom door. Fernando knocks and says they're ready for him in the dining room. Alex collects Diane's pistol from the nightstand and tucks it into his waistband at the small of his back.

The others are gathered at the kitchen table, and Alex balks at the sight of Alejandro seated between Catalina and Fernando.

"Did you sleep well?" Alejandro asks.

"How's our friend?"

"Ricardo's cleaning him up," Fernando says. "A few stitches, fresh clothes for the journey."

"Which ends where?" Alex asks.

"I need to have a word with him," Alejandro says, "and then we'll take him to La Línea, south of here, near Gibraltar. The negotiations are finished, the shipment is on its way. The boat he planned to leave on will meet us to collect him."

"Who's 'us'?" Alex asks.

Catalina glances nervously at Fernando, then at Alex, while Diane stares into the cup between her hands.

"You and I," Alejandro says.

"No," Alex says. "Not happening. We gave him to you on a silver fucking platter. Let the kids go. We're done here."

"I need someone with me for the swap. Unless we have a volunteer, it falls to you. I'll make the call about the children from the boat. It will be our pleasure to release them then, but not before."

Alex draws the pistol from his waistband and aims it between Alejandro's eyes.

"Easy, easy," Fernando says, pushing back from the table and raising a hand to ineffectually shield his wife.

"That's not happening," Alex says. "Not part of the deal."

"Neither was the shootout, which happened thanks to your choice of driver." Alejandro sips his coffee. "What good would it do to kill me now?"

"Juan Carlos has a friend in La Línea with a boat for you," Fernando says. "It's been arranged. Put the gun away, for God's sake. No one gets killed at my table."

Heads turn as Ricardo comes in from the backyard.

"*Listo,*" he says, wiping his hands on his pants.

"*Bueno, gracias,*" Alejandro says. Then to Alex, "Come see your prize."

"I'm coming too," Diane says.

They follow Ricardo up the hill behind the house to a red utility shed with a steel-plated door that the gardener opens to reveal Li—blindfolded under a pair of harsh fluorescent tubes, bound to a chair, and dressed like a country angler in quick-dry khaki pants and a safari shirt. He flinches at the creaking of the door and the footsteps that follow. Alex and Diane lean against the wall while Alejandro walks a tight circle around the chair. Li follows the sound, his head moving back and forth like someone watching tennis.

"You watch a lot of American movies in China, no?" Alejandro says. "There's a line from one—I forget the title now—but a man, a stockbroker, says, 'Greed is good. Greed works.' Have you seen this film?"

Li shakes his head.

"But that's something you believe."

Another, tighter headshake.

"That's not the impression you gave us. Greed is not good, my friend. It works in the sense that it brought you here, put a hole in your leg. What a story to tell your friends in Shanghai. You could call it a hunting accident, since you were being hunted." Alejandro walks to the workbench against the wall and picks up a handsaw, its long steel blade speckled with rust. "How many times were you warned?"

Li turns his head and says, "Once."

"Once? No." Alejandro opens the safari shirt and rests the blade against Li's trapezius muscle, between his neck and his shoulder, eliciting a shiver and a series of short, shallow gasps. "You were warned and then you were taxed and still you let your greed control you. You were paid very well in exchange for exclusivity. We expected you to honor that. Selling to the competition, delaying our shipments: What were you thinking?"

Li is stammering an unintelligible mix of Mandarin and English when Alejandro draws the saw slowly toward himself, letting the weight of the blade do the work, its teeth biting through Li's skin and into the muscle. Alejandro lifts the blade and repeats the process, opening cut after cut, each one deeper than the last, moving up the neck until the saw rests at a ninety-degree angle over the carotid artery. Li's screams dissolve into hyperventilation. Alex turns to Diane, who's staring at the saw, wide-eyed and unmoving.

"Tell me what you learned," Alejandro says.

"What? What—What—Whatever you want."

"Which is only what we asked, what you agreed to. Commitments are important. Honor them. And if you don't, we can reach you anytime, anywhere. Do you know your daughter goes for long runs by herself at night along the Charles River? Long, dark stretches of path, earbuds in her ears. A thing to do if you have no enemies, if your father has done nothing greedy."

"Please," Li says, weeping now, the blade still in his skin. "I understand."

"I believe you," Alejandro says. He places the saw on the workbench and carefully, almost tenderly, blots the blood on Li's neck with the collar of Fernando's shirt. "In a few hours you'll be safely on your boat. Let the scars be a reminder: Greed isn't good for you."

An hour later, they assemble at the back bumper of the clean white sedan Alejandro arrived in. Ricardo opens the trunk to reveal Li, who appears to be sleeping peacefully in spite of the zip ties on his wrists and the duct tape over his mouth.

"Está dormido?" Alex asks.

Ricardo shakes his head and hands Alex five short intramuscular syringes and a small glass vial.

"Ketamine?" Alex says, examining the label. *"Ketamina?"*

"Sí, exactamente. Sabes cómo usarla?"

"Sí," Alex says. *"Yo sé."*

Ricardo wishes him luck and heads back up the hill; Alejandro and Juan Carlos are already in the car. Catalina and Fernando say goodbye, leaving Alex alone with Diane.

"What's the opposite of 'can't take you anywhere'?" he says.

"Happy to help."

"Stay put for real this time."

"I will. How do you feel?"

"Tired. Scared."

"Good," she says. "This is scary. I said it this morning, I'll say it again: Go. Get this done." No quiver in her voice this time, no wringing of the hands. She grabs his head and pulls him in for a quick, hard kiss. "Get out of here," she says. "Home stretch. Cakewalk. Go."

They take the back roads, a long run of narrow switchbacks high above the Carretera Nacional, which is clogged with roadblocks and crawling with police. Juan Carlos sent one of his roommates ahead of them to make sure the mountain route is clear. Alex drives through the early-morning darkness with Alejandro beside him while the young torero navigates from the back seat. Between directives, Juan Carlos explains that Javi, his friend with the boat, is a Moroccan Gypsy who lives on the water and moves things between his homeland and adopted country. He's hosting a party with Gypsy flamenco musicians at his apartment, but Juan Carlos assures Alex that the crowd won't be a problem because Gypsies don't talk to the Guardia Civil. They'll be launching from the dock attached to Javi's building, and the bribe they're bringing will guarantee that the coast guard ignores their boat and the one coming to meet it. They're miles south of Marbella when Juan Carlos guides them down out of the mountains, across an empty highway, and onto an unmarked road. The asphalt turns to dirt after half a mile, and ends at a parking lot above a block of apartments built into a steep hill that runs down to the water. Alex backs the car into a dark corner of the lot, and the three men gather by the trunk. Li is still unconscious, undisturbed by the drive. Alex fills a syringe and injects him in the shoulder as a precautionary measure before he shuts the trunk.

Juan Carlos leads the way down a narrow staircase and along a path that hugs the shoreline. The units on the lower level of the complex are all dark except for one, where people come and go through a sliding glass door. Alex hands Juan Carlos a pack of Marlboros containing two cigarettes and three thousand euros, and the boy disappears into the haze of hookah smoke. The Gypsy flamenco band is set up just inside the door. Alex expected middle-aged musicians in frilly blouses and high-heeled boots, but finds himself facing a trio of teenagers in tight jeans and tee shirts, one male and one female guitarist, possibly brother and sister, with a boy on box drum between them. The

music floating through the open door is unlike anything Alex
has heard, a mournful, hypnotic, communal effort in which the
vocal part moves around the room at random, each voice adding
a verse to an endless narrative of love, loss, and redemption. The
girl on guitar—birdlike and beautiful, her head shaved except
for a blade-like forelock of black hair over her left eye—catches
Alex staring through the glass. The musicians take a break as
Juan Carlos emerges from the apartment, gives a thumbs-up,
and leads Alex and Alejandro down to the water. Alex knows
from the map that La Línea is just north of Gibraltar, but he's
surprised to see the low, dry mountains of another continent
across the water against the brightening sky. At the end of a
small dock sits their boat, a white dinghy with a freshly painted
blue interior and outboard motor.

"*Está bien?*" Juan Carlos asks.

Alejandro nods. "They'll meet us at that point in an hour,"
he says, pointing to a rocky outcrop of land with a single light
at its tip.

All three men turn as someone steps onto the dock. It's the
guitar player, walking toward them with an unlit cigarette dangling from her lips.

"Do you have fire?" she asks Alex, who shakes his head.

Juan Carlos hands her matches and the girl thanks him
without taking her eyes off the tall American.

"Enjoying the music?" she asks.

"Yeah," Alex says. "I was. Are those songs everyone knows
or are people making it up?"

"Both. You can sing something you know or something you
feel."

"What was that last one you were singing?"

"That was both," the girl says with a smile. "It's about a
woman who asks the Sirens to come on board her ship, to be her
captains. *Vente conmigo y serás capitana de mi barco.*"

"How does that work out for her?"

"Not well in the end. She thinks they'll be less dangerous if she brings them close."

"That won't save you," Alex says.

The girl gives him a puzzled look as she exhales. "Nothing will save you," she says.

As she walks back to the apartment, Alejandro asks Juan Carlos to keep the dock clear for the next few minutes while they bring their package down to the boat.

In the parking lot, Alejandro pops the trunk and leans back to dodge a cloud of acrid body odor mixed with the sweet reek of urine. The sight of a bound and gagged middle-aged man in a fetal curl and borrowed clothes awakens something close to sympathy in Alex. They extract Li feetfirst and sit him upright on the bumper. He's groggy and unsteady but cooperative as they guide him down the stairs toward the water, one arm over Alejandro's shoulders to compensate for his injured leg. Slowly, haltingly, they get Li aboard and situate him on the center bench. Alex lowers himself onto the small triangular bow seat while Alejandro starts the engine. Juan Carlos salutes ironically and stands on the dock until the boat disappears from sight.

AT THE small wrought-iron table by Fernando's pool, Diane and Catalina watch the sunrise over cold coffee and cigarettes, a fresh phone from Fernando between them. The dogs doze at their feet, lifting their heads now and again to stretch their jaws and sniff the air.

"How does Diego deal with this?" Diane asks. "With what you do, I mean."

"He shuts himself in his studio and works like a madman when I'm on a job," Catalina says. "Comes out only to eat. It's hard on him, but he's accepted it. Doesn't ask me to change, knows better than that."

"I didn't ask anyone to change, if that's what you're implying."

Catalina smiles. "That wouldn't have worked. It's been on his mind for a while. I felt it. But I ignored it, because I didn't want it to be true."

"What about you? You're going to keep doing this? After what happened to Ben?"

"It's what I do."

"What will Christian do now?"

"One night when he was very drunk he whispered to me that he knew things would end badly for Ben, that he was terrified, but couldn't say anything to anyone, certainly not to Ben. He begged me never to repeat that, said he had to tell someone, that it was eating him alive. I told him—"

On the table between them, Catalina's new phone spins slowly as it vibrates with a call. She laughs at the number displayed on the screen.

"Alex?" Diane asks.

"No, Diego. I left him a voice mail earlier. *Mi amor?* I need to keep the line clear in case— What? Diego, slow down." Catalina flinches. "What's— Where's this coming from? You heard—what? It's a rumor, bad information. I don't know what to tell— Okay, I'm listening. Diego, I said I'm listening to you." The confusion in her face hardens into grave concern as she rises slowly to her feet. "I need you to tell me where this is coming from. No. Bullshit. That's bullshit, Diego. She's retired. Yes, she is. For years now." Diane can hear Diego now, yelling in Catalina's ear. "Diego, listen to me, please. Help me understand. Who's coming to take him off our hands, then?" Catalina scans the sliver of ocean on the horizon, then lowers the phone with Diego still shouting on the line.

"What?" Diane asks. "What is it?"

"Oh my God," she says.

THE SUN has just cleared the horizon in La Línea, and morning light sparkles on a wide stretch of olive-drab Atlantic.

Alejandro scoops up a handful of seawater, wets his face, and palms his neck.

"Where are they?" Alex asks.

"We should see them any minute."

"Pretty quick negotiation."

"Our point was made, the shipment was paid for. Nothing to discuss. How are you feeling?"

"Fine," Alex says, leaning forward to examine Li, who's slumped on the bench with his chin on his chest, in and out of consciousness, twitching to avoid collapse. "Better than him."

"I wonder where he was for the last few hours. It's strong medicine, ketamine. You can get it from veterinary supply stores quite easily in Mexico. We used it when I was younger—a group of us, lying on the floor, going on a journey. Have you tried it?"

"Yeah," Alex says. "In a group, on a floor. A doctor friend of mine gets it."

"You and I have more in common than the name."

"Someone else told me that recently."

"Who was that?"

"Doesn't matter," Alex says, "because it's bullshit. We've got nothing else in common. Taking people's kids is a few rungs below pedophilia in my book. I'd kill you nice and slow if I wasn't retired."

"This is the end for you?"

"Absolutely." Alex takes his phone from his pocket to check in with Catalina, but the battery, which he forgot to charge before they left the house, is dead. "I've had all the fun I can stand."

"It's surprising to me that you ever did this kind of work. You're not who I expected to meet that night at Palm Trees."

"What does that mean?"

"You struck me as someone in the wrong profession, in spite of your abilities. It's something I recognize, being in the wrong profession also. I'm curious—do you justify it somehow? Are there things you tell yourself?"

"I'm out," Alex says. "I'm not telling myself anything."

Alejandro shrugs and scans the horizon. The breeze is picking up. A small black bird drops out of the sky and perches on the starboard gunwale. It cocks its head to eye the occupants of the boat—the captain, the semiconscious passenger, the tall man perched awkwardly on the bow—before it takes off and continues toward land.

"One of my first jobs was in Las Vegas," Alex says. "Some Saudi prince roughed up a hooker, threw a bunch of cash at her, kicked her out of his suite. A few months later, he came back to town, and one of his guys called the same escort service, probably by mistake. Or maybe you can burn call girls with a curling iron and get a second date where they're from, who knows. The girl's madam tipped off Ben, told him that the prince traveled with a lot of cash and valuables, that the girl could get us in the room. The madam didn't even want a finder's fee. 'Just put the fear of our Christian God into that motherfucker.' So that's what we did. I brought a camera with me and we staged a little photo shoot before we left. The prince with the girl, the prince cutting up a pile of cocaine. I told him if he made a peep, we'd send the photos to his wives, his kids, his embassy, his enemies, every newspaper on earth. We didn't even wear masks, just baseball caps and sunglasses. Robbed him blind and leveraged his fake religious piety to keep his mouth shut. That made more sense to me than anything I'd ever done."

"Baseball caps and sunglasses in hotels is a theme for you, no? Is there always some higher purpose? What about your last job in Las Vegas?"

"Graff jewelers? Blood-diamond dealer to the stars since 1960? We hit them and they turn around and pass their losses on to some insurance carrier that's also robbing everybody blind. Everyone gets made whole except our friend here, who's getting rich off high school kids overdosing in Appalachia. Ethically speaking, I'd say that one was a wash. I don't really need the tidy moral calculus, to be honest. That Robin Hood speech is for cocktail parties. It was never really about that for me."

"What was it about?"

"Control. Order out of chaos. Or inside it."

"Calm in the eye of the storm."

"Sure."

"Was your childhood chaotic?"

"Wasn't the smoothest ride."

"So you create chaos in other people's lives. Pass on what was visited on you."

"Not anymore, amigo. Groundbreaking insight, by the way. You should consider social work if you're sick of this."

"It's an old story. I came to this differently. I was—"

The sound of an engine reaches them as a yacht emerges from the far side of the point, a mile from the dinghy. Alejandro shades his eyes and starts the outboard motor. "Exactly on time. When we get there—"

"Wait," Alex says, "hang on a second. What did you just say?"

"That you should let me do the talking when we get there."

"No, before that. Baseball caps and sunglasses in hotels, that being a thing of mine. I wore that on one other job, my first job. Who told you about that?"

"You did, no?"

"No," Alex says. "I never told you that."

"Then Ben must have."

"Ben wasn't there. And I was with you two the whole time. Ben didn't tell you anything. Where'd you hear that?"

Alejandro shrugs. "Part of your legend. Folklore."

"Who told you that story?"

Alejandro looks over Alex's shoulder at the approaching yacht and says, "I don't remember."

"Bullshit. Four people know that story. Two of them are dead and one of them is me. Answer my question."

"I heard it somewhere. What does it matter?"

"I know who you heard that from. And you know why it matters."

"Do I?"

"Why is Maricel Sandoval telling you about the night we met? She told me she didn't know you."

"I don't know what you mean."

"Give me your phone." The boat is half a mile away when, for the second time this morning, Alex draws on Alejandro. "Give me the phone in your pocket."

"Enough with the gun already, Alex. You want to explain a dead man in the boat to these people?"

"I don't think they'll give a shit as long as he's okay. In fact, I'll take those odds if you don't hand it over." Alex cocks the hammer. "Stop fucking stalling."

Alejandro shakes his head as he complies. Phone in one hand, gun in the other, Alex pulls up the call history and dials the first Mexican number he finds, eyes flitting between the approaching yacht and Alejandro. No answer, no voice mail, nothing. When he dials the second number, a woman picks up after three rings.

"Bueno? Alejandro?"

A voice that Alex would know anywhere. There's a strong wind on the other end and Alex imagines Maricel standing on the balcony off her bedroom in the moonlight.

"Alejandro?" she says. *"Todo bien?"*

"Tell her yourself," Alejandro says. "Is she on the line? Tell her it's finished."

"We're done here," Alex says.

"Who is this?"

"Take a wild guess."

A pause. "I see. It's finished? Last I heard there was some trouble."

"That's resolved."

"Very well, then. Could you pass me to Alejandro?"

Alex hands over the phone without lowering the gun and listens as Alejandro assures Maricel that collateral is no longer necessary.

"You were her first suggestion," Alejandro says as he hangs up. "'The perfect implement.' She thinks very highly of you."

"Turn the boat around," Alex says, glancing at the yacht over his shoulder. "Get us back to shore."

"And undo your end of this?"

"Who's on that boat? Who's coming for him?"

"The people who were meant to protect him. You think they'll touch us after you showed them what we can do? Relax. Everything has been negotiated. These men are professionals, agnostics. They take delivery and we're finished here."

"And you know that how? From her?"

"Yes."

"If she'd sell me out, she'd sell you out too."

"I don't think so."

"Turn the fucking boat around."

"Let it happen, Alex. Let it end."

The approaching engine dies and the yacht glides to a stop beside the dinghy, water rushing down the hull. No one on the deck or bridge. A ghost ship. Alex climbs onto the center bench behind Li, wraps an arm around his neck, and puts the pistol to his temple as Derrick steps onto the aft deck, smiling and unarmed.

"Hi, Alex," he says. "You won't be needing that."

"You know each other?" Alejandro asks.

"Old friends," Derrick says. He points to Li. "Drugs or shock?"

"A sedative," Alejandro says. "He'll be himself in a few minutes. Alex, let him go."

"I need the other thing," Derrick says. "They said you'd have it for us."

"What other thing?" Alex asks.

Alejandro pulls a green felt jewelry bag from the pocket of his pants and tosses it to Derrick, whose eyes go wide as it arcs over the water between boats.

"What the fuck is that?" Alex asks.

Derrick carefully extracts the necklace, a cascade of white and Champagne diamonds stolen two months ago in Las Vegas, and holds it up in the clear morning light.

"The tax I mentioned," Alejandro says, "which you helped us to collect."

"One more thing," Derrick says. "I know he promised to stop selling to the competition, but he's only selling to them now."

Alex spots the gun barrel in the nearest porthole just before a three-round burst rips into Alejandro's chest and stomach, driving him back on the bench. He clutches his gut as a second burst snaps his head back with a puff of blood and sends him over the side. Derrick hits the deck as Alex opens fire, shattering the window and punching holes in the fiberglass around it. Li, startled by the shooting, spits out garbled Mandarin and squirms against Alex's hold.

"Easy, cowboy," Derrick says, standing up to show Alex his empty hands. "You've got what, two left in there? Three? Just let him go. You think I'm gonna shoot you? I could have done that back in town. Let us have him and get the fuck out of here, like I asked you. This ain't even your show."

"Okay," Alex says. "All yours. I'm gone. You'll never hear from me again."

He lays the pistol on the bench behind him. Derrick throws a line into the boat.

"Good man," he says as Alex reels it in. "I'm not gonna shoot you, Alex. He is."

Alex doesn't see the gun as he dives sideways but the first shots ring in his ears as the lights go out.

Forty-One

He wakes up choking as a mix of blood and bile floods his nose and mouth. The sun is almost overhead now, scorching his skin. He's lying in the bottom of the boat, wedged tightly between the center bench and the bow, calves resting on the seat cushion, chin pressed into his chest. The rounds his vest caught broke his ribs, stifling his breath. His spine sits in what he hopes is sun-warmed water, but the creases in his shirtfront are filled with blood, and sharp pain pulses from an entry wound above his hip. A breeze brings the boat slowly about, and Alex finds himself facing the sun, a white disk in the cloudless sky.

He raises his right hand to shield his face and discovers that his palm is split almost in half, his pinky and ring finger dangling near his wrist, swaying with his movement and the rocking of the boat. He wonders why it doesn't hurt and then it does—intense aching pain shooting down his arm and branching out across his chest and shoulder. He yells but the sound catches in his constricted throat, where it rattles and dies. No voice, no phone. No boats on the horizon. This, he thinks, is what the end looks like.

Alex is staring at a strange lump on his thigh when he remembers the ketamine in his pants pocket, salvation from the pain, if nothing else. He inches the vial down his leg, extracts it carefully, and grips it by the neck between his bloody thumb and forefinger. He uncaps a syringe with his teeth and, with his good hand, guides the needle through the rubber membrane. What's left of his right hand is quickly losing feeling, and the liquid in the barrel is two milliliters shy of what he wants when the vial slips out of his grasp and bangs against the bottom of the boat. Gripping the syringe, he hovers his fist over his thigh and lets it fall. The needle penetrates his pants and then his flesh. Alex feels the liquid flood the muscle as he drives the plunger home.

He wonders, as he lies there, if he'll see an image of his body torn apart when his body is already shot to pieces. Alex tries to focus on his breath, hoping he has enough blood left to get the drug into his brain. He opens his eyes at the sound of a helicopter, but it's patrolling the coastline, flying due south, and soon it's out of sight. The patter of the rotors echoes on the water like a drumbeat. Alex thinks of Paola playing music in Tulum, then of Paola and Diane dancing with their fingers intertwined over the turntables. As his mind begins to cloud, Alex deeply regrets the injection and fights to hold on to that image. He opens his eyes again, hoping to sober up, to stay a little longer. The sun looks unsteady, expanding and contracting or advancing and receding—Alex can't be sure. Then the sky begins to darken at the edges of his vision, a creeping blue-black that slowly obscures everything. Alex blinks and tries to focus, unsure now if his eyes are closed or open. All that's left in his field of vision is a distant, jittery pinprick of light. The train again, he thinks. This time the light goes out.

The fishermen brought fresh tuna this morning, which Ernesto prepared with a key lime cream sauce. Lunch was served when Maricel and her bodyguards returned from her walk on the beach. No wine with the meal today—her doctor is concerned about her blood sugar—but Ernesto promised something special for dessert, *algo delicioso pero no muy dulce*. Maricel hears him washing dishes in the kitchen while she eats. She's due for a call with her eldest daughter after lunch. Two days ago, as Juliana walked from her car to her condo in La Jolla, someone threw her to the sidewalk from behind. Sabrina, Maricel's four-year-old granddaughter, started screaming when her mother's hand was torn from hers. Juliana rolled over to find a man in a motorcycle helmet with a pistol leveled at her head. He ripped the crocodile handbag off her broken wrist, jumped on his bike, and roared off down Romero Drive. Maricel has been trying to sell her daughter on personal security for years; now she'll insist. She's rehearsing her argument when a steel pan clangs against the kitchen's tiled floor. Maricel pauses with her fork in her food and calls Ernesto's name. She's halfway out of her seat when Diane strolls into the dining room and sweeps her hair back with the hand that's not holding a gun.

"Hi," Diane says. "Don't get up." She sits opposite Maricel and sets the pistol on the glass tabletop.

There's a loud grunt and then another from the kitchen as a body slams into the wall and then the floor. Maricel catches a glimpse of Catalina as her eyes flit between the doors to the dining room, and Diane watches the older woman realize that the barriers have all been breached, that nothing will save her now. The flash of panic is followed by acceptance, calm.

"I was very sorry to hear about Alex," Maricel says.

"Were you? That's nice."

"How was it to see your children again?"

"Like you did that out of the goodness of your heart. You had no choice after everything went to shit. The only problem bigger than the one you created would have been two dead kids."

Maricel cuts a bite of tuna with her fork, swipes it through the sauce, chews slowly. The fish slides down her throat.

"How is that?" Diane asks.

"Very good. There's more in the kitchen, but you'll have to serve yourself."

"I'm having lunch after this, but thank you. I gotta ask: Why jump back in? Boredom? Legacy? I gotta hand it to you, recruiting Alejandro was a good idea. Even if it didn't quite work out for him."

Maricel continues eating.

"Ripping off that necklace in Vegas was what? A shot across the bow? A little warning to your Chinese friend? But they ignored you, stopped your shipment. So you took it up a notch and went after Li personally. Only people like that don't take kindly to your third-world cartel bullshit, so they killed Alejandro and cut you off completely. That kidnapping was a pretty big miscalculation, I'd say. Seems like you lost your edge."

Maricel adds a dab of sauce to the fish on her fork with a dull silver knife.

"You killed Clay, didn't you," Diane says.

The older woman finally looks up from her food.

"You wanted to keep Alex close, but Clay and Alex were a package deal back then, so you killed his friend and made it look like highway robbery."

"The operation at the airport went on for many years," Maricel says. "With a change of staff, of course. I found other uses for Alex."

"Other uses?"

"He worked for me on and off for years without realizing it. The airport was too valuable to be run by the people who offered it to us, so we dispensed with them, including Clay. I let Alex live because I thought he might be useful. I was right. You should have seen him when he came to me in Mexico after I had your son's father removed. Unsure where to turn, afraid of his own shadow. He jumped at the opportunity to join up with Ben. They were very good, that little crew. So I started feeding jobs to them. It still amazes me that Alex never saw it. He had had this foolish idea of independence, of making a life on his own terms. It was almost heartbreaking to watch. They did everything I asked without knowing who was asking. Anyone can buy an army. What's more valuable is a crew that can pick off the diversified assets—bonds, boats, jewelry, art—things men in this business put their money into when the cash becomes too much. That's where Alex and his little band of thieves came in. They made all our rivals feel unsafe, including Li Jianrong."

"Why turn on him after all these years?"

"Did he tell you how we met?"

Diane nods.

"I never understood why he thought he could steal from me and get away with it, why I would ever act in his best interests after he broke into a hotel room to take things that belonged to me. He wanted so badly to believe someone was looking out for him. No one had before. A blind spot, perhaps the only one. Unfortunately it cost him everything."

"Almost."

Maricel sets her silverware down.

"Oh, I'm sorry," Diane says, "you still think he's dead. He's here. He couldn't promise me he wouldn't kill you, so I had him wait outside."

"You're lying."

"Am I?"

"So how is he?" Maricel asks, unconvinced.

"How's your daughter? How's her arm?"

Maricel retains her composure except for a twitch at the corners of her eyes.

"Oh, honey," Diane says. "You thought that was a coincidence? Some purse snatcher jumps your little girl ten days after what went down in Spain? I gave that bag of hers to a girlfriend, but this you can have." She tosses a red leather wallet onto the table. "We knew where to find her, obviously. I know where all your children live. I know which doggie day care Juliana uses, where Raúl plays golf on Sunday when he's not with his hippie teenage girlfriend in Topanga. I know about your children's children too. I'm new to this, so every day is full of surprises, but you know what absolutely floored me? How much it costs to have kids killed professionally. Kids and politicians, right? I mean, it's doable, but the prices are appalling."

"You wouldn't do that. Kill children. A child."

"You made the rules. The way we've set things up, I won't have to lift a finger, because if anything happens to any of us, someone will start killing off your family automatically. Think of it as estate planning." Diane can almost hear the whirring of Maricel's mind in the tiny movements of her eyes. "Sure, you could circle the wagons, uproot your kids and their families, wreck their lives. I'll still get to them eventually. I'll make it my life's work."

"I don't think it will come to that."

"Not if you keep up your end. You still owe us for Spain. The original fee is fine, plus five million for Ben's partner. You have forty-eight hours."

"You think I have access to that kind of money?"

"You know what? I don't think about it at all. It's not my problem. That's what you owe. Sell some furniture. Pass the hat. Maybe one of your kids can explain GoFundMe to you. Either we see that payment, or your family starts getting smaller. I probably won't kill your grandkids over money, but your kids are fair game, because ours were. Two days should be plenty."

When Maricel picks up her knife and fork, Diane raises the pistol, which Maricel pretends not to notice.

"Who am I kidding, right?" Diane says. "I barely know how to use this thing."

A mishap during a catered luncheon taught Diane a lesson about large glass tabletops: Drop something exactly in their center and they shatter. She leans across the table and brings the gun butt down on its midpoint. The glass turns as white as a snow-covered pond, then crumbles to the floor. Diane walks across the wreckage to where Maricel sits, eyes closed, hands trembling, her lap full of shards. With the tip of the gun barrel, she raises Maricel's chin until their eyes meet.

"Think of your children," Diane says. "I know I did."

She leaves by the front door and finds Catalina sitting on the wide white steps. Leaning on a column in the shadow of the house is Alex, his right hand covered by a bulky bandage, his left hand holding a pistol equipped with a silencer that reaches to his knee. The bridge of his nose is pale and peeling from a second-degree sunburn. Six hours after the shooting on the water, Juan Carlos commandeered a second dinghy and found Alex lying in the bottom of the first, bleeding heavily and barely breathing, his vest pocked with brass-coated lead, his skin cold to the touch even as it blistered in the sun. His right hand, a swollen mitt of exposed flesh and shattered bone that a moonlighting surgeon nearly amputated, will never be the same.

"No last words for her?" Diane asks. "She's primed."

"You covered all the bases, right?"

She nods.

"Nothing else to say," Alex says. "Let's go."

He kisses Diane on the mouth, then walks to the guardhouse and steps over the body on the floor to hit the button that rolls back the gate.

The road is empty in both directions, and the only sound is the soft clacking of palm fronds overhead. Diane tucks the pistol into the waistband of her jeans and lights a cigarette as the three of them walk side by side. A hundred yards down the road, a mid-sized silver rental car is hidden in the jungle beside Catalina's motorcycle.

"Call me from the airport," Catalina says as she pulls on her helmet.

In the car, Diane draws on her cigarette and lets a plume of smoke like a question mark slip through her lips. Smoking in the rental triggers an automatic cleaning fee, which Alex decides not to mention when she takes another drag.

"You okay?" he asks.

"We never tried that restaurant."

"What restaurant?"

"The seafood place near Xcacel. You don't remember? We were on our way to lunch that day."

"That's right," Alex says, "we were."

"Let's go there."

"You want to eat right now?"

"That's exactly what I want to do."

"Okay," Alex says. He starts the car. "Let's eat."

Acknowledgments

To my agent, the best agent, Julie Barer, for her saintly patience and inspired advocacy. To my editor, Jason Kaufman, for his patience, vision, editorial advice, and steady hand. To everyone at Doubleday, especially Todd Doughty, Lauren Weber, Tricia Cave, and Carolyn Williams, for their tireless work on behalf of this book. To Angus Cargill and everyone at Faber and Faber for the same. To the DJs and producers whose music sustained me through long days of writing, especially Avalon Emerson, Roi Perez, Job Jobse, DJ Tennis, Jane Fitz, Andrew Weatherall, Four Tet, Midland, and Blondes. To Greg Greenberg and Nate Goralink, great lawyers and great readers. To Eric Sullivan for his sharp and sometimes shouted notes. To Matthew Sharpe for a helpful edit. To Alexander Chee for keeping the faith. To Alison Roman for the inspiring tough love. To Claude Hillel for his healing powers. To Charles Jolley for a place to write and an important lesson. To Courtney Wilk-Mandel for her kindness and good counsel. To Anna Sánchez Bendahan for unwavering support and familial inspiration. To Hari Nef for many things. To my New York crew, especially Bart Higgins, Carla Robertson, Julie Schuck, Peter Szollosi, Michael McKnight, and Shibon Kennedy, incredible friends and ports in a storm. To Matthew Haar, without whom this would not have happened. To the Jersey boys who fucking saved my ass, especially Mike Hokenson, Pete Martin, Kyle Burke, and Chris MacFarland. To my parents, cousins, aunts and uncles, Nonna, and my siblings, especially my sister, for being the family everybody envies. And to my great friend Jim Salant, a supernaturally gifted editor and reader. Jim stepped in when I was lost and, with fierce intelligence and wild generosity of spirit, helped me find my way. He passed away suddenly just as we finished working on the manuscript. This book is dedicated to his memory.

About the Author

Stan Parish is the former editor in chief of *The Future of Everything* at *The Wall Street Journal* and the author of the novel *Down the Shore*. His writing has appeared in *GQ, Esquire, Surface, The New York Times,* and *The New York Times Magazine,* among other publications. He holds a brown belt in Brazilian Jiu Jitsu and lives in Los Angeles.